Sarah Alderson is a London-born, LA-based writer whose previous books include *Friends Like These* (Mulholland), *In Her Eyes* (Mulholland), *The Weekend Away* (HarperCollins) and *The Stalker* (HarperCollins). Sarah is also a screenwriter; her adaptation of *The Weekend Away* is now streaming on Netflix.

You can follow @sarahalderson on Twitter and @sarahaldersonauthor on Instagram.

D0784826

Also by Sarah Alderson

The Weekend Away
The Stalker

THE
CABIN
IN THE
WOODS

SARAH ALDERSON

avon.

HarperCollins*Publishers*
1 London Bridge Street
London SE1 9GF

www.harpercollins.co.uk

HarperCollins*Publishers*
1st Floor, Watermarque Building, Ringsend Road
Dublin 4, Ireland

A Paperback Original 2022
1

First published in Great Britain by HarperCollins*Publishers* 2022

A catalogue copy of this book is available from the British Library.

ISBN (UK): 978-0-00-853158-4
ISBN (US): 978-0-00-855111-7

This novel is entirely a work of fiction.
The names, characters and incidents portrayed in it are
the work of the author's imagination. Any resemblance to
actual persons, living or dead, events or localities is
entirely coincidental.

Typeset in Sabon LT Std by Palimpsest Book Production Limited,
Falkirk, Stirlingshire

Printed and bound in the UK using 100% renewable electricity
at CPI Group (UK) Ltd

MIX
Paper from
responsible sources
FSC™ C007454

This book is produced from independently certified FSC™ paper to ensure
responsible forest management.

For more information visit: www.harpercollins.co.uk/green

For Alby

'Police are using cadaver dogs to scour several square miles of woods in the Hardscrabble Wilderness Area. Officials have not yet commented on whether a body has been found, but a team of forensic specialists was spotted removing what looked to be several trash bags from the area and tagging them as evidence.

'A source within the Westchester police department has revealed that the Reids' eight-bedroom home is currently being cordoned off, as police prepare to conduct a thorough search of the house and grounds.

'Detective Lim, who has been leading the investigation into Rose Reid's disappearance, has so far refused to comment on whether they are any closer to finding her or a body.

'While too early to speculate, it seems that the search for Rose Reid, who vanished without trace two days before Christmas, could finally be over.'

ALASTAIR BALL
OPR NEWS, LIVE BROADCAST
Westchester, NY

Chapter One

Present

Someone is watching me. Like a deer with a gun trained on it, I freeze, the axe dangling from my hand, half-expecting to hear a shotgun blast ring out and to find myself flung forwards onto the frost-speckled ground.

My ears strain to catch the cock of a gun or the snap of a twig, but all I can hear is my own quick, shallow breathing and the hush of leaves in the highest branches of the trees. My senses are blaring a five-alarm warning that someone is out there, lurking in the forested dark, spying on me – but a voice in my head tells me that I'm being paranoid. The nearest neighbor is a couple of miles from here as the crow flies and no one should be hiking or hunting in the area, thanks to the 'Private Property, No Trespassing' signs, which are posted so frequently throughout the woods that you'd have to be blind to miss them.

I spin around and scan the forest behind me, but it's impossible to make anything out beyond the thick tangle of trees. It would be easy enough for someone to take cover out here, to hunker down among the bushes and foliage and watch from afar. I used to spend whole days like that with my grandfather when I was a kid, squatting inside his hide, passing a dented flask of black coffee laced with bourbon back and forth, as we cradled our guns and waited for a deer to wander by.

Missourian hunters were only permitted to shoot two un-antlered deer a year, but my grandfather believed it was his God-given right to shoot as many as he liked, which meant we spent a lot of time in that hide. But I didn't mind; even as a child I had an affinity for silence and for being outside in nature. I appreciated the grandness of it, the vastness, and how it made everyone small and insignificant, not just me. I also understood that the woods were a perfect place to disappear. So long as you had survival skills, that is, and knew how to hunt, kill and dress animals. My skills are a little rusty after years of neglect, but I know if I'm to survive out here, I need to hone them fast.

The feeling of being watched vanishes like my breath into the cold air. Perhaps it was an animal.

Or maybe it was nothing at all. My mind is playing non-stop tricks on me these days: I've started hearing things. Not just the usual sounds you get out in the woods – bird calls and creaking tree limbs – but voices, sometimes so real that I could swear someone is standing right beside me, whispering into my ear.

Last night I startled awake having heard someone call my name. I sat up in the dark, heart hammering, convinced I could hear footsteps pitter-pattering away across the wooden floor of the cabin. In the daylight I've seen things out of the corner of my eye – flashes of movement that make me whip my head around – though never in time to catch sight of anyone.

Maybe it's an angry ghost, haunting me.

Or I could just be paranoid.

The wind whips up and I bend quickly to gather an armful of the wood I just chopped. I hurry back to the cabin with it, slowed by my aching knee and sore back. There's snow on the way: I can taste it like iron, like blood on my tongue. I step carefully over the string of empty, rusting cans that I've hung between two trees as a rudimentary alarm system, and head toward the cabin. Nudging open the creaking screen door with my foot, I shoulder my way inside, shivering even more as I enter the chilly interior. Winter is closing in, and the place is full of cracks, through which the wind whistles and the cold creeps like a witch's fingers. The furnace is ancient and doesn't work.

I throw the wood down and then check the little box beside the stone fireplace. Inside I discover an empty packet of firelighters and a pile of yellowing newspaper. The date on the newspaper is March 2006, and the headlines are all about the Iraq War.

The newspaper helps explain the years of dust and cobwebs decorating the cabin and I wonder why the place has been left to decay for so long. Tired, I drag myself to my feet and trudge through into the kitchen.

I open the cupboards despite already knowing what I'll find inside: cobwebs, instant coffee, a bag of sugar, packets of noodles, a kilo bag of rice and several boxes of spaghetti. I reason that I could last for a couple more weeks – I'm barely eating anyway – but, as I gaze through the window at the lake glinting through the trees, I know it's too risky: if I don't make the journey soon, I will shortly have no means of getting any supplies at all. This morning when I went down to the lakeshore I noticed that the water had turned syrupy, thickening toward ice. It won't be long before it freezes over and then I'll wind up stranded, unless I want to hike the twenty-three miles around the lake's circumference to the nearest store.

Even so, I hover by the front door, chewing a fingernail. I'm nervous to venture beyond the strict boundaries I've set for myself – roughly two hundred meters beyond the front door in all directions – but needs must. It's not just food; without matches or firelighters I won't be able to light the fire, and without heating I could easily freeze to death out here. My grandfather taught me how to strike together two rocks to get a spark, but it's difficult and I'd have to find some rocks. Matches and firelighters will make things a lot easier. The batteries on the flashlight are running low too. I don't want to be left in the dark, especially not at night, when the nightmares come. Out here, away from the city, it gets so blindingly dark that it's like startling awake from one nightmare and finding yourself in another.

After dithering for a few minutes, I take down the hunting jacket from the hook beside the door. It's a man's jacket and far too big for me but it's warm and waterproof. I dig a woolen hat and a pair of old fleece-lined gloves from the pockets and pull them on too.

Glancing in the dirty mirror hanging on the wall, I am relieved to see that I look nothing like my old self, and I'm amazed how a few months can make such a difference: my cheeks are hollow, and my cheekbones have sharpened and are blotched red from the cold; my eyes are sunken and ringed by such dark circles that even if I had foundation and concealer I would still struggle to hide them. My skin is pale and dry, my lips cracked. My eyebrows are no longer carefully tweezed but have grown out and now form two strong dark arches. I look less like the groomed, perfectly coiffed, designer-clad woman I was six months ago, and more like the grubby, dirt-poor and starving child that I used to be. It almost makes me smile to see the remnants of my scrappy younger self staring back at me. Almost.

A few strands of hastily bleached white-blonde hair poke out from under my hat and I tuck them out of sight. I may not be that recognizable facially, but there's nothing I can do to hide my height. At five foot ten I've always stood out in a crowd.

Being recognized will depend, I suppose, on if I'm still making headlines and if the police are still looking for me.

Chapter Two

Past

Twenty-Two Years Ago

'Where are you?'

My head flies up and Daisy's eyes go round with fear. Her body, scrawny as a scarecrow's, starts to quiver.

'Girls?!' our dad yells. There's a loud crash as he trips over something. 'Damn!' he curses.

He's heading this way. I leap to my feet and snatch Daisy's hand, yanking her up out of the nest of dirty blankets, and shoving her into the closet. Moving quickly, I push her down and pile clothes on top of her, then I press my finger to my lips in warning, but she doesn't need telling. Though her bottom lip trembles, she doesn't make a peep.

'It'll be OK,' I mouth but I am shaking too.

Our dad found some work today, helping shift gravel and rocks at the quarry. I thought that would mean Daisy and I would have a whole day to ourselves, that we could relax, but something must have happened as he's home early. Dread fills me. If he's been fired then he probably hasn't been paid, which means he won't have enough money to buy drugs, which means he's now likely on a comedown. And when he needs a fix is when he's most dangerous.

'Where are you, Rose?' my dad shouts in a singsong lilt. He's outside the door to the small bedroom Daisy and I share at the back of the trailer.

As I go to close the closet door on Daisy, ready to face my father – to take whatever is coming in order to protect her from it – she reaches out and yanks me back inside.

I barely manage to slide the closet shut before the bedroom door flies open. Holding my breath, Daisy's sweaty, grubby hand in mine, I stare through the louvered slats, as our father scans the room, looking for us.

Like an ogre from a fairy tale, he stops and sniffs as if he's trying to hunt us down on scent alone. But the trailer is full of ugly smells: stale beer, cigarettes, a blocked toilet and an overflowing septic tank, burned crumbs, urine-soaked sheets that have dried stiff and yellow and now stink. Two unwashed girls amongst all that are hard to sniff out.

I can read his body language enough to know I was right about him being on a comedown. His eyes are glittery with rage. He's jitterbugging away, his foot tapping, and his hands scratch at invisible fleas. He wants something to take his mood out on. He wants us.

He glances at the unmade twin bed Daisy and I share, and kicks at the pile of blankets on the floor where we were just playing cards, before his head swivels toward the closet. His eyes seem to lock on mine and I feel my heart drop out of my chest and hit the ground.

Daisy's hand grips mine even tighter in terror. I squeeze back. My mouth is dry as I watch my father step closer and closer. I decide that when he opens the door, I'll throw myself forward, push him with all my might, and hopefully buy us enough time to escape, or at least Daisy. But just a few feet from us, he gets distracted by something he's noticed sitting in the detritus. I curse to myself as I follow his gaze to the photograph in the silver frame lying on the ground; I should have hidden it again after I took it out to show Daisy. It's too late now. He's picking it up, frowning at it. It's a photo of our mom, her arms around Daisy and me. He's probably wondering where I got it. The truth is I stole it off

11

the coffin at her funeral and I've kept it hidden from him for the last three years, knowing he would hawk the silver frame if he ever found it. I watch him stare at the photograph for a few moments longer, then he turns, muttering to himself, and slinks out of the room with it.

I want to run after him and demand he give it back. It's the only photograph we have of our mom. Daisy was three when she died, and I was six. I barely remember her – only as a vague shape in my mind – and Daisy doesn't at all. I take it out often, whenever Dad isn't around, and tell my little sister stories about our mom; about how she was the best mom in the world, and loved us more than anything. I sing the songs she used to sing to us, stupid made-up songs, and describe the grilled cheese sandwiches she'd make for us, and the beautiful flower crowns she'd weave for us in the summer. I tell Daisy about all the adventures we went on before she died in a car crash, including the time she took us to Disney World.

It's all lies of course. We never went to Disney World. We never went anywhere outside the trailer park. She never sung us so much as a nursery rhyme and I was making my own grilled cheese from when I was old enough to haul a chair to the stove and lift a frying pan. My mom was definitely not going to win the world's best mom award. She was strung out all the time and she died of an overdose, not in a car accident. Even though the adults around me tried to tell me she had gotten sick and died from a fever, I knew the truth. I wasn't blind; I had seen her and my dad crushing up small white pills into a powder and snorting it. I had seen them both passed out on the sofa, so out of it I couldn't even wake them when the toaster oven caught fire one time. Five years old and I put the fire out myself with a bottle of Kool-Aid. I had watched my mom shoot up heroin many times and had learned to keep the syringes away from Daisy's roaming toddler hands.

But Daisy doesn't need to know any of this.

I sink down to the floor beside her in the closet, my shoulders hunched, and I punch my knee with my fist. I don't know why I care that he took the photo. It's not like I have good memories of our mom. But I wanted Daisy to and now she's upset, tears streaming down her face.

'Why did he take it?' she asks.

He's probably going to take it to the pawn shop, get whatever dollars they offer him for it and then trade them for a baggie of heroin. The photo will end up tossed in the trash. I don't tell her that. I reassure her that we'll get it back.

A minute later we hear the door to the trailer slam and a few seconds after that I let out the breath I've been holding.

'Rose?' Daisy whispers.

'What?' I answer, trying to keep my anger out of my voice.

'I did a pee.'

I look down at the patch of urine that's darkened her pajama bottoms and I sigh.

'It's fine,' I tell her, the acrid smell of it hitting my nostrils. 'Don't worry.'

'I'm sorry,' she says again, her voice quavering.

'It doesn't matter,' I tell her.

I lead her out of the closet and help her undress. I toss the wet pajamas and underwear aside and dig out a pair that aren't clean but aren't stinking either, and help her put them on. Then I find a pair of leggings that have dirt stains on the knees, but will have to do. We're all out of clean clothes. I don't know the last time we went to the laundromat. Maybe I could borrow some money off Jeanie, our neighbor, and haul a bag of dirty clothes there. But I worry that if I start asking for money off the neighbors, the next thing we'll have the social services people showing up on the doorstep and if that happens I know they'll split Daisy and I up and put us in foster care. It's what happened to a kid I go to school with: Abby Watts and her three brothers and sisters. They were all put in separate foster homes and the younger sister got adopted and now Abby cries all the time and when I asked her if her foster parents were nice, she showed me the bruises on the insides of her arms.

Sometimes I think maybe it's worth the risk. Maybe we wouldn't get split up and we'd get nice foster parents. Daisy could get adopted by a kind family, one with a big house and a pool, and enough money to buy her pretty dresses and dolls and even a pony. She wants a pony. And she's still young enough and pretty enough that a family might want her, even though she's not a baby.

I know I'm far too old to ever get adopted. I might even end up in a group home. It would still be better than living here in this trailer with our dad, but the thought of losing Daisy stops me short. What if she didn't get adopted? What if she ended up in a foster home like Abby Watts and I wasn't there to look after her? At least here we have each other and I can look out for her and protect her. Round and round these thoughts go, and I can't ever decide what to do.

I wish I was all grown up already and I could find a place to live – just us two. A real home with real walls and our own bedrooms, though we'd probably end up sharing anyways because Daisy likes to sleep pressed up against me. But I'm only nine so there's a while to go until I'm old enough to get a place on my own and I'll need a job first. And that means finishing school.

'I'm hungry,' Daisy says as soon as she's dressed.

I nod. I am too. I'm always hungry. My stomach

growls almost constantly. There's no food in the trailer; I hunted around earlier, searching for anything to stave off the hunger pangs and all I dug up was half a stale pretzel, lodged in the toaster oven and forgotten about for who knows how long. I warmed it up and gave it to Daisy for breakfast, making do myself with licking the salt it left on my fingers.

'OK,' I say, standing up. 'Let's go.'

'Where are we going?' she asks as I lead her over to where our boots are.

'On an adventure,' I tell her, and we leave the trailer, letting the door swing shut behind us.

It's a two-mile walk to town and I need to distract her or she'll whine the whole way so I start telling her a story, one about an ogre who eats little girls. But these two girls find a magic spell book and place a curse on the ogre, sending him to sleep for a hundred years.

'Why don't they kill him?' Daisy wonders.

I shrug. 'They don't want to,' I answer, though she has a good point. Leave the ogre alive and in one hundred years he's only going to wake up and go eat more children.

By then, we're outside the Pay Less Discount supermarket in town. The parking lot is pretty busy, which is a good thing. More people means it's easier to shoplift without anyone noticing. I set Daisy down and give my back a stretch. Even though she's skinny as a stick she felt heavy enough after the first quarter of a mile.

We time our entry into the store so we're following a woman inside who could pass as our mom if anyone were paying attention. As she grabs a shopping cart, she gives us a funny look, so I pull Daisy quickly down the aisle with the hot dog wieners. I grab a packet and, checking to make sure no one is watching, shove it quickly up inside my sweater. Next, I sneak a pack of six hot dog buns inside my coat pocket.

I decide that's enough for now, but as we make for the door, Daisy digs her heels in, noticing the candy by the checkout. I shake my head at her but she makes her eyes all big and puppy-like and so I relent. 'Go do that thing,' I whisper to her.

She grins and slips free of my hand then runs up an aisle yelling 'mommy!' like she's lost or having a tantrum. The checkout lady and half the store turn to see what's happening, and I snatch a packet of Sour Patch Kids and cram it under my sweater alongside the hot dogs. Then I make for the door.

'Oi!'

I freeze.

'You, kid!'

I look back over my shoulder. The checkout lady is pointing a finger at me. 'I saw you. You just stole some candy!'

I take off running, colliding with a shopping cart

being pushed by the woman who now I see her up close looks nothing like our mom. I almost take a tumble but manage to right myself, as well as keep hold of the hot dog wieners that are slipping out from under my sweater. As I keep running, I turn to look for Daisy, spotting her pelting after me, her arms and legs flying.

'Stop!'

A security guard is trying to cut me off, but Daisy shoves her little body sideways into a display of apple cider and pumpkins. The bottles go crashing to the ground and the pumpkins roll like bowling balls, tripping the man up. He lunges to grab her but Daisy ducks him, shrieking.

We meet up by the door and I grab her hand and we run until we are out of breath and then we collapse in fits of laughter. I pull out the wieners and the buns and we picnic right there on a scrap of wasteland behind the old elementary school.

Chapter Three

Present

Making sure I have my envelope of money stuffed in the inner pocket of my jacket, I step outside. I pause on the front stoop, taking care to lock the door behind me and to wedge a tiny pebble in the rim of the screen door so I will know if anyone has tried to enter the cabin in my absence.

Training my attention on the forest, I wait for a few minutes longer, paranoia making me wary, before I hurry toward the lake. My grandpa used to joke that just because you're paranoid, doesn't mean they aren't out to get you, and I try to imagine what he'd tell me to do if he were still alive. He'd say: *Keep your wits about you and make sure you don't get caught.* But he never did have much respect for the law. I guess in that sense, we are now very similar.

The kayak is resting on a rack by the shore. It's heavy but I manage to lift it down and drag it over to the edge of the jetty. There's no knowing if it's watertight. I should have checked before now but I haven't had the energy or the inclination to do anything since I got here. It was only this morning that I finally forced myself up and staggered outside to chop wood, propelled less by the cold and the damp encroaching on the cabin, and more by the promise I'd made to myself to see this through. This isn't the end. Not yet.

Gathering my strength, I push the small boat into the water, keeping a grip on it as I wait to see whether or not it will sink.

It stays buoyant so I gather the paddle and gingerly climb in, praying I don't flip it. I can't imagine how I'd ever get warm again if I fell in. The boat rocks dangerously, splashing water onto my lap, but I manage not to overturn it and so I push off – navigating slowly until I get the hang of the paddling – making toward the opposite shore, which is a couple of miles away and barely visible.

I glance over my shoulder back at the jetty, wanting to imprint the location on my memory for my return journey, and using reference points – a strand of very tall firs, a boulder at the water's edge – to help orient me. The cabin itself is invisible from the water, nestled as it is among the trees, and that gives me comfort.

It doesn't take long before my muscles – unused to exercise – start to ache and sweat begins to trickle down my back. I press on though, enjoying after a time how the ache blots all else from my mind and the repetitive motion of the blades slicing through the water silences the thoughts in my head. The afternoon sun glints off the surface of the lake and the trees spring up like sentinels around its edge. It doesn't escape me that the setting is beautiful, breathtaking even, and I realize that's the first time in months I've noticed the beauty in anything. It feels wrong. Unearned. The world should never be beautiful to me again and a sharp pang of guilt assails me. I look down at my knees and keep paddling.

A handful of geese erupt suddenly up into the whipped sky, making me startle and look back up. They take off flapping, brushing the water before gaining elevation and soaring over the tips of the pines in their flight to who knows where. I am jealous of those birds and their freedom, their ability to fly off to wherever they like, and so I cut my gaze from them and focus back on my knees.

I've studied the fusty map that I found in a drawer back at the cabin and it's tucked in my jeans' pocket just in case I need it. Directly opposite from the cabin there is a channel that narrows into a stream and that's where I am heading.

After what seems like hours, I approach the channel

entrance. I am so tired from paddling that I have to dig deep to find the reserves of energy to fight the wind and steer the kayak in the right direction.

Here the wind dies down, and I feel an alertness come over me. I'm closer to civilization now, to people, to danger. I can only hope no one is out in this bitter cold and that if I do run into anyone they won't think it strange to see a woman alone in a kayak in this weather. Rounding a curve, I spot a thin stretch of beach and behind that a hill, on which sit several concrete picnic tables. That must be the state park. There's a camping ground too nearby, but I'm praying that it's closed for the winter.

Though I don't see anyone, which reassures me, I keep going, past the beach and on a bit further until I see a patch of shoreline that's barely six feet long and backed by undergrowth. I glide toward it, jolting as the kayak hits the gravelly bottom. After standing up carefully, I leap onto dry land, then haul the boat up behind me, covering it with some branches and looking around anxiously as I do to make sure I'm not being watched.

It's a mile-and-a-half hike to the store, and then I need to make the reverse journey, and it will be dark by around four thirty. I need to get a move on if I'm to make it back in daylight.

I scramble up the bank and look around, fixing the location in my head. There's a trail just ahead of me and I follow it in the direction that leads toward the park entrance. Worried that a park ranger might be on duty, or some foolhardy hikers or campers might be taking advantage of the wintry beauty and isolation of the place, I keep to the path only a little way before turning off and tramping through the forest for another mile. The trees are dense, and I'm starting to panic that I've veered off course when I catch the thundering growl of a semi-truck some way in the distance. I hurry toward the sound and sure enough, within minutes, I've hit the highway.

Relieved, I glance to my left and see the gas station and general store is visible on a bend in the road up ahead. As I get close, I tuck my hair nervously beneath my hat and think through what I'll say if anyone asks questions about what I'm doing out here without a car.

My stomach is a ball of knots and for a moment, as I approach the door, I think about turning around and walking away, but I steel myself. I think about the freezing cold cabin and the fading flashlight, and my desire for matches and batteries trumps the urge to flee. I've come this far.

There are no cars parked outside and I don't know whether it's better or worse to be the only customer. I might be more memorable that way but then it also means there are fewer people around to notice me.

The door dings as I enter and I wince. Get in and

get out, I tell myself, keeping my head down and darting down the nearest aisle, away from the counter.

I hear a woman call out; 'Good afternoon!' and I halt, a tremor of fear running through me.

'Hi,' I manage to grunt, my voice rusty from lack of use. I don't turn around, not wanting to show my face, and instead I hurry further in amongst the neatly stacked shelves, trying to remember the grocery list I compiled in my head on the way here, not having any pen or paper at the cabin.

'Let me know if you need help!' the woman calls after me.

I ignore her and scan the place. The store is well stocked, with groceries but also items campers might need, like bug spray, headlamps, water bottles. Out of the corner of my eye, I notice a bait and tackle section with hunting supplies too.

I grab a box of candles, some matches and fire-lighters and then move quickly on. Knowing I won't be able to carry too much with me on the hike back, I opt for packets of noodles over heavy cans, then throw in trail mix, jerky, and a handful of high-calorie protein bars. As I make my way to the counter, I come upon a box of apples. I stare at them like they're rare jewels, a memory popping into my head of the time I went apple picking last year. Nostalgia hits me like a shotgun blast, cutting through the fog of

24

my mind like a shard of light. I can sense the dappled sun on my face, can hear laughter ringing in my ears, feel the weight of the wicker basket as it fills up with golden green fruit.

'Did you find everything?'

I startle and turn around. It's the woman – the store owner I presume. She's about sixty-five, short and with the stocky build and plaid shirt of a lumberjack. She has silver hair and a weathered face that suggests she's spent a lot of time outside. I make eye contact only briefly before returning my gaze to the shelves. 'Um, do you have batteries?' I mumble. I worry I'm too furtive-seeming and so I force myself to look back at her.

'Right over here,' she says and leads me to the display.

Affecting what I hope is the nonchalance of an average customer, I search for the right size, scanning the prices as I do.

'You're not camping in this weather, are you?' the woman asks.

'No,' I say, hoping she won't press me for any more information.

'You didn't drive here either,' she comments, cocking her head to one side. 'Where are you staying?'

My palms start to sweat. 'Um, in a cabin not far from here.'

'Oh, right,' she says, appraising me with curiosity.

25

'Whose cabin is that, then? I know everyone around here.'

Just my luck, I groan silently to myself. I should have told her I was camping. 'Er, I don't actually know the owner,' I say, grabbing the double A's I need. 'It belongs to the friend of a friend.'

God, I'm digging a hole for myself and I know it so I hurry over to the checkout, hoping to pay quickly and get out, before she can ask any more questions. She follows me and squeezes in behind the countertop. I can feel her eyes on me as she rings up my purchases, and so I angle myself away from her and pretend to study the candy bars to my right.

'Eighteen dollars and twelve cents,' she says.

I snatch a Snickers bar and throw it down with my other groceries. 'And that, please,' I reply. I reason I'll need the calories in order to row myself back across the lake, but to be honest I also felt a sudden urge for something sweet. It's been months since I ate chocolate.

She retallies as I forage in my jacket for my envelope of money, and I inwardly curse my lack of foresight when she eyes that curiously too, no doubt wondering why I don't have a proper wallet or a bag with me, and why I'm dressed like a vagrant, in mismatched items of clothing clearly pulled from a donation bin.

'How long are you staying for then?' she inquires when I hand her the money.

'I don't know,' I mumble. Why is she so nosy? 'Not long.'

'Snow on the way,' the woman continues as she hands me back my change.

I murmur agreement, watching her bag my items incredibly slowly, and having to resist the urge to snatch them from her hands and race for the door.

'Where are you from?'

'Missouri,' I answer, before kicking myself. 'Originally,' I add. Shit.

'Cold winters there too,' she says. 'And lots of woods. So I guess you'll be feeling right at home.'

Brusquely, I nod, though in my head I'm thinking that I'll never feel at home anywhere ever again. I'll never be able to stay in one place or settle long enough to put down roots. From now on I'll always have to keep moving.

She finally finishes, pushing the brown paper bag across to me, and I grab it and make quickly for the exit. But just before I reach it, I almost trip, my gaze snagged by the rack of newspapers and magazines to the left of the door.

My own face leaps out at me from the front page of the *New York Times*, and the shock of seeing myself is violent – stealing my breath and almost knocking me to my knees.

'Here, let me get that for you.'

My heart stutters. I realize the woman thinks I've stopped as I have no hands free to open the door, and she's coming to help me. Quickly, as she moves around the counter and her back is momentarily turned away, I snatch up a copy of the paper and shove it inside my open jacket, wedging it beneath my arm.

The woman appears at my side and I pray she didn't see. I pray even more that she doesn't glance sideways and notice the photo of me staring out at her from the newspaper rack. She opens the door, letting in a gust of icy air, and I step outside, my whole body trembling, though not from the cold.

'Bye,' she trills. 'Take care.'

'Bye,' I manage to murmur in reply.

Without looking back, I make my way in the opposite direction to the one I came from because I know that she is watching me from the doorway – I can feel the heat of her gaze like a sniper rifle on my back.

I walk for a quarter of a mile in the wrong direction until I round a bend and when I'm finally sure that I'm out of sight I rush across the road and dive back into the welcome shadows of the forest. With adrenaline still pumping through my body and my hands shaking, I set my bag of groceries down on the frost-bitten ground and pull the paper out from inside my jacket.

Clumsily, I unfold it and stare at myself for a long moment, and at the headline written above it: 'NYC SOCIALITE, ROSE REID, STILL MISSING'.

Chapter Four

Past

Eight Years Ago

'Rose, any chance you could do a double shift?' Rory, my manager pleads. 'Joey's called in sick again.'

I glance at my watch. It's just gone twelve. 'I can't,' I tell him with an apologetic shrug. 'I have to run. I'm late for class.'

'Please? It's a big table. It'll be a good tip.'

I turn to look at table four. A bunch of suits, probably lawyers or hedge-fund managers by the looks of it, are being seated by the maître d' who then hands them the wine list. They're probably on a business lunch, expensing it. I could make a hundred dollars in tips easily, I calculate. But then I think about the short story that I sweated blood and tears over all week – a tale about a feral child who grows up in the woods and befriends a wolf – and which I'm due to receive feedback on today from my creative writing professor: an enthusiastic, middle-aged woman called Lynn, an actual published author, who's pulled me aside more than once to tell me I've got potential but that I'm in danger of flunking because of how many classes I've skipped. I'm torn, but in the end the fact my bank balance is in the red wins out and I nod at Rory.

'Thanks,' he says, squeezing my arm. 'You're a star.'

I head over to table four, trying to tamp down the disappointment blooming in my chest. Recently, I've started to wonder if I've bitten off more than I can chew; I was stupid to think that I – a kid of two addicts, raised in a trailer park in a shithole town in nowhereville, Missouri – could ever make it in New York. I'm like a catfish swimming in a shark tank. I have no place being here. My inner voice keeps telling me that I should pack my bags and head home on the next Greyhound bus.

But every time I almost do, I think of the small classroom on the third floor of the humanities building at Columbia, where every week I meet with a dozen other students and my professor, to talk about writing and to share what we've written. That's what keeps me going – stops me from throwing in the towel – it's the only place where I feel I belong. When I'm writing,

I feel like I can tell the truth. I put pen to paper and it's like all the secrets I've been hiding, even from myself, come tumbling out.

As I reach the table, I straighten my skirt, smooth my hair and plaster on a smile. One thing I know I'm good at is waitressing. I've been doing it since I was fifteen. Although this place, Locanda, is a five-star restaurant with gleaming cutlery, blisteringly white tablecloths, and a stroppy French chef who constantly reminds anyone who happens to be in earshot that he has a Michelin star to his name, and the diner where I waitressed back home has plastic wipe-down tables, a cracked lino floor slippery as an ice rink thanks to the decades of grease dripped onto it, and a short-order chef called Hank who can cook anything, so long as it's deep-fat fried.

'Good afternoon, my name's Rose,' I say, handing out menus to the table. 'I'll be serving you today. Can I get you anything t-to . . . drink?'

I stumble on my words as I catch the eye of the man at the head of the table. He's watching me with a half-smile on his face, his electric blue eyes dancing with what looks like a mixture of curiosity and amusement. The clatter of the dining room dulls in my ears. The blood rushes to my face and I see his smile widen as he notices. I can barely drag my gaze off him to address the other customers at the table who are starting to call out their drink orders. No exaggeration, this man with the dancing blue eyes is the most attractive man I've ever seen.

Admittedly, that's not hard. I've come from a place where most of the adult male population are either meth users or alcoholics, or else backwoods types with unkempt beards and trucker caps glued to their heads. No one in the history of my town has ever worn a suit, not even to their own wedding or funeral. The standard uniform is a flannel shirt, jeans and workmen's boots.

Whereas this man is clean-shaven, with tanned but unlined skin, perfect white teeth and the confident smile of a movie star. I'm guessing he's about thirty-two, maybe a few years older, so at least a decade older than me.

Someone touches my arm and I startle. It's one of the men at the table. He's gesturing to the wine menu and asking me something about the pinot noir. Flustered, my cheeks burning, I mumble something about fetching the sommelier and hurry off. At the bar, I risk a glance back. The man is watching, and my pulse skitters. And when I finally pull myself together enough to return for their orders, I'm so aware of him that I have to concentrate extra hard to remember what the specials are.

I hadn't heard of half the items on the menu before I started this job – aioli, burrata, osso buco – and spent an entire afternoon, with the help of Google, looking everything up and memorizing it all. When I'm done explaining to the table exactly how the veal and the pan-fried sea bass are prepared, the man with the blue eyes asks me what I would recommend. His voice is deep and warm – the kind of voice you could wrap yourself up in like a blanket.

I tell him my favorite dish is the pasta arrabbiata and when he orders it I feel a stupid rush of pleasure that he's taken my recommendation.

But I regret my choice as I place his food in front of him ten minutes later, as my hands are shaking so badly that a dollop of tomato sauce splatters across the pristine tablecloth and his suit trousers.

'I'm so sorry,' I say, aghast. Oh my God. Did Rory, the manager, see? I cannot afford to be fired. I need this job. It's the only thing keeping me in college and Rory fired a waitress last week for dropping a panna cotta on a customer's lap. Panicking, I grab a napkin and dab at the splotch on the man's thigh, before I realize what I am doing and that I'm perilously close to a sexual harassment charge.

His hand settles on top of mine. 'It's fine,' he says, quietly, taking the napkin from me. 'I've got it.'

His touch is electric and it takes me a second before I pull my own hand out from under his. 'I'm sorry,' I mumble. 'I'll pay for your dry cleaning.'

'No, don't worry. I didn't like this suit anyway,' he says, laughing.

I risk a look at his face. He's still wearing the same easygoing smile as before. I can't be sure but it seems like something passes between us.

The restaurant is buzzing now with the lunch crowd and I'm covering a dozen tables. As I work I try not to look at the man, because every time I do I get distracted and almost drop plates, but I'm aware of him anyway, out of the corner of my eye, and I feel a flutter of butterflies, as I imagine him being also aware of me.

When I bring the check, he signals that I should leave it with him and, as he hands me his card, I take a peek at the name embossed on it: Ryan Reid.

Smiling broadly, I return with the receipt, but Ryan takes it without a word or a glance in my direction and I feel a kick of disappointment and then embarrassment. As if he'd notice me. He's probably married or has a girlfriend anyway. I'm being a fool.

After he's left, I start to clear the table and it's then I see the pile of notes he's tucked under his plate. I gather them up and do a double take. Normally, I get an average twenty percent tip from customers, but this is easily a thousand dollars in hundred-dollar bills. He's added a one hundred percent gratuity. I spin around, wondering if I should chase after him and give it back. Surely, it's a mistake? But he's nowhere in sight. In a daze, I stuff the money in my back pocket, feeling light-headed with gratitude. That will cover my bills for the next couple of months.

Later, when I clock off, I decide to walk the twenty blocks back to my dorm to enjoy the warm evening air. I haven't gone half a block when someone steps in front of me. It's Ryan.

'Hi,' he says.

I blink at him in surprise. Where did he come from?

'I was waiting over the road in that coffee shop for you to finish work,' he tells me, obviously intuiting my question.

I raise my eyebrows but find myself speechless.

'That makes me sound like a stalker, doesn't it?' He laughs. 'I'm not,' he reassures me quickly. 'I just er . . . I wondered if I could take you to dinner sometime?'

My tongue is still tied.

'Is that too presumptuous of me?' Ryan asks, his smile morphing into a frown.

'Yes,' I manage to blurt.

His face falls.

'I mean, yes, I'll go to dinner with you,' I correct myself.

He grins with relief. 'Ryan,' he says, offering me his hand.

I take it, feeling the warmth and strength in it, as it encompasses my own. 'Rose,' I say.

'I know,' he tells me. 'You introduced yourself at the table. It's lovely to meet you, Rose.'

For my whole life I've felt like a rickety boat, sailing on stormy seas, always on the verge of capsizing or sinking, but as he holds my hand, the boat stills and the sea turns placid. When he lets go, I feel strangely unmoored. I fight the urge to grab hold of him again just to regain some ballast.

He hands me his card and tells me to call him, and then he leaves me standing there on the corner. I watch him walk away, feeling that life just took a sudden, unexpected turn.

Chapter Five

Present

From trailer trash to NYC socialite. That's how the
story goes. Although now I suppose every story about
me will lead with something else, something far more
derogatory than trailer trash.

I am still standing in the woods, scanning the article,
when the snap of a branch makes my head fly up. I
glance nervously around, my ears pricked. Is someone
out there, watching me? The trees creak in the wind,
and there's a rustling of leaves. Feeling spooked, I
quickly stuff the paper back in my bag and move off.

By the time I make it back to the cabin, night
has fallen and I have to pick my way by the milky
light of the moon toward the front door where I
kneel down and feel with numb hands for the little
stone that I wedged in the screen door. It's still there,

reassuring me that no one has tried to enter while I've been gone.

I step inside and without even stopping to put the groceries away I head for the fireplace where I quickly stack the wood I chopped earlier and take out the firelighters and matches. I worry briefly about the chimney, that the smoke might act like a signal to anyone looking. But it's night and I doubt anyone will see it and besides, I'm too frozen to care.

It takes me less than a minute to get a fire going and I silently thank my grandpa for teaching me how to lay one. I have a lot to thank him for besides that. Namely, for taking us in after our dad died. Our grandpa hadn't had contact with our mom for years, and didn't even know she'd had kids until social services showed up on his doorstep and asked if he'd take us. He did so without any hesitation, and though he had no idea how to raise two young, half-feral girls, he did love us in his own taciturn way. He took care of us, fed us, clothed us and taught us what he termed essential life skills – how to change a tire, how to shoot and dress an animal, how to make a bed army-style, and how to cook a mean beef stew.

I sit cross-legged in front of the fire, holding out my hands until they're warmed through and my body begins to thaw. I would kill for one of his beef stews right now. I would kill for a hot bath too. In fact, I would kill for a lot of things. I smile darkly to myself:

that's not the best choice of words. My mind drifts to my old bathroom, with its stand-alone tub, marble floors, rain shower and heated towel rails. What a world away it is now. It feels like a memory of a movie I once watched. Even further in the past is that bathroom in the trailer – the one with the blocked toilet, backed up thanks to an overflowing septic tank. I remember the mold in the shower and creeping along the ceiling over our bed like dark tendrils. I have gone from rags to riches and back to rags. Likely, it was inevitable: I was always living on borrowed time.

Brushing aside the past, I take out the candles and light one, dripping wax onto a plate and then securing the candle in it and setting it on the coffee table.

The room, already warmed by the fire, takes on a coziness hitherto absent, even though the shabbiness of the worn sofa and threadbare rugs, and the cobwebs in the corners are now on display.

The rumbling of my stomach reminds me that I haven't eaten all day, besides the Snickers bar, which tasted even better than I remembered, so I head through into the kitchen, lighting another candle in here and drawing the curtains across the window, out of an abundance of caution. I put a pot of water on to boil over the little camp stove. It's the first time my appetite has made itself known in a long time, and I attribute it to all the exercise I did today.

As the noodles cook, I head into the bathroom, bringing one of the candles with me. I move to open the cabinet above the sink, catching a glimpse of my reflection in the mirror as I do.

I pull off my hat and eye the jagged scar running across the side of my head, which my hair only partly hides. It looks like someone clumsy has tried to open me up with a can opener. I run my fingers over the still-tender pink skin for a moment and then I shuffle back into the kitchen, rescuing my noodles just as they are about to boil over. I empty the sauce packet over them and sit down in front of the fire to eat, shoveling them into my mouth without much thought.

When I'm done, I put the rest of the groceries away, noticing with surprise that there's an apple in the bottom of the bag. I take it out and stare at it. How did that get in there? I had considered buying some but then I got distracted by the woman asking me something. Perhaps she noticed me looking at them. It's strange though that she would do that.

Still, I take a bite, remembering too late the story of the witch in *Snow White*. But the apple is sweet and crisp and juicy, and the flavor is a delicious shock to my taste buds. I savor every bite, devouring it in seconds, and then I lick my fingers, slowly, trying to summon some courage. I can't put it off any longer. I walk back into the living room and sit down by the

42

fire and then I take the newspaper that I stole and unfold it.

'NYC SOCIALITE STILL MISSING'. The shock of seeing my face splashed across the front page has still not worn off.

There I am, wearing a cashmere sweater and diamond stud earrings, standing in front of a roaring fire and a marble mantelpiece, which I'd decorated with a hand-made Christmas garland of eucalyptus and red berries. Every holiday season the house looked like something out of a Martha Stewart TV special. Taking a deep breath, I steel myself and move on to the article.

'Rose Reid, 31, who was reported missing eight days ago, has still not been found. Rags-to-riches Reid, a glamorous fixture in Manhattan's elite circles, caused a scandal by marrying Ryan Reid, the son of Patrick Reid, the hotelier and real-estate magnate, after a whirlwind romance.

'By the time Rose Reid was eleven, her heroin-addicted parents had both died of drug overdoses, and Rose was taken in by her maternal grandfather.'

I grip the paper tightly. How dare they dig through my life like this? I scan the paragraph. The reporter has done their research on my childhood, and there are lurid details of my parents' deaths. The tone revels in my journey from opium-riddled backwoods town to glamorous New York socialite and wife of the famous Ryan Reid. There's even a picture of the trailer I grew up in, juxtaposed beside the mansion in Westchester where I lived until only a few months ago. Angry, I keep on reading, skipping over the part about Ryan's run for the governorship and his illustrious career, first as district attorney and then attorney general. I know all the details of his rise to politics. I was there for most of it. Once I'm done reading, I return to the beginning and read the end of the first paragraph again:

'Reid escaped eight days ago from Crosshill Psychiatric Hospital in New York State, where she was an inmate.

'Connecticut police have warned people not to approach Reid, who is considered a danger both to the public and to herself.'

Chapter Six

Past

Seven and a Half Years Ago

Ryan knew that it would be embarrassing for me to have a grand society wedding where half the church – my half – would be empty, so he whisked me off to paradise instead. We married at sunset on a beach in the Bahamas, where his family own a hotel. It was just the two of us saying our vows to each other, and it was perfect, magical even, like a fairy tale. I had to pinch myself throughout the day, half-expecting to wake up and find myself back in my dorm room, having dreamed the entire thing.

Ever since then, I regularly find myself spinning the huge diamond ring and wedding band on my finger, to reassure myself that I am in fact married, that I am now Rose Reid. Six months ago, I was a penniless, working-class nobody, and then along came Ryan. He rescued me like Prince Charming, carrying me off to an enchanted castle – a huge mansion in Westchester.

There is even a wicked witch in the story – Ryan's mother, Gloria, who took against me the moment she met me and shows every sign of never accepting me. I am not good enough for her son. She has told me as much. Ryan tells me not to take it personally; no woman would ever be good enough for Gloria, not even if she was the heir to the English throne. But secretly, I know Gloria is right. I'm not good enough for Ryan. I don't admit it out loud, though. I'm too scared he might agree and decide to divorce me. And, although we've only been together six months, I can't imagine my life without him.

To say that Ryan is Gloria's pride and joy would be an understatement. He is the sun in her universe. She worships the ground he walks on and he, in return, adores her, though I have no idea how he can love such a vicious crone. I keep that opinion to myself too, obviously. I'm very good at keeping things to myself, having spent a childhood lying to teachers that yes, everything was great at home and to Daisy that yes, our mother was the best mother that ever lived.

I've told Ryan very little about my past, only that I come from a small town in Missouri and that both my parents died when I was young, and that the grandpa who went on to raise me, is also now dead, of lung cancer.

And, though he knows I grew up poor, I don't know if he *really* understands what poverty is, or can really envisage it. He's certainly never stepped foot inside a trailer. He's never had to worry about staying warm in winter or had to wear dirty socks on his hands to stave off frostbite, has never been so hungry that he's fainted.

Ryan grew up surrounded by extreme wealth. He has never flown on a regular plane, only a private jet. Needless to say, he's never taken a Greyhound bus, and he's definitely never shopped at a dollar store or had to shoplift from one because he didn't have a dollar to his name.

The day he invited me to dinner, the day we first met, I returned to my dorm room and Googled him, discovering that he was worth billions, a fact that totally blew my mind, having never had more than a few hundred dollars to my name.

I sat there for hours, reading everything I could find about him and his family, learning that he'd been educated privately, studied law at Harvard and was now a partner for a firm in Manhattan specializing in acquisitions. There were already rumors swirling online that he was thinking of running for attorney general.

I also learned from Google that he was thirty-two, the only son of Gloria Reid – a philanthropist and patron of the arts. The family money came through real estate: his great-grandfather had bought up half of Manhattan in the early twentieth century, and had also established a well-known luxury hotel chain. Ryan's father had died when Ryan was eight, in a plane crash. His mother had never remarried.

As I carried on digging, I discovered that Ryan had never been married, although he had been linked, albeit never officially, to several incredibly beautiful women whose photographs I obsessively pored over. All of them had names like Aubrey or Lucinda, and all of them seemed to come from similarly wealthy families to Ryan's. By the time I was finished with my research, I was readily considering ripping up the business card he'd given me, but something stopped me: the lingering feeling of his hand gripping mine and the sensation I'd had, standing on that street, of the seas around me calming and the boat I was in, settling.

It took a week to work up the courage to call him. He picked up on the first ring and sounded relieved when he heard my voice, as if he'd been waiting with the phone in his hand for me to call.

On our first date he took me to a small French restaurant on the Upper East Side. I remember studying the menu and worrying that he would expect me to go halves, because the cheapest starter was thirty dollars – an insane amount of money for a plate of lettuce – but Ryan told me that he was paying and asked if I minded if he ordered for both of us. I didn't mind at all. In fact, I found it liberating to let Ryan take control. I still do. I also didn't want to embarrass myself trying to pronounce the things on the menu, as it was all in French.

Since marrying Ryan, for the first time in my life, I don't have to be in charge. I can sit back and let someone else make the decisions. The anxiety that has constantly hummed discordantly through my body since I was a kid has ceased, because everything is now taken care of. *I* am taken care of.

Ryan ordered steak tartare and a tarte Tatin for dessert on that first date, neither of which I'd ever eaten before. When I told him so, he shook his head in fascination, as though he was in the company of a tribesperson from the Amazon who had not yet encountered civilization. Since that moment, he has made it his mission to seek out things that I've never tried and watch me experience them for the first time.

It started with food – caviar and oysters and scallops and lobster – and then clothes. He bought me an entire drawer's worth of silk underwear after he saw my own cheap cotton bra and panties, and then a brand-new Apple laptop when he saw the exercise books I was writing my stories in. Whenever I protested at his generosity, he told me that he'd grown up with so much wealth that he'd always taken it for granted. Having the opportunity to spoil me and see the world through new eyes was good for him; it helped him appreciate what he had all the more.

And when he found out no one had ever bought me flowers, he sent me a fresh bouquet every single day, until I begged him to stop as my dorm room was too small to accommodate them – at which point Ryan told me the only solution was for me to move in with him.

I hesitated before I said yes because I worried that things were moving too fast, but after spending a weekend lying in his arms in his king-size bed, looking out over a majestic view of Central Park, I knew I'd never be going back to the dorm. It wasn't that the apartment Ryan lived in was beautiful – although it was certainly the most luxurious place I'd ever stepped foot in – or that his fridge was full of food that I was welcome to at any time. It was because lying in his arms I felt safer than I'd ever felt. That feeling of peace I experienced with him was what I fell in love with first.

It has become like a drug that I cannot do without and that I'd do anything to keep getting a hit of. And, well, addiction runs in my family.

When I wondered out loud how he was still single, Ryan shrugged it off, telling me that the women in his social circles were all the same – rich and entitled and honestly, quite boring, his words not mine. He liked that I was different. When I asked him what he meant by that, worrying that he thought I was some unsophisticated hillbilly, he told me that I had an innocence those women didn't.

I am far from innocent. But I didn't tell him that then, and I haven't since. I want him to believe I am everything he thinks I am.

'How are you feeling?' he asks me now, kissing my bare shoulder, his hand sliding around my waist, gripping me with a possessiveness that thrills me.

I force a smile, nerves bubbling up in my stomach, making me nauseous, but I don't let on. Ryan's mother has insisted on throwing a big party to celebrate our wedding, with five hundred guests – none of whom I know – and I don't want to let Ryan down. My grandpa used to say you should never show fear in the face of a predator. Never, ever turn your back, he warned. He was talking about bears and wolves, but as I scan the ballroom, swarming with wealthy white people, in black tie and couture evening dresses, I think the lesson stands.

The men appraise me openly and give Ryan nods of approval that make me both grit my teeth and, much to my chagrin, also make me proud to have met their approval.

The women in the ballroom smile at me too, but

their eyes betray them. They are like hyenas. I have no doubt that given the opportunity they would tear into me the second the opportunity arose; I wouldn't even have to be dead, just a little injured, and they'd descend en masse to finish me off.

As I gaze around the room, I silently vow to never give them the chance.

I know that all of these women are wondering how I've managed to bag the most eligible bachelor in Manhattan and are trying to guess what magical powers I must possess to have successfully entrapped him. All evening, as Ryan has guided me around, steering me from one set of guests to the next, I've been catching snippets of conversation wafting after me.

'He met her in a restaurant.'
'She was waitressing.'
'She slipped him her number with the bill.'
'How brazen.'

I glance over at Gloria, holding court, hiding her disappointment behind a wide smile and a graciousness that could win her an Oscar. I know she's acting, because four months ago, she showed up unexpectedly at Locanda for lunch and insisted on being seated in my area. I had no idea who she was until I asked her what she would like to order and she told me she wasn't there to eat but to invite me to remove my hooks from her son. She let me know that Ryan was on a fast track to the governorship, that I was a nobody who would ruin his prospects, and that if I had any care for him, I would break up with him immediately. As she left, she handed me an envelope stuffed with five thousand dollars. A payoff.

I didn't tell Ryan. Instead, I returned the money, mailing it to her the next day. Afterwards I ignored Ryan's calls and texts. I did care about him, I loved him in fact, and I conceded that much as I hated Gloria, she was right: I was ruining his prospects. But like any addict I spent the days of our estrangement writhing in agony in bed, sobbing into a pillow, jonesing for my next hit.

Luckily, I didn't have to go fully cold turkey. Ryan's response to my week-long silence was to show up at my dorm room, with a three-carat diamond ring and a declaration of love. We could face the world together he said. He wanted no one but me at his side. At that point all my reservations crumbled. Nothing could have made me say no to him. Not even Gloria.

After Ryan proposed to me, Gloria dropped around to the apartment when he was at work, swooping in like a hawk and using her own key, to let me know, without any preamble, that there would be a water-tight prenup for when we inevitably divorced. She wagered that we wouldn't last two years.

I kept this visit from Ryan too, not wanting to drive a wedge between him and his mother. I don't want to give Gloria any more reason to hate me. But, despite my silence, Ryan clearly knows she objects to me as he didn't invite her to the wedding on the beach. I imagine that she is only throwing us this party grudgingly, for appearance's sake. Everything is about appearance with Gloria.

'Come on,' Ryan says to me now, taking me by the wrist and pulling me toward the door.

'What? Where are we going?' I ask.

He doesn't answer. He just moves smoothly between guests, politely avoiding all attempts to waylay us, and hustles us out of the ballroom. He walks briskly down one of the hotel hallways until he finds a dark alcove. He pulls me into it, crushing me against his chest and his hands slide greedily down the silk of my dress to circle my waist. 'That's better,' he murmurs. 'God, you're beautiful.'

In one swift movement, he hitches up my dress. I draw in a sharp breath. Though I'm worried someone will see us his lips on my skin are leaving a trail of fire and within seconds I've forgotten all about where we are and am reaching to undo his belt. Ryan responds by tearing at the lace and silk underwear I'm wearing and within seconds he's inside of me.

I have only had two lovers, Ryan being the second. The first was a high school boyfriend who knew nothing, and Ryan is an expert. I didn't know sex could be anything like this.

'I love you,' he whispers against my lips as he pushes me against the wall, hooking my thigh over his arm. He's usually tender, but in this moment he's rougher than normal, urgency infusing his actions. His fingers grip hard enough to leave bruises, and my back slams against the wall. I don't mind though. I like how much he wants me. It feels like in this one instance, the power slides to me.

'We should get back,' I say breathlessly, after we're finished and he's collapsed against my shoulder, panting.

'Screw them,' he says with a grin, kissing me on the lips. 'Screw all of them.' But he does pull away, reluctantly and with a sigh. I shimmy down my dress and smooth my mussed-up hair, wondering what I must look like. Is it obvious that I've just been ravished? Ryan takes my hand, leading me back toward the ballroom.

'How many of these women have you dated?' I ask him as we enter the room and note the glittering steel gazes of all the hyena women, circling us.

Ryan squeezes my hand. 'Don't think about that. I married you. I chose you,' he tells me.

It isn't really an answer, but I don't press him, too thrilled by his words. *He chose me.*

'I don't think they like me,' I whisper, noting a

striking, dark-haired woman in a black dress, shooting me daggers as we pass by. 'Everyone's giving me dirty looks.'

'That's just Di – ignore her.' Ryan laughs, taking a glass of champagne from a passing waiter and handing it to me. 'Everyone's just jealous. You're the most beautiful woman here and they can't stand it.'

I give him a smile but then something distracts me. The energy in the room has shifted. A circle is forming around the dance floor and all attention seems to be turned toward it. A gap opens up in the crowd and I see that the object of fascination is a woman gyrating like a drunk pole dancer in the middle of the floor.

My heart drops, smashing into the floor with a boom. It's my sister, Daisy.

Chapter Seven

Present

I burst awake and sit bolt upright in the bed. Sweat coats every inch of my body and blood pounds like a drum in my ears. Instinctively I put a hand to my head, to feel my scar – a reminder that it actually happened, that the nightmare is real – then I swing my legs over the side of the bed and take a few deep breaths, trying to steady myself and chase away the lingering remnants of my dream, but the images of the tree leaping out of the darkness, of the splash of red in the road, of the knife – they linger in my mind's eye.

Fumbling for the flashlight by the side of the bed I turn it on and see the blankets are strewn across the floor. I must have tossed them aside. It's freezing in the room and I start to shiver, less from the cooling sweat on my body and more from the aftershocks of the nightmare I just woke up from. I gather a blanket and wrap it around my shoulders. And then I cock my head toward the window and freeze.

A dull tinkling sound has caught my attention. It was only brief though, and I wonder if I imagined it. My pulse is thrumming still and my head is foggy but then it comes again, clear as a bell this time – the unmistakable rattle of cans. Maybe that was what woke me from my dream.

With trembling hands, I switch off the flashlight and for several seconds I sit in the pitch-darkness. Adrenaline rushes through my bloodstream but I can't move. I'm paralyzed by fear. I've been over the plan of what to do should I ever hear that sound, but now, in the moment, in the dead of night, panic has taken over.

I force myself to snap out of it and move. I slide my hand beneath one of the fusty old pillows on the bed and retrieve the fire poker that I sleep with. Gripping it tightly, I tiptoe to the bedroom door and open it as quietly as I can. What if it's the police? That woman at the store might have called them and told them she thought she recognized me. Why would she not, considering who I am and what I've done?

What if the cops are surrounding the cabin right now, ready to kick the door down and storm inside to arrest me?

The cabin is eerily still and quiet. It's as if it's holding its breath. Not even the wind can be heard sliding through gaps like it usually does to rattle the doors and windows.

Stepping into the hallway, I wince as the wooden floorboards creak beneath my socked feet. I stare straight ahead at the front door, waiting for it to burst open, but nothing happens. I inch forwards slowly, my head swiveling toward the kitchen and the back door. They could come that way too. Either way I'm trapped.

Chapter Eight

Past

Seven and a Half Years Ago

Daisy is wearing a tiny, sequined dress and high heels and she's whooping and hollering, holding an arm in the air like she's riding a rodeo bull. In the other hand she clutches an empty champagne flute. She's drunk and even from here I can tell that she's high. The guests in the ballroom, all five hundred, are staring at her slack-jawed.

I am too. I thought she was in jail. We haven't spoken in almost three years, not since the day before our grandfather's funeral. A week after we buried him, I moved to New York and then, not long after that, I heard from a friend back in Missouri that Daisy had been arrested for possession and dealing.

She was denied bail. I was happy because I thought that being locked up would help her get clean. Though I've tried to help her over the years, and got her into rehab once, she's never been able to stay off drugs for very long.

She started using when she was just fourteen. She's now twenty-one. First it was weed, then pills, now heroin. I blame her boyfriend at fourteen for dragging her into it, but maybe the damage had been done far earlier. Maybe it was my fault, for not getting her out of that trailer sooner. Or for neglecting her once we moved in with Grandpa. I know I was happy to finally be able to hand over the responsibility for taking care of her to someone else. If I hadn't, I often wonder, would Daisy be clean now? Would she be standing here beside me as my maid of honor, rather than gyrating like a stripper?

How did she even find out I was getting married? There was a mention of our engagement in the newspaper but I'm fairly sure she doesn't have a subscription to the *New York Times*. It must have been via Hank, the short-order cook at the diner where I used to work. I keep in touch with him sporadically. He must have been the one to update Daisy.

She spots me just then. 'Rose!' she screams in delight, staggering toward me across the dance floor.

The eyes of the entire room swivel in my direction,

as though a spotlight has lit me up. I want the ground to open up and devour me.

'You know her?' Ryan asks, turning to me with a frown on his face.

I want to run. I want to disappear. I want to die.

'There's my sister!' Daisy yells as she reaches me. 'My invite got lost in the mail.' She smirks. 'But I made it! Surprise!' She throws her arms around me. She's thin as a rail, but her grip is hard as a vise and I sense she wants to crush me.

I can't look at Ryan, I'm so humiliated. He knows that I have a sister, but I told him we were estranged. I didn't tell him she was a drug addict.

'You didn't visit me in jail,' Daisy says now in a voice so loud the entire ballroom can hear. I wince. I didn't tell Ryan about that either. And what the hell must Gloria be thinking? I dare not look at the people standing around us, staring in shock.

'I guess you were too busy,' Daisy says, gesturing with one arm around the room. 'I mean, good for you! Check this place out! It's the fucking bomb. I've never seen so many rich people all in one place. Is Oprah here? How about Bill Gates?'

I want to reach out and strangle her to make her stop talking but Ryan interrupts before I can.

'Hi,' he says, holding out his hand. 'I'm Ryan.'

Glancing at him, I am surprised to see a warm smile on his face. He doesn't seem the slightest bit perturbed by Daisy's appearance, though a quick look around at the people surrounding us confirms my worst fears. Everyone is eating this up.

'You must be the husband!' Daisy pronounces, letting go of me and taking Ryan's outstretched hand. 'I'm the sister.' She tries to curtsy and almost falls over.

Tears blur my eyes.

'I've heard all about you,' Ryan replies, still smiling at Daisy.

'Is that so?' Daisy laughs, cutting her gaze in my direction before turning back and giving him an appraising once-over. 'Did she tell you everything?'

'Only the good parts,' Ryan answers smoothly. He takes her by the elbow. 'Shall we step outside where it's quieter?' he murmurs in his most charming voice. 'I'd love to get to know you better, without everyone else eavesdropping.' He smirks as he says this, gesturing with his head toward the crowd gathered around us as though he isn't one of them, but rather, an interloper, like her.

Daisy narrows her eyes at him suspiciously, but his gaze is so sincere that she lets him steer her toward the exit. Ryan throws me a reassuring, conspiratorial smile, and I trail after them, head down, my face flaming with humiliation.

'Watch yourself,' someone hisses at me as I bump into them.

I look up. It's the woman in the black dress from earlier, the one who was shooting me daggers. I blink at her, mumble an apology, then hurry on.

In the lobby, I find Ryan pulling a large amount of cash from his wallet. For a moment I don't understand what is happening and I watch as Ryan says something quietly to Daisy. Whatever he says seems to sober her up. She grabs for the money. Ryan holds on to it for a beat until she nods, and then he lets her take it. He's paying her off.

Ryan gestures at one of the venue's security staff, who comes and escorts Daisy by the elbow toward the exit. She squints back at me as she goes, clutching the money in her fist like a prizefighter's winnings. 'Good luck!' she yells.

I am vibrating with shock, dizzy with shame, but Ryan is suddenly there, in front of me. He takes my hand, grounding me, and leads me back toward the ballroom. I resist, not wanting to show my face to the guests who've just witnessed my humiliation. 'I can't,' I protest, tears slipping down my cheeks.

He stops and turns me around to face him. 'Yes, you can,' he says to me gently. 'Who gives a damn what they think? You walk in there and you face them down. Dare them to say something. Trust me, they won't.'

'How do you know?' I ask, still digging my heels in, terrified of the thought of walking back into that vipers' nest.

'Because . . .' he says, wiping away my tears with his thumb. 'I'm Ryan Reid.'

I don't quite understand what he means but I let him guide me back inside. When we enter everyone turns to us and the hiss of gossip stills. I see Gloria standing in the center of the room, struggling despite her best efforts to hide her own mortification, and I look down at the floor in abject misery.

I need to get out of here. I don't belong. I can't do this. It was all a mistake: marrying him, thinking I could pretend to be something I'm not. But Ryan tugs me onto the dance floor, twirling me in front of everyone with a big grin on his face.

I see the pleasure he gets from it, the kick from showing them all that he doesn't care what they think. He draws me against his chest, and I press my cheek to his shoulder and laugh despite everything.

To my amazement, he's right. No one dares say anything, not to our faces, and I am able to tune out the whispers when I'm in his arms. I am no longer the girl in the filthy clothes, with the matted hair. I am no longer the kid who is being bullied at school, or having to run from security guards with wiener hot dogs stuffed up my sweater.

I am Rose Reid. Nothing can touch me now.

Chapter Nine

Present

Heart hammering, I slip into the bathroom and close the door behind me. It's the only room in the cabin with a lock on the door. I slide the catch across. It wouldn't hold anyone back for long, but it gives some sense of safety. It might not be the police outside, I try to reassure myself: it could be a stranger, someone who lives out here in the wilderness. I came across men like that when I was out hunting with my grandfather, people who were living off-grid in the national forest, keeping to themselves for either criminal or antisocial reasons. They scared me. My grandfather warned me to steer clear of them. But out here, in upstate New York, it seems less likely there will be people hiding out. It's too close to civilization. Having said that, isn't that what I'm doing out here? Running from the law?

I sit on the edge of the aging bathtub, clutching the fire poker in both hands and I wait, my teeth chattering from the cold and my limbs stiffening from the tension and the awkward position I'm in. Hours pass, and it's only when the first flickers of dawn start to make their way into the room through a small window above the bathtub that, still wrapped in the blanket, I stand up slowly, my body protesting.

My legs are stiff from sitting for so long in the dark, primed and waiting for someone to kick down the door. After I married Ryan and went to live in Westchester, I became a Pilates and yoga queen, keen at first to emulate the other women in his world and then because I didn't have much else to do but exercise. I'm so out of shape now though, and my shoulders and arms ache from yesterday's activity chopping the wood and rowing across the lake.

I set the poker down on the toilet seat, starting to feel stupid in the cold light of day. It was probably an animal that set the cans off. A racoon most likely. Once the sun is up, I decide I'll go outside and see if I can find any clues that might help set my mind at rest.

Exhausted, I drag myself into the kitchen to make coffee.

There's a strange hush in the air – a stillness as if the world has stopped turning and time has stood still – and I recognize it, not with the thrill of a child waking up to the year's first snowfall and bursting with excitement over the thought of sledding, but with the stomach-gripping anxiety of a child who knows that snow means being stuck inside a trailer that's as cold as a meat locker, with no food and no heating and two parents on a comedown that will definitely end in fists flying or worse. Even this many years later, the sight of snow makes me fearful, makes me want to huddle beneath a blanket in a dark corner and hide.

I pull back the curtain in the kitchen and see that I'm right: snow has fallen in the night and the world is coated in a thick, white carpet of the stuff. Beyond the trees, I can see the surface of the lake is also coated with snow. It must have iced over, allowing the powder to settle like royal icing on a cake. My breath billows in front of me with each exhalation and a thin layer of ice crystals glazes the inside of the windows.

I decide to boil some extra water to wash with. Until now I haven't bothered to wash because of the effort, but I feel the urge. My clothes are grimy, my skin tacky from days-old sweat. My hair is so greasy that the platinum blonde is looking dark brown.

I briefly wonder what all of Ryan's friends and family would say if they could see me now. I'm sure their Botoxed-smooth brows would furrow in disgust.

When I think of them, I hear their voices in my head:

'There was always something off about her, something strange.'

'She didn't fit in.'

'Of course, he only married her for her looks.'

'She only married him for his money.'

'What do you expect? She's trailer trash.'

'Weren't her parents both heroin addicts? Or was it meth?'

'Same thing isn't it?'

'She was an addict too. They hushed it up.'

And they were right about most of it: my parents, the addiction, not fitting in. I could never have fitted in among women like them; all privately educated, able to trace their WASP families back to the *Mayflower*, most with their own impressive careers, even if they'd set them aside in the name of producing the next heirs of America.

I tried at first to be one of them, to make friends with the hyenas, though Ryan warned me not to bother, that none of them were worth befriending. That they would bore me senseless with all their talk about Martha's Vineyard vacations, who was having an affair with whom, which museum boards they were being begged to sit on, and which pre-schools they had bought their way into.

I wanted to make an effort though. To show Ryan I wanted to be part of his world. But he was right: I was completely out of my depth. I didn't even know Martha's Vineyard was an island and had only stepped foot in a museum one time, much less been invited to sit on the board of one. And anyway, even if I had been able to join the conversation, the women ignored me, or shot me sour stares, like that woman Di at the party.

If they'd talked about books or about current affairs I might have been able to contribute. I spent a lot of my time reading, but these women weren't interested in anything but gossip.

So, after going to a few of these calorie-light brunches in Westchester and the city (no one appeared to ever eat lunch), I was happy to call it quits and go back to my own safe little bubble, which happily consisted of just Ryan and me, and my books.

It's possible the fault was mine. I'd never had friends, so I didn't know how to make them, and I gave up too quickly, my insecurities triggered by their sophistication and confidence. Things might have been different if I had tried a little harder.

The water is boiling furiously and I'm still standing here, staring into space, thinking about those women and about Ryan and our marriage. I wonder, if things had turned out differently, if I'd never attended that fundraiser, whether we would have gone on to be married for fifty years. Who's to know? I have a sliding-doors moment as I pour the water over my instant coffee granules, wondering how my life took such a dramatic, violent turn.

In a parallel world, maybe I'm standing in my kitchen right this moment, making coffee on my five-thousand-dollar espresso machine and then carrying it through to Ryan in his study. I am setting it on his leather-topped desk and he is reaching to pull me into his lap, setting aside his piles of work to nuzzle my neck and tell me how much he loves me. The sun is slanting through the windows and our dog, Toby, has followed me in and is lying at Ryan's feet.

In that universe, everyone is still alive.

I stir my cup of instant coffee, shaking my head, trying to dislodge the memories. There's no point in dwelling on the past or on what's happened. I did what I did. I can't take it back now.

After I drink my coffee, I start another fire in the fireplace, deciding that the smoke from the chimney is a risk I'm willing to take in these temperatures. Hopefully, any smoke won't be too visible against the bleak white of the sky.

Once the fire is going, I bring in a bowl of hot water that I've heated over the camp stove and set it down on the floor in front of me. Then I brace myself and strip naked. My body trembles from the piercing cold but I ignore the goose bumps as best I can and use soap and a flannel to give myself what my grandfather used to call a spit bath. I even stand over the sink in the kitchen and rinse my filthy hair.

As small children, Daisy and I would go weeks without washing, with no adult to tell us to or to run us a bath or even to wipe our faces of crusted snot. At school we would get teased in the playground. At six or seven years old, children understand irony and they would make fun of us, calling us Dirty Daisy and Revolting Rose. They'd hold their noses whenever we came near. Even the teachers would look at us pityingly, though none of them ever did anything like call social services, perhaps because no matter what we looked like, we were always at school. I made sure of it. Because, despite the bullying, it was a safer place than the trailer. It was warm, and I could always steal food from someone's backpack to feed us, there was running water, and the toilet wasn't blocked. There were books too, and, to be honest, I actually liked school. I liked learning. It was one thing I was good at – besides shoplifting, which I did start to excel at after a time.

After I've washed myself, I peel off the bandages on my arms. My left arm is starting to heal – the knife wounds have scabbed over – but the ones on my right are inflamed and pus oozes from them. I have a small first aid kit in my bag and I search through it, finding a tube of antiseptic and some clean gauze.

Once I've cleaned and dressed both wounds, I put on some clothes: underwear, a pair of leggings that bag around the knees and then, over those, I pull on a pair of sweatpants. I layer a cotton long-sleeved T-shirt with a plaid shirt and two sweaters. Lastly, I put on a pair of wool socks, grateful that I have them, and then I wonder how I'll go about washing the dirty things without hot water or laundry soap or a dryer. There's nothing for it. I guess I'll just have to smell. There's an irony to how full circle I've come, and I would laugh, if I was able to laugh at anything anymore.

After stuffing my feet into my boots and throwing on my jacket and hat, I step out into the brisk morning. I stand for a moment in the doorway, looking down at the snow that is buffering the door: it's about five inches deep and there are no footprints anywhere that I can see, which makes me relax slightly.

I set off, relishing the pleasing crunch as my feet sink through the crisp snow, in the direction of the strand of cans.

The cans are half buried beneath snow but they're visible; the leaves I covered them with have been knocked off. I stop and survey the ground all around, as my grandfather taught me to do when tracking animals, spotting paw prints immediately. I crouch down to get a better look at them. They're big, too big to be a racoon. A wolf perhaps? Or a mountain lion? Do they have those out here?

It was just an animal though. It's reassuring, but it makes me feel like even more of a fool for spending half the night huddled in the bathroom clutching a poker. Satisfied, I stand up, deciding to spend the rest of the morning chopping more wood. If another load of snow comes, I want to be prepared. But, really, I also just want something to do to take my mind off things, so I stop counting the days, so I stop thinking of that night. I worry I might go mad sometimes and there have been some mornings when I've woken from a nightmare and wished to God I was back at Crosshill, if only for the blissful sedation that kept all my memories blurry and impossible to reach.

As I turn to head toward the axe and the chopping stump, I see something that makes me stop abruptly in my tracks. It's a footprint in the snow, not ten feet away from where I'm standing. There are several I see now, stopping just short of the string of cans and then turning and heading away, back into the woods. Judging from the look of them, they were made by a man's boots: large with a heavy tread.

My blood mixing sharply with a fizz of adrenaline, I whip my head left to right, scanning the forest. Is someone out there now, watching me? Was it them who rattled the cans in the night, or was it the animal?

Paranoid that I'm being watched, and forgetting all about the wood, I flee back toward the cabin, slowed by the snow, which drags against my boots. I make it inside and shut the door behind me, sinking to the floor, where I sit, arms wrapped around my knees, shaking, wondering who the hell is out there and what they were doing watching the cabin in the middle of the night.

Chapter Ten

Past

Four Years, Nine Months Ago

In true Daisy fashion, she shows up unannounced again. It has been almost three years since the wedding. Daisy has somehow tracked down our address in Westchester, which is not that difficult as Ryan has earned a lot of publicity recently in his run for office and only last month we appeared in *Tatler* together, posing in the living room.

I'm riding the Peloton that Ryan gave me for my birthday, staring out the window vacantly, when Marie, the housekeeper, appears to tell me there's a young woman asking for me at the door. I'm surprised to hear this because no one ever drops by. I haven't made any friends in the neighborhood. So, I'm curious but also wary, when I open the door.

When I see Daisy, I almost slam it in her face, but something stops me. It's her appearance. She's thin but not skeletal. Her skin is pale and lined but her cheeks aren't blotched and her eyes aren't bloodshot either. Her hair is lank but it's at least seen a brush. She seems sober.

'What do you want?' I say, aware of Marie dusting in the living room within earshot.

'I wanted to see you,' she says. 'I'm clean,' she adds, and I catch a glimmer of what looks like shame in the way she ducks her head and looks down at the ground.

I frown, studying her. I'm not sure whether to believe her. She's played me so many times before, tried to convince me she's sober, and it's always because she's looking to trick me into giving her money.

'I wanted to come and see you before now, but I was too ashamed,' she says, still staring at her feet. I don't answer and she risks a peek up at me and I'm taken aback by the vulnerability on her face. The armor cladding around my heart starts to rust. I warn myself sternly not to fall for it. This is what she always does. She knows how to play a part, as well as I do. We spent our whole childhood stealing and lying and pretending. Daisy's skilled in deception. But still, the shadow of the child she was lingers in her face and for a second I want to reach for her and hug her.

'I know you don't believe me,' Daisy says. 'But it's true. I'm not here to ask anything of you, nor do I expect you to forgive me, but I needed to apologize. So . . . I'm sorry.'

I grit my teeth. Anger's much easier to hold on to than it is to let go of. I've been carrying mine around for years like a sack full of lead, alongside my shame, letting them both weigh me down. Ryan has no idea how much I carry from my other life before I met him. I thought marrying him would mean I could ditch those sacks overboard, but it hasn't worked like that, much to my unhappiness.

'Nice house,' Daisy says now, a small smirk playing at the corners of her mouth.

'Thank you,' I say, testily. She's mocking me and I'm sensitive to it. I have spent two years decorating. It was the first time in my life I had the chance to set down roots and create a home, and I took the opportunity and ran with it.

I worked with interior designers. I never had the chance to acquire any taste, so it was something of a relief to have someone else steering me. The style is very classic, I'm told. Nothing too modern or gauche. There are antiques and gilt mirrors and a neutral color scheme. I don't know if I like it, but Ryan does, and that's all that matters.

'I'll go,' Daisy says, shifting her gaze to the garden. 'I shouldn't have come. I could have written instead. I just wanted to see you. See how you were doing. I'm glad you're doing well.'

I don't answer her.

'Are you?' she asks, frowning at me.

'Yes,' I tell her, bristling at her inquiry. 'I'm very well.'

She nods then starts to turn away, her shoulders slumped, and I get a flash of a memory of her as a little girl, trudging ahead of me toward the trailer, her head bowed low as though walking up the steps to the guillotine.

'Don't go!' I call out, surprising myself.

She stops and looks back toward me.

I open the door and she smiles, sheepish, and walks inside. She hesitates in the hallway, her eyes widening as she takes it in. I try to see it from her perspective, this house with its grand staircase and gleaming marble floors, the entryway table with the vase of lilies on it. The Louis XIV mirror and the expensive art on the walls.

Worried she'll make a snide comment, I lead her through into the kitchen before she can say anything. She follows, unexpectedly meek and seemingly a little awed, like a visitor to the Vatican, and stands uncomfortably as I move around the room, filling the kettle and opening the fridge.

I can see her gaze darting from the gleaming surfaces, empty of anything except the state-of-the-art appliances that Ryan has a fondness for, to the rows of organic produce in the fridge that gets delivered in a box every week, and then, at last, settling on me, weighing me and assessing me in my Lululemon workout gear. I'm sweating from the prickle of her gaze more than the exercise.

Can she see through this façade? Can she sense that I don't belong in this world? Has she guessed my inner fear: that no matter how good I look, no matter how I carry myself, no matter how expensive my highlights and my clothes, inside I am and will always be that starving, desperate kid stealing and lying to survive? If anyone will see through it, it's Daisy.

Still unable to think of anything to say, I put the mug of tea down on the table in front of her, and she sits, perching on the kitchen chair. Her fingers play with the cup handle. I take a seat opposite and meet her gaze. Strangely enough, I want to see if the old me is still inside, recognizable to the one person who would remember her.

'You look good,' she tells me. 'Great, in fact. You polish up real well.'

I press my lips together, feeling a little disappointed and also prickling at the notion she's mocking me.

I take a sip of tea, watching her over the rim of

my cup, surreptitiously checking her for signs of drug use. She's wearing long sleeves so I can't see if there are track marks up her arms. 'How long have you been clean?' I ask, finally.

'Eighteen months,' she says, and I note the vulnerability again showing beneath the tough veneer. 'It's hard.'

I don't answer. I am feeling her out, as she is me. We are two strangers, prowling around each other, sniffing for danger. I can glimpse traces of my sister in this young, brittle woman with the premature lines around her mouth and the angular jut of her chin, and I can even see myself in her; a hardscrabble version of myself with chewed fingernails, dull hair and rough, uneven skin. I feel self-conscious of my own good health, my unlined face – the result of an expensive skincare regime and regular facials.

She breaks the silence. 'Where's Ryan?'

'He's at work.'

'And you?' she continues. 'You don't work?'

I shake my head.

She raises her eyebrows, as though amused to find me a housewife. 'Did you finish college?'

I shake my head again.

'Why not?' She doesn't attempt to hide her surprise.

I shrug. 'There wasn't much point. I was busy.' It's what I told myself at the time, but I can hear the lie when I say it out loud to Daisy. The truth is that Ryan couldn't understand why I'd continue studying full time when I didn't need a job, and then we moved to Westchester after we married, and it was too far to commute.

'College was all you cared about,' Daisy says now, bewildered. 'All you ever wanted was to be a writer and live in New York.'

'I'm close to New York,' I say, hearing the pathetic note in my voice.

She looks out the window at our manicured lawn. 'Not really,' she says.

'I still write,' I add, though that's a lie too, and I'm sure she can tell because Daisy knows me better than anyone. The last time I put pen to paper was before I married Ryan.

'What are you writing now?' she probes.

'A story,' I lie. 'It's still a first draft.'

She doesn't press but I think she knows I'm lying. 'You were always such a good writer,' she says with a sigh. 'It's a shame.'

Anger rises up inside me then, hot and sharp. How dare she come here into my house and question my choices?

'What about you? What have you been up to?' I ask, wanting to turn the tables.

'I spend a lot of time at meetings,' she tells me, wryly.

'Twelve steps, huh?' I mutter, a little snidely. I know

all about AA and NA and the twelve steps, as our parents tried it a couple of times, never to any success.

Daisy shrugs, her smile turning rueful.

'So what step are you on? The one where you have to make amends?'

'Yeah,' she answers.

So that's why she's here. I decide to get this over with quickly. 'OK. I'm listening,' I tell her. 'What exactly are you sorry for?' Instinctively, I cross my arms over my chest.

She squirms a little in her seat. 'Mainly for being a total asshole,' she admits. 'The wedding party wasn't my finest hour.'

I take a deep breath as the embers of humiliation from that night stir in me.

I have forgiven her for almost everything else: for the teenage arrests for possession and the bar fights and other brawls, even for stealing my waitressing wages when I was in high school so she could buy drugs and beer. I have forgiven her for the way she treated our grandfather and for not showing up to his funeral because she was on a bender that day, but I find it nearly impossible to excuse her for what she did at the party, showing me up like that in front of Ryan and his friends and Gloria, whose disdain of me reached another level after that night.

'But, I guess,' Daisy adds, 'mostly, I'm sorry about the letter. I shouldn't have hidden it from you.'

Stonily, I set down my cup of tea and stare at her. The letter she is referring to is my college acceptance letter from Columbia and the offer with it of a full scholarship. I never knew about it until three years later. It was the only place that offered me full financial aid and when I didn't get it, broken-hearted, I'd decided to accept my lot in life and stay put, waitressing at the local diner. My grandpa had become ill around the same time and I decided it was all for the best anyway as I wanted to stay and take care of him.

'That scholarship would have changed my life,' I tell her, thinking of how I could have deferred it at least, if I'd known about it.

'I know,' she says and for the first time in a long time I see regret and honesty in her eyes. 'I didn't want you to go. I didn't want you escaping, not without me.' She sighs loudly. 'I always felt like it was unfair. That all the good things only ever happened to you. Never to me.'

I pause to consider this. It isn't true but from her point of view, especially sitting here in this kitchen, I can see how she could think that. I soften toward her. I never expected an apology for that.

'Will you forgive me?' she asks. 'You don't have to. I'd understand if you can't.'

I feel angry with her for putting me on the spot, but in the end, I nod. She's my little sister. The kid I practically raised. The kid I would have died for. The kid I would kill for.

I will always love her to the depths of my being and then some. And, looking for silver linings, if things had played out differently, if I had gone to Columbia earlier I would never have met Ryan.

Daisy gives me a weak smile, relief washing over her and the last of the armor around my heart falls away.

'You made it in the end,' she says. 'You got out.'

I bow my head. She's right: I did get out. My grandfather had been as disappointed as me when I didn't get that scholarship and he made me promise that, after he was gone, I would reapply for college. So I did, and was surprised to discover from the Columbia admissions office that I had been accepted three years prior and even offered a scholarship. That's when I realized what Daisy had done. I confronted her over it and she admitted it, though without any remorse.

To her credit, now she's sober, she does seem to have discovered some.

'Where are you living?' I ask, changing the subject.

She looks down at her coffee and shrugs. 'Here and there,' she says. 'A halfway house for a while.'

It's news to me. A halfway house must mean she's been in prison again since I last saw her. Maybe that's where she got clean.

'Actually, at the moment I'm sort of homeless,' she confesses, giving me a quick glance.

So that's why she's here. I knew there would be something. She must notice the look on my face because she grimaces and blurts: 'That's not why I came. I'm fine. I've got friends. Places I can go.'

I doubt that very much, but I bite my lip. She isn't my problem. Not anymore. I've tried so many times to save Daisy and every time I've ended up regretting it. I will myself not to fall back into the same trap.

She finishes her tea and looks at the clock on the stove. 'In fact,' she says, 'I should probably go. I have to catch the bus. They don't run that often out here. I guess no one takes public transport. Everyone has a Mercedes or a Tesla.'

'I can give you a ride to the bus station,' I offer.

'It's fine,' she says, standing up so quickly she almost knocks her seat over. 'I don't mind the walk.'

I get to my feet too. She zips up her hoodie, which is two sizes too big and has frayed cuffs and I have to fight the urge to reach over and fold the cuffs up over her hands, like I used to when we were kids.

'Do you want to stay here?' I blurt, surprising myself. I spoke the words without thinking. Immediately, I wish I could take it back, but the hopeful look that lights her face makes it impossible to.

'Are you sure?' she asks me.

'Yes,' I say, still kicking myself for offering. 'I mean,

for a few days. That's all.' What was I thinking? But how can I throw her out, when she doesn't have a place to stay?

'Ryan won't mind?' Daisy pushes, anxiously.

'No, of course not,' I tell her, though the truth is I'm not so sure. We rarely have guests and never ones who stay over, even though we have seven spare bedrooms and could easily accommodate them. I should have talked to him before inviting her, but I can't imagine him saying no.

After Daisy's appearance at the wedding, I came clean to Ryan about my childhood – or some of it. I told him that our parents died when we were young and we went to live with our grandpa, how Daisy started getting into trouble at fourteen, first drinking and then playing truant, and then finally, falling in with a bad crowd and taking drugs. I told him how I'd tried and tried to help my sister and had finally given up and how I could never forgive myself for letting her fall down that slope into addiction. I think that's why, when I call Ryan later to tell him, a little nervous about his reaction, he tells me he understands and is fine with her staying a few days.

When he comes home from work that night and discovers Daisy at the kitchen table watching me make dinner and teasing me about how I've learned to cook something more than packet noodles, he is charming and welcoming.

He kisses her on the cheek then comes over to me at the stove, his arm sliding around my waist. 'What are you cooking?' He nuzzles my neck. 'It smells amazing.'

'Pasta arrabbiata,' I tell him, leaning into him.

It's what I make for him on special occasions. I have become quite the chef these days, having set my mind to the task. Ryan takes the wooden spoon from my hand and tastes the sauce, then kisses me again on the lips. Then he steps away, tugging his tie loose, and moves to get a sparkling water from the fridge. Usually, he drinks a whiskey in the evening, and wine at dinner. I think he's being deliberately thoughtful of Daisy and her sobriety and it makes my throat tighten.

The two of them start talking about politics, and Daisy is surprised by Ryan's liberal stances toward social care and progressive causes like support for single mothers and drug users. He starts telling her about the platform he is running on for attorney general and asking her questions about her time behind bars. He is genuinely curious about prison life and Daisy, after a while, starts to warm to her audience, telling tales about her fellow inmates and the guards that have us both roaring with laughter.

'She's great,' Ryan whispers in my ear later as Daisy loads the dishwasher. 'She can stay as long as she likes.'

I squeeze his hand. 'Thanks,' I reply, hope blossoming in me. Perhaps this time Daisy really will stay clean. I could help get her a job, find her a place to stay, somewhere nearby even.

I show Daisy into one of the guest rooms and she hugs me goodnight, and whilst she's in the bathroom I leave a pair of blue silk pajamas on the bed.

I go to bed feeling a spark of hope igniting in me. Daisy is clean. She is sober. And she is here. My kid sister is with me. And things might finally be about to change for the better.

But when I wake up the next day she's gone. And so are the pajamas.

Chapter Eleven

Present

Despite my certainty that the snow would stick around, an unexpected warm spell over the last two days has caused most of it to melt, taking the footprints with it. I am glad to see them go, but also anxious because the snow has acted as a warning system for me, almost like fingerprint dust. Every morning I've been able to inspect the boundaries of the property to see if anyone has approached the cabin in the night or been sniffing around while my back has been turned. I haven't seen any more footprints, though I've had sleepless nights lying awake, listening, convinced I can hear someone sneaking up the porch steps and trying the doors and windows.

Now, I push the kayak off the jetty and onto the water, cracking the thin layer of ice still on the surface, like a spoon on crème caramel. My nerves are frayed and the voice in my head argues with me once again that I'm being reckless going out, but I can't wait. The wound on my right arm isn't getting better. It has started to throb and the skin around it is inflamed. There's no paracetamol or painkillers in the first aid kit. I need to go into town again and get some, and some iodine too, as the antiseptic clearly isn't working. I pat my pockets to make sure I've got my envelope of cash and, once I'm reassured that I have everything, I start rowing, ignoring the pain that shoots up my arm with every stroke.

My senses are on high alert the whole way. The weather is better and I'm worried more people might be out enjoying the lake or the national forest. Luckily though, I don't spot anyone. I stop at the same place as before but spend more time covering the kayak up with branches, just to be careful – I don't want someone taking it and stranding me – and then I hike through the forest until I reach the road and see the store up ahead.

There's a pickup truck parked outside, and I decide that's a good thing. Hopefully, the owner will be dealing with another customer this time. The door dings as I enter, and I throw a quick glance toward the counter. The woman from before isn't there and, relieved, I pick up a basket and hurry over to the newspaper stand. My intention had been to grab the paper as fast as possible before moving to the grocery aisle, but the front page of the *New York Post* puts paid to that idea. Even though I had steeled myself for the possibilities, I find myself frozen at the sight of the photograph they've used. I can't breathe. All I can do is stand and stare in shock.

'Hunt for missing socialite continues,' the headline reads. 'Family offers $50,000 reward.'

It's the same photo as before – the Christmas portrait – but instead of cropping it, they've printed the entire thing this time; no one is cut out – and that has sucker-punched me.

My body starts to shake and blood roars in my ears. I snatch up a copy of the paper and shove it face-down into my basket, before hastily moving a hunting magazine in front of the remaining copies of the *Post*.

'How are you?'

I almost jump out of my skin. Turning, I find the storeowner standing behind me, smiling.

'Fine,' I mumble, before hurrying past her toward the food aisle. I grab for the nearest items I see, not even registering what they are, just tossing them into the basket. I feel like I'm wearing a flashing neon sign that screams 'FUGITIVE'. I don't want to look up to see if she's staring at me and I warn myself to stay calm, to try not to draw attention. I walk the whole length of the store as though I'm casually perusing groceries, before I stroll over to the counter.

'Is that everything?' the woman asks.

'Um, do you have any iodine?'

She points to the far corner of the store. 'Over there, on the end with the rest of the first aid,' she tells me.

I hurry over but I can't focus and everything in front of me is a blur. As I try to make sense of the labels, I become aware of someone watching me and I look up. A man is standing in the parallel aisle staring at me over the top of the shelves. He's about thirty-five, with a scruffy black beard and a sharp, angular face. He's wearing a red plaid hunter's cap and a padded jacket and he's eyeing me like he's sizing up prey.

I break eye contact and grab the first ointment I see, as well as a roll of gauze, and then I rush back to the counter.

'I thought you wanted iodine?' the woman says.

I look down and see I've grabbed a bottle of nail polish remover.

'What's it for?' the woman asks.

'Oh,' I say, caught out. 'I cut myself. Nothing serious.'

'Let me get you the right thing.' She moves off around the counter and heads toward the first aid section. I shift nervously, anxiety building as the man comes to stand behind me, waiting his turn in line. I can feel his eyes on the back of my head and I touch my hat, pushing a strand of loose hair beneath it.

I'm paranoid that he's recognized me, that he knows who I am. I'm a fugitive criminal from a mental asylum. My gaze skips to the newspaper sitting in my basket. Shit. The photo of me is visible. I nudge it, so the paper is hidden from view.

The woman returns a moment later with iodine. 'There you are,' she says, setting it down on the counter.

'Thank you,' I say.

She starts ringing me up again and, as she picks up the newspaper and the headline stares me in the face for several seconds while she scans it for the price, my whole body tenses.

'How's it going?' The woman smiles. 'How's the cabin?'

'Great,' I reply, forcing a smile as I watch her put the paper in the bag. 'I'm writing a book so it's the perfect getaway. I'm on a deadline actually.'

'You're a writer?' she asks.

'Mmm,' I mumble.

It was the story I came up with to try to throw her off the scent in case she drilled me with questions again, something I thought would sound realistic, but now I'm starting to regret it, as well as my decision to come here.

'What kind of book are you writing?'

I hear the man behind me clear his throat, impatiently.

'Er, fiction,' I blurt. 'Crime. A mystery.'

'Those are my favorite!' she says, delighted. 'Have you published anything? Would I know your name?'

'No,' I say, handing her the money in my hand.

'Oh, well, good luck with it.'

I grab the paper bag of groceries. 'Thanks,' I say, already turning away.

I bump into the man who seems to have deliberately arranged himself to block my path. He gives me a hard stare before I dart around him. I'm reminded of what it was like when I was a kid and I would steal from the dollar store: the clammy palms, the pounding heart, the fear gripping my insides as I shoved a box of mac and cheese or a chocolate bar inside my jacket and then raced for the exit. I recall the moment of euphoria I'd have when I looked back and saw no one was coming after me and that I'd got away with it.

Once I'm outside the store I walk briskly up the road, feeling none of that old elation. Instead, I feel faint and nauseous from adrenaline. I want to dive across the road and into the forest on the other side but I'm anxious that I'll be seen, and I need to keep up the ruse that the cabin is in the opposite direction to where it actually is, so I head toward the bend in the road up ahead, deciding that I will do what I did last time and wait until I am around it and out of sight.

When I reach it, I start to cross, and that's when I hear a truck heading my way at speed. I don't know what to do and I waver for a moment in the middle of the road, clutching my groceries, before I keep going, hoping to make it down the embankment and into the shadow and safety of the trees before I'm spotted, but I'm only halfway down, stumbling over hidden roots, when the truck rushes past. When I look back over my shoulder, I see the man from the store looking sideways through the window, right at me.

Damn. I march back toward the kayak, angry tears welling up. I fight them back. I can't cry. If I start, I won't stop, so I keep on, head down, refusing to stop and look at the paper, even though it's nagging at me.

It's only when I'm back at the cabin two hours later, that I pull it out and collapse in front of the cold fireplace to read it.

The sight of that photograph cuts like a knife. There's Ryan standing beside me, his arm around my shoulder, smiling his movie-star smile.

And there, between us, glowing and vibrant, is our daughter, Sienna.

Chapter Twelve

Past

Four Years Ago

When my waters break, Ryan drives me at speed to the hospital, one hand on the wheel and the other gripping mine. He is exhilarated but I am terrified. It feels like I am giving birth to Edward Scissorhands. It is trying to rip its way out of me with razor claws.

Ryan wanted a baby desperately, claiming he wasn't getting any younger and that we would make brilliant parents. I was quietly resistant to the idea, not sure I was ready for the responsibility, and truthfully, not believing I would be a good mother – but Ryan got his way.

I wanted to make him happy, so I set aside my trepidations and silenced the doubting voice in my head.

Ryan gives me everything, and having a baby felt like the only thing that I had the power to grant him in return. But now, as another bolt of eviscerating pain hits me, I am very much regretting the decision.

I had only been off the pill for a couple of weeks when I fell pregnant. It was the same week Daisy came to see me and then vanished without so much as a goodbye. Following our conversation about college, I'd started to have second thoughts about the baby idea and was excitedly pondering a return to college instead – I had even tried to think up an argument to present to Ryan as to why it was a good idea to complete my education (children of two college-educated parents are more likely to go to college themselves), but, as if the universe wanted to shatter that dream once and for all, I fell pregnant.

Four weeks later, sitting on the edge of the bathtub, grimly holding the test in my hand, staring at the two blue lines, I let my dreams of college drift away, like ashes on the wind. Ryan's joy at the sight of the positive test almost made up for my own disappointment.

He looks slightly less happy at the moment. He looks worried, though he's trying to hide it. 'Push,' he urges, mopping my sweating brow. I have to resist the urge to punch him in the face.

'I am pushing,' I hiss through gritted teeth, furious at him. He was the one who encouraged me to have a natural birth.

I feel like a failure and am quickly reaching the point of surrender. 'I can't do this,' I tell Ryan, flopping back on the bed in the twenty-second respite between contractions.

'Yes, you can,' he tells me. It's more of an order than a motivational speech.

He's been telling me this same thing for the last nine months, reassuring me that all will be fine. The pregnancy was a difficult one from the beginning. I had terrible morning sickness and spent most of the first four months in bed or heaving over the toilet. Then just as the nausea subsided, I was diagnosed with high blood pressure and the doctor ordered me to rest up as much as possible.

While Ryan was in awe of my growing bump, lying beside me, resting his head on it, I felt like I was being invaded by a body snatcher. Watching his love for the tiny alien inside of me made me anxious. Why didn't I feel the same way as him? He seems utterly besotted already, whereas I just feel resentful and angry at what it's put me through.

Another excruciating bolt of pain shoots through me and I strain and bear down like the midwife is encouraging me to but it's half-hearted. I'm so tired. I can't keep pushing. I just want to give up. But my body keeps being racked by contractions. I collapse, panting back on the bed, and notice Ryan in the corner of the room, talking to the doctor. I strain to hear and catch mention of the words *emergency C-section*. I register the terror on Ryan's face, but I feel none of it myself. Yes, I want to say. Sign me up. Get this thing out of me. I'm done with this. Why is the doctor not asking my opinion?

'Will the baby be OK?' Ryan is questioning him.

'Let's get your wife into theater,' the doctor replies, avoiding the question.

I'm so relieved when they wheel me off to be operated on. It will be over soon.

As they push me along on the gurney, another contraction hits and I scream. A nurse rolls me onto my side and I am told to lie still as they insert a needle into my spine. Yet another contraction hits and I bellow like a cow but then a blissful numbness washes over me as the anesthetic works its magic. I am rolled onto my back and smile beatifically at the anesthetist who has performed this miracle of pain relief.

They draw a blue curtain across my abdomen and get to work with their scalpels. I feel nothing, just a strange tugging sensation like my organs are being rearranged. And I feel nothing when a minute later I hear a loud cry and a nurse places a tiny baby, covered in sticky vernix and blood, in my arms.

I stare at the squished, red face of this alien creature. Did it come from inside of me? After all those hours of relentless torture, I feel oddly removed from the experience of birth. I didn't feel it come out of me. I didn't see it come out of me. Is it really my baby? I don't know what to make of it.

Ryan appears just then, at my side, scrubbed up and looking like a surgeon. He hesitates, looking down at this object in my arms and his expression transforms into one of wonder and amazement. It's as if he's witnessing a miracle. The love in his eyes is enough to melt the hardest heart, but all it does is make me feel even more removed from the situation. Why am I not feeling the same way? Shouldn't I be looking at it with the same sense of wonder and awe?

I am relieved when he takes the baby from my arms. I am so tired. I just want to sleep.

And sleep I do. When we get home a day later, my abdomen puffed up with stitches and bruised from surgery, I take to bed. Ryan spends every moment holding the baby – a girl we've named Sienna – soothing her, walking her up and down to shush her colicky cries, marveling at every particle of her being. He hands her to me to feed, and I grit my teeth as she latches on like a vampire, and I try to pretend to Ryan that I am happy and contented, but behind my smile is a rictus grin of terror. I do not know how to be a mother.

My instinct was right. I should never have gotten pregnant.

But it's too late now.

Chapter Thirteen

Present

The photo of Sienna stares out at me from the front page of the paper.

There are nights I wake up having heard her cries. I will startle and look around for her. Sometimes it takes me several seconds to face reality and accept it's only in my imagination. I have to remind myself that she's dead and each time I do the grief hits me all over again. It doesn't get better with time, like they say it does. I'm just better at managing it.

Swallowing down the lump in my throat and blinking back tears, I force myself to drag my attention from Sienna's smile and read the article.

'Hunt for fugitive socialite continues'.

My jaw clenches. One moment they're calling me trailer trash and the next a socialite, but the truth is

I was never the latter. I would attend a few fundraisers with Ryan every now and then, but that was all.

I keep on reading.

'Rose Reid, the wife of Ryan Reid, has been missing for almost two weeks, since escaping from Crosshill Psychiatric Hospital in Utica, New York, where she was an inmate.'

My hands are shaking as I read, and nausea churns in my belly. My breathing is fast to the point of hyperventilating and it's several minutes before I can calm myself and move on.

'Police are concentrating their search for the missing woman in the area of the family's $8 million mansion in Westchester, and have also alerted local police in Missouri, where Reid is originally from, believing that she may return to the area.'

That's good, I think to myself with relief, they're not looking for me here, in upstate New York. There's nothing that links me to the area. Still, I don't feel completely reassured. My encounter with that hunter earlier today and the woman at the store have left me unsettled. I make a vow to stay put and to not venture out again, not until it's time.

I keep on reading:

'An unnamed source confirms that Reid spent time in an institution prior to her incarceration at Crosshill, being treated for addiction. The same person, who spoke on condition of anonymity because they weren't authorized to speak, suggested it's possible Reid may try to take her own life. "She has a long history of mental illness," they said. "That's why she was sent to Crosshill."

'They also confirmed that Reid was suicidal at the time of her disappearance and the police aren't sure if they will find her alive.'

Who's the unnamed source, I wonder? My history of mental illness has never been made public before. Ryan made sure of that. He was running for attorney general at the time and couldn't afford the scandal. I don't know how many people he paid off to keep it quiet but I'm sure it took watertight non-disclosure agreements and God knows how much money. He's New York's attorney general now, so whatever he paid was worth it.

'Gloria Reid, Ryan's mother, is offering a $50,000 reward to anyone who can provide any informa-tion on Rose's whereabouts. "Rose has committed

terrible crimes and she must face the conse-quences," she said.'

Fifty thousand dollars. That's a huge amount of money. Who wouldn't turn in a stranger for fifty thousand dollars – especially one who has done what I have done?

Chapter Fourteen

Past

Three Years, Eight Months Ago

'She's your goddamn daughter!' Ryan yells. 'You're her mother! Start acting like it.'

His words only push me deeper into the dark well of depression I've sunk into. The shame is shoveled on top of me like dirt, obliterating the light. I feel dead inside. I wish I actually was dead.

I stare at my daughter lying on the bed beside me, yelling her outrage, and I can barely lift my head to look at her, let alone do anything to comfort her.

At first, Ryan assumed I was an overwhelmed new mother, recovering from a traumatic birth, and didn't notice my repulsion toward our daughter. He hired a night nurse to help and, when he returned to work he assumed that I would be OK managing on my own in the daytime, with Marie in the house to do all the chores and lend a helping hand. But it was a disaster. It still is.

I cannot soothe the baby when she cries, which seems to be all the time. I don't know how to comfort her because nothing I try – singing, rocking, bouncing – seems to work. It only makes her scream louder. I have started to hate her because she so clearly hates me. Frustrated by the agony of breastfeeding I quickly turned to formula, handing the task of feeding Sienna over to Marie, who now glares at me openly and purses her lips in judgment every time we're in the same room.

Marie must have reported back to Ryan on my struggles, because he started to work from home more often, and to observe me more closely when I was with the baby. In those moments I worked hard to hide my true feelings but after a week he suggested hiring a nanny to help in the day too, and I took him up on the offer, trying not to seem too keen.

She started a few months ago. A no-nonsense middle-aged woman called Jan who, rather irritatingly, but also much to my relief, can make Sienna stop crying just by talking to her in a singsong voice. She has a gift that I clearly do not possess.

'Are you just going to lie there, watching her cry?' Ryan asks. He's doing up his tie, glancing at his Rolex.

'I need to get to work, Rose. You need to take her until the nanny gets here.'

I don't respond. I don't want to touch her. I won't be able to stop her crying. In fact, she'll only cry more if I go near her. I roll over instead and drag the covers over my head. I hear Ryan mumbling something angry, before his tone switches. Soothing the baby, he murmurs softly to her and picks her up. He always speaks to Sienna in a much more gentle tone than he does me. Not that I blame him. A moment later I hear him leave the room with her and I let out a huge sigh of relief.

I bury my head under a pillow to drown out the sounds of my child's screams, which reverberate through the house. Eventually I hear the doorbell – the nanny arriving – and Marie letting her in. I hear the sound of Ryan's car tearing down the drive. I don't move. I don't sleep though. I can't – I have forgotten how to. My mind is exhausted, my body too, but I cannot sleep. I just lie there, and the dark thoughts rattle around my head like a rollercoaster on an endless loop.

After what must be hours of this, I throw back the covers and I blink in the gloom and crane my head to listen. I can't hear Sienna screaming. The nanny must have gotten her down for her mid-morning nap. Without knowing what I'm doing, I throw back the covers and drag myself out of bed. On autopilot I shuffle in my pajamas down the hallway toward Sienna's nursery and poke my head in the door. She's there in the crib, fussing but not crying.

Willing myself to feel something – a pang of maternal instinct – I step closer. I feel nothing and in that moment I realize that's why I'm here. I'm testing myself to see if any love might have grown in the night. But it hasn't.

I take another step closer and stop, standing over the crib. She stares up at me like I'm a stranger. She's holding on to her feet with her little hands and now she lets go and gives me a suspicious glare. It's enough to make me want to return to bed, but instead, I force myself to reach for her, intending to pick her up, but as soon as I touch her, her face puckers with rage and she lets out a scream. I draw back, at a loss.

Turning to flee, I spot the teddy bear that Gloria gave her lying on the ground as though it has been tossed out of the crib. I bend and pick it up. As I'm reaching to offer it to her, I hesitate.

Marie walks in just then. She finds me holding the teddy bear just above Sienna's face – and she swoops in with a bottle and picks the baby up, giving me a fearful glance as she does.

I wasn't going to do anything, I want to tell her, but I'm afraid that by voicing it I will be admitting out loud that I thought about it.

Chapter Fifteen

Present

I finish reading the article, avoiding the paragraphs that go into detail about Ryan and Sienna, then I read it several more times before putting the paper down and sitting in silence, staring into space and thinking.

I don't know how long I sit there for but it's time enough that the shadows are beginning to stretch and the light in the room is dimming. Eventually the chill in the air gets to me and I stand up and arrange some logs in the fireplace.

As the fire crackles, I carry the grocery bag through into the kitchen and unpack it, bewildered to discover that in my panic I bought a can of kidney beans, which I hate, a can of Spam and a box of Rice-a-Roni. I push the groceries aside and pick up the gauze and the iodine.

In the bathroom I look in the mirror and see how wan and exhausted I look, like I am made of tracing paper. When I was a child, looking after Daisy pretty much on my own, before we moved in with our grandfather, I felt this way most of the time – bone-tired and fragile-skinned – although it was mainly from hunger back then, less from grief.

I give up and turn my attention to the job at hand, pulling up my sleeves and unwinding the bandages wrapped around my right wrist, wincing as I do and then biting my lip as I peel them away from the raw, red wounds running across my inner arms.

The skin is still inflamed around the slash marks and it's hot to the touch. The scabs are still wet and oozing. Clearly, the infection is getting worse. I wash both arms with soap and water, sucking air through my teeth as I do. Afterwards, I pat them dry and then dab iodine all over them, the searing pain of it making me cry out. I wonder if I should keep my wrists unbandaged for now and decide I should try it.

I go back into the living room to be near the fire where it's warm and I look around. I've spent the last few days cleaning and scrubbing the floors and the skirting, dusting the cobwebs out of the corners and beating dirt out of the rugs. I found an old mop in the cupboard and some ancient cleaner and set about the task with total dedication, needing something to occupy myself with. The alternative had been lying on the sofa staring into the flames, waiting for a knock on the door.

The cabin looks much more homey now, thanks to all my hard work, and I almost regret the fact I'm going to have to leave here at some point. Two more weeks at the most. I can't stay any longer. But where will I go next?

A knock on the door interrupts that thought.

Chapter Sixteen

Past

Three Years, Four Months Ago

When Sienna is eight months old, I wake up and find Ryan sitting in a chair by the bed, watching me. I squint at the clock, bleary-eyed. It's nearly eleven in the morning but I am still not sleeping well, despite my exhaustion. I find myself awake long into the night, my mind turning circles, insidious voices whispering in my ear that I'm a terrible mother. I must have fallen asleep around dawn as I remember the light starting to creep its way into the bedroom.

I sit up, confused to see him there. 'What's wrong?' I stammer. Ryan should be at work. He usually leaves by seven, sometimes earlier. Is it the weekend?

'Where did you get these?' he asks, holding up a bottle of Ambien.

I draw a breath. How did he find them? I hid them in my bedside drawer. Did Marie find them when cleaning and tell him?

'The doctor prescribed them,' I stammer. 'Your mother's doctor.'

He seems surprised by that. I never told him about Gloria's visit a few months ago. He was out when she waltzed into the bedroom where I was lying staring into the void and yanked back the bedcovers. 'Time to get up,' she crowed.

I rolled over onto my side and ignored her. But a moment later I felt her birdlike weight depress the mattress as she came to perch on the edge of the bed. 'I know motherhood can feel challenging,' she admitted to me. 'It's not easy. Being a mother doesn't come naturally to everyone – that's a giant fallacy. But you have a healthy, beautiful daughter. And she needs you.'

I didn't respond.

'I've made an appointment for you with my doctor – he's a psychiatrist,' she told me. 'It's in an hour. Get up. Get showered. I'll take you.' She poked me with a sharp finger when I didn't budge.

'If you don't want Ryan to start looking elsewhere, you'll do as I say.'

Those words were the fuel that finally got me

moving. The thought had already been keeping me awake at night and Gloria voicing that worry stirred something in me: a paralyzing fear that Ryan would soon tire of me and ask for a divorce.

Doing Gloria's bidding, I dragged myself out of bed and into the shower. After I'd washed, I pulled on some sweatpants and a hoodie and followed Gloria out the door, head hanging low.

We didn't speak on the way to the doctor's office. I was too exhausted. I leaned my head against the car window and closed my eyes. I was an animal dragged out of a burrow in the midst of hibernation. The world felt hostile and overwhelming. I wondered why Gloria, who had made no attempt to disguise her loathing of me, was bothering to help me, then it occurred to me that it wasn't out of care for me or my marriage. She was only doing it to protect Ryan's image, which had been burnished thanks to the new publicity strategy portraying him as a devoted family man. Gloria was worried that image might shatter in the event our marriage fell apart, and that he might not make it all the way to the governor's mansion as a result.

The doctor saw me for five minutes, informed me I had the baby blues and handed me a prescription for antidepressants and Ambien to help me sleep.

I started taking the antidepressants that same day and when Ryan came home from work, he found me in the kitchen, dressed and cooking dinner with Sienna asleep in her bouncy chair by the table. It took a monumental effort on my part to play the role of contented wife and happy mother, but I was determined.

I took an Ambien that night and I slept for twelve blissful hours. Very quickly, I fell into the habit of needing it in order to sleep, and then not just at night but to keep me calm during the day. The antidepressants kicked in after a few weeks and helped mute the thoughts looping eternally in my head: that I was a bad mother, that I didn't love my daughter, that I wished she had never been born.

They mute the thoughts, but they haven't made them entirely go away.

'It's eleven in the morning,' Ryan reminds me now, shaking the Ambien bottle in my face. 'I couldn't wake you. How many of these did you take?'

'I don't know,' I stutter, though that's a lie. I took two last night before bed.

'Are you only taking them at night to sleep?'

I swallow. 'Sometimes in the day too,' I admit.

He glowers at me and I feel a rush of shame. 'You're addicted.'

'I'm not,' I argue, on the verge of tears, but I look at the Ambien and start to wonder. I am taking more than the recommended dose on the label. I like the way it makes me feel, how it helps me get through the days without falling apart. How it stops Sienna's wails from sounding like nails on a blackboard. The thought of going without it terrifies me. I have also hidden it from him. These are all the behaviors of an addict.

'Addiction runs in your family,' he tells me tersely.

I have no comeback to that. 'I've got it under control,' I tell him, starting to panic at the thought he might take the bottle away.

He gives me an arch look and I realize that's exactly what an addict would say.

'I've arranged for you to spend some time in rehab,' he tells me, standing up. 'Getting treatment.'

'Treatment?'

'For this and for your depression. You've not been yourself since the baby.'

'But . . .' I start, my mind frantically trying to clear a path to reason. All this talk of rehab is shockingly out of the blue and sudden. I feel like we need to pump the brakes and talk about it some more. I can quit. I will swear never to take them again, even though the idea terrifies me.

'You don't want it to become a bigger problem, do you?' Ryan says gently, and his look stills me. He seems to be implying that I am becoming a problem for him. And I know how important it is that I don't mess up or do anything that might jeopardize his career.

'It's more like a spa,' he reassures me, taking my hand and speaking more gently now that he's received my acquiescence. 'It'll be good for you. Think of it as a much-needed vacation.'

I bite my tongue and blink back tears.

It's lies though; it isn't a spa. It's a psychiatric hospital – albeit a fancy private one called the Sanctuary. The marketing people must have thought that making it sound like a yoga retreat would take the stink off with its rich clientele.

Is has en-suite rooms, beautifully landscaped grounds and a restaurant on site that would put Locanda to shame, but they cannot disguise the fact it has locks on all the doors, bars on all the windows and more security than a maximum-security jail.

And, though the people who greet me and walk me inside for the intake session tell me I am a patient, it's not true. I am a prisoner.

Chapter Seventeen

Present

There's another knock on the door.

I stand there in the middle of the cabin, braced for the kick to the door and a stampede of men in uniform coming to arrest me. I close my eyes, accepting that this is the way it will end. But nothing happens. Instead, whoever it is, knocks again.

My eyes fly open. Who the hell could it be? I consider ducking down behind the sofa and hiding until they go away but I'm also curious to know who's found me. I hesitate, adrenaline coursing, unsure what to do. And then someone calls out 'Hello?' and immediately I recognize the voice.

I unglue my feet and walk into the kitchen. As I reach for the door I pause and yank down my sleeves to cover my wrists, then I try to arrange my face into what I hope is an expression of casual innocence, before I open it.

'Hi,' I say.

It's the woman from the store. What is she doing here? And, more to the point, how did she find me? Surreptitiously, I scan the woods behind her, wondering if she's come alone, but there's no sign of anyone else and no cars or police vehicles either.

'Someone saw you out in the kayak,' she says, as though she has read my thoughts. 'And there aren't too many cabins on this side of the lake. I know most of the owners, so I put my detective cap on.'

It takes a monumental effort to keep smiling at her.

'I parked on the road,' she goes on, jerking her head in the direction of the gravel track that cuts through the forest about a mile north from here, in the opposite direction to the lake. 'Saw the smoke.'

My smile falters. I turn my head to the sky and see the fat cloud of smoke wafting up from the chimney stack into the brilliant blue sky above. I should have thought twice before lighting that fire. I look back at the woman, still unsure what she's doing here.

She thrusts her hand toward me. 'You forgot your change,' she says with a smile.

In her palm are four dollars and an assortment of coins. I was in such a fluster earlier I must have forgotten to take it.

'You didn't need to do that,' I answer.

'Yes, I did,' she says. 'I would have come sooner but I had to wait until someone could take over for me at the store.'

She pours the money into my palm. When I look up, I see she's watching me like a hawk, and my stomach flips with anxiety. I feel certain she knows who I am, or at least suspects, and is here to verify those suspicions. My mind flashes back to the newspaper article and to the fifty-thousand-dollar reward Ryan's family have offered. Has she heard about it?

Pinpricks of sweat break out all over my body and across my hairline. My instinct is to try to get rid of her, but I'm afraid that will look even more suspicious. In a split second, I make a decision. 'Do you want to come in?' I ask with a smile.

She looks surprised. 'Are you sure?'

'Yes,' I say. 'Have a cup of coffee. You came all this way. It's the least I can do.'

She steps inside, looking around, as though scoping for clues to who I am.

'I'm sorry, the place is a little rustic,' I say, wondering why I'm apologizing. It's not as if the place is mine.

She shuts the back door and shrugs. 'Well, it's been empty for a while now. Since old Kurt passed away. When was that?' she muses, frowning to herself. 'Must have been 2005 or so. Nice fella. I wasn't sure what happened to the cabin after he died. I heard it passed to someone in the family, but we never saw anyone come by. Not until you. Figured they'd forgotten all about the place.'

I busy myself making coffee, my hands shaking a little as I fill the kettle and set it on the stovetop. I don't want her asking how I know the family. 'I'm sorry,' I say, trying to change the direction of the conversation. 'I only have instant. And I don't have any milk.'

'No mind, I like it black,' she says.

I reach for the jar of coffee in the cupboard and when I turn back, I see she's staring at me with a curious expression on her face, like she's trying to place me. My mind races for something to say to distract her.

'How long have you lived out here?' I blurt.

'Seventy-one years.'

My eyebrows shoot up. 'Wow.'

'My whole life,' she says, proudly. 'Store belonged to my daddy. I took it over when he died.'

'You must like it out here, then?'

She nods. 'It's a small community. Swells in the summer of course with the tourists, but yes, I like it. It's nice to know all of your neighbors. Feels good knowing that there are people looking out for you, and vice versa.'

I make a murmuring sound of agreement.

'You don't get that in the city, I don't imagine.'

'No,' I say, spooning the coffee into mugs. 'I guess not.'

She's fishing for information. It's obvious. I think through what lies to tell her about myself that might throw her off the scent.

'I'm Gwen by the way,' she says before I can say anything. I spin round and find her holding out a hand.

'Emma,' I answer quickly, shaking hers.

'Nice to meet you, Emma.' She says the name with what looks like a twitch of a smile.

My stomach tightens and all my muscles tense as I try to force a smile in return.

Unable to hold her gaze any longer I extract my hand from hers and pour the not yet boiling water into the mugs, then I busy myself stirring the coffee granules. I don't know what to do, how to brazen this out. Should I try telling her some lies, hoping it will be enough to cast doubt on her assumptions? Or should I come clean and admit who I am? But that's taking a huge gamble. What can I say or tell her that would outweigh a reward of fifty thousand dollars? Nothing.

Instead, I hand her the drink.

'It's a shame they've let this place go,' Gwen comments, taking the mug and moving to peer into the hallway. 'Although I thought it would be a lot worse. There's nothing a coat of paint and some general maintenance wouldn't fix.'

I eye her warily, my pulse racing and my mind spinning out as I try to figure out what to do. She walks out into the hallway and I follow her, startled at her boldness as she keeps going and walks right into the living room. 'At least the chimney is clear,' she comments. 'You're lucky. I've seen cabins burned to the ground by owners who never get around to sweeping them. Next thing you know they've lit a fire in the grate and the whole place goes up in flames.'

I grit my teeth as I watch her inspect the living room. Too late, I notice the paper sitting on the footstool by the fire. I move to stand in front of it before she can notice the front page and the photo of myself, Ryan and Sienna smiling happily into the camera.

'Are you managing to get much writing done?' she asks.

I stare at her blankly for a split second before I remember my previous lie about being a writer. 'Er, yeah, I am,' I say.

She studies me over the rim of her mug as she takes a sip of her coffee.

'I was actually right in the middle of it,' I add, nerves jangling.

'Oh,' Gwen gasps. 'Sorry. You should have said. I don't want to interrupt you while you're working.'

'It's OK,' I say. 'I invited you in. It's nice to have company.'

'Are you using that?' she inquires, tipping her head toward a typewriter in the corner of the room.

I glance at it. I've noticed it before, obviously; I even wiped the dust off it during my cleaning spree the other day, but I've not really paid it any mind. 'Oh no,' I reply, shaking my head. 'That was here before. I don't think it works. I've been writing by hand.'

'It's peaceful out here,' Gwen offers. 'I can imagine it's the perfect place to write. No distractions, apart from strange old ladies interrupting you.'

My forced laugh sounds strangled.

'How are you managing without any electricity?' she asks, pointing at the candles.

I hope my voice doesn't betray my panic. 'It's fun,' I tell her. 'It's like camping.' I think about how many times my parents forgot to pay the electricity bill or just used the money for drugs instead, and we were cut off.

Gwen studies me curiously. 'Where is it you said you came from?' she probes. 'Missouri, wasn't it?'

Damn it. I should never have mentioned where I came from.

'That's a long drive,' she says, looking impressed.

I don't contradict her. I'm too furious at myself for screwing things up so badly. I should never have gone to the store.

She crosses to the window and peels back the curtain. 'I parked on the forest road as I wasn't sure the track in would be clear. There used to be one all the way to the cabin, a driveway of sorts, but it's grown over now. And there are a couple of trees down too, I noticed.'

'Right,' I murmur.

'How did you get here?' She lets the curtain drop and turns back to face me. 'I didn't see a car anywhere around.'

'A friend dropped me off.'

'The friend who owns the place?' There's no mistaking the edge in her tone. This woman is worse than a detective.

'His girlfriend.'

'That's nice of her.'

Her eyes keep searching the room. She spots something and her gaze lifts to meet mine and with a sinking feeling I know she's seen the newspaper. She steps closer and I feel like a bug caught in a spider web.

Gwen studies the tabloid and shakes her head. 'Awful story, that,' she says, tutting under her breath. 'Such a tragedy.'

I swallow again, trying to dislodge the thorny mass in my throat. For one brief, terrible moment I think about lashing out, grabbing the woman, hitting her, doing whatever it takes to stop her from saying another word.

An idea springs into my mind of locking her in the bathroom, tying her up somehow, and buying myself enough time to flee before anyone comes looking for her. But if I do that, then I'll be giving myself away. The whole plan will be ruined.

I cast a sideways look at the poker standing beside the fireplace.

'I wonder what made her do it.'

My eyes jump back to Gwen. Her expression has altered. She looks almost sympathetic. I watch her take another swallow of tepid coffee. My own is growing cold in my hand.

Realizing she's waiting for me to say something, I make a grunting sound in the back of my throat in response. My heart is pounding in my ears. Gwen continues to stare at the paper and then looks back at me. 'If you like,' she says, 'I'd be happy to drop groceries by if you need me to. Save you the trip. It's a long way for you to come to the store without a car.'

I bite my lip. It feels like another coded message – but how can I know for certain? Am I reading into it?

'Thanks, but I'm OK,' I say.

'Are you sure?' she asks, her eyebrows rising. 'It's not a bother. I'd like to help.'

I don't know how to answer her. It would save me the danger of running into someone, like the man in the truck, but at the same time I don't know if I can trust her. Does she know who I am? Has she figured it out?

'OK,' I finally say. 'But I don't have a landline and I don't have cell phone service out here either, so I don't know how I'd get in touch to let you know what I needed.'

'You could write me a list now, and I can bring it in a few days' time.'

I hesitate. I don't have any paper, but I've just told her I've been writing my book by hand. Having said that, if she knows who I am then she knows I'm lying about being a writer so what does it matter?

She waits for me to move or say something and when I don't she digs in her purse and pulls out a scrap of paper and a pen, offering them to me. 'Here, use this,' she says with a small smile tweaking the edge of her mouth.

I put my coffee cup down on the mantelpiece and take the pen and paper from her, my mind drawing a blank. I can't think what to write. Paranoia buzzes around my head, convincing me this is somehow a trick, that I'm making a mistake trusting her. Why would she not report there was a killer living in the woods?

She gestures at the pen in my hand. 'Are you done with the list?'

I look down at the blank scrap of paper.

Apples, I scrawl, before adding a few more items, including milk. I hand the list back to her and she takes it and pops it in her bag.

'I'll come by Thursday,' she tells me. 'Thanks for the coffee,' she says, draining what's left of it. She moves for the door. 'I'll let you get back to your book,' she says. And with that she walks out.

Chapter Eighteen

Past

Two Years, Four Months Ago

I have been home from the Sanctuary for six months and Ryan still hasn't touched me. Previously, our love life was active, but when I do the math, I calculate with shock that he has not been near me since before I gave birth.

I have never been the one to initiate things – he prefers taking the lead – and so I have waited, trying to be patient, aware that I needed to rebuild trust, but he has made no effort to reach for me and I have started to worry that perhaps he no longer desires me or worse, no longer loves me. Not that I would blame him. For a while there I was not myself.

The doctors at the Sanctuary officially diagnosed

me with postpartum psychosis but I have climbed out of the dark well of despair and back into the light of day thanks to the right medication and hours of therapy, a lot of it focused on my own early childhood trauma, and I know now that a lot of long-buried emotions had been triggered by the birth of my own child.

Once the chemicals in my brain were balanced and I was weaned off my reliance on Ambien, I couldn't believe the difference. It was night and day. I was flooded with disbelief and shame that I ever looked at my baby with revulsion or wished she'd never been born. It's something I'm still struggling with, though as my therapists reminded me, shame is the most damaging of emotions.

I have been focusing for the last six months on bonding with Sienna, making up for lost time. The moment I returned home, and saw the nanny holding Sienna's hand, I was overcome with a heady rush of love. It felt as if the whole time it had been there, but trapped behind a dam, but the wall had finally given way. Since then, it's only grown.

I spent days getting to know her, feeding her, playing with her, reading to her. Ryan even let the nanny go after a few months, after I convinced him that I was capable and things seem to have returned to a more normal state of affairs. He goes to work. I stay home with Sienna, under Marie's watchful eye. We go to the park, we play in the garden, we go to the library, we read books together, we nap together. Sienna and I are doing well. But Ryan and I are not.

Though he visited me every week while I was in rehab, and called me every day to check in, there is a huge distance between us. He is not unkind but he is not his old tender, loving self either.

The thought terrifies me that while I was away he found someone else. It's a possibility, though one I've been trying to ignore. But he is an attractive man. And I'm sure all those hyenas caught wind of my situation and were instantly scratching at the door to be let in. Would Ryan have been tempted by any of them?

As soon as I got home from the Sanctuary, I was determined to win him back. I started to exercise daily even more than I used to. I have had my hair cut and colored. I have made a big effort with my appearance, but to no avail. He doesn't even seem to notice when I wear his favorite dress or cook his favorite dish – pasta arrabbiata – or when I wear only a silk negligee and perfume to bed.

This morning, I have decided to finally address things. While part of me would prefer to remain in blissful ignorance, the other part needs to know. The moment he leaves for work I put Sienna down for a nap and then I head into our walk-in closet and search the pockets of his suits, rifling through them all, looking for clues – for receipts he might have left, or for a lipstick stain on his collar.

I find nothing in his pockets and so I go downstairs and slip into his study when Marie is occupied in the kitchen, and I search his desk. I find no evidence there either, that he is being unfaithful. Sitting back on my haunches, I let out a sigh of relief and shake my head. I'm being paranoid. I just need to give it time and work harder at being better.

Ryan comes home on time that evening and to my surprise he finally reaches for me. He kisses me on the lips as I stand at the stove making dinner, and asks what I'm making. My knees weaken with relief.

Later that night we make love for the first time since Sienna's birth and it's amazing; the sweetest, most tender love I think we've ever made. I wipe away a tear afterwards, as I lie with my head on his chest, and he strokes my hair.

'Do you forgive me?' I ask him.

'Of course,' he replies, kissing my forehead. 'You weren't well. You weren't yourself.'

'I love you,' I whisper.

'I love you too,' he says, kissing me. He rolls over and gets up, out of bed and I watch him go. And that's when I notice the scratch marks on his back.

Chapter Nineteen

Present

I watch Gwen vanish into the dusk, heading back to her car. The minute she's gone the voice in my head yells at me to get moving before it's too late. She knows who I am and is luring me into a trap. She came out here to the cabin to get a better look at me and to confirm her suspicions. She's right now about to drive to cell phone coverage and then she's going to call the police and rat me out.

I weigh up the options. If I stay, there's potential that Gwen might turn me in, but there's also a chance that she hasn't figured out who I am at all and I'm being paranoid. If I leave, there's a big chance I will be seen by someone, recognized, and probably captured by the police.

But I still run to the bedroom, grab my backpack

from under the bed and start tossing clothes into it in a flurry of panic. I am willing to take the risk.

I've had this feeling so many times before that it feels familiar. The instinct to run is twisted into my DNA: a survival mechanism from childhood that's never fully left me. I guess it started with me running from the dollar store before I could get caught for shoplifting. Then, as a teenager I applied to every college that I could, desperate to get out of the small town where we lived, terrified if I stayed I'd turn out like my parents or like Daisy.

I ran from the past. I ran away from Crosshill, too.

I flee from problems. That's what I do. I had a therapist once tell me that I'm running away from the trailer that I grew up in, and from my father's dead body. And she was probably right. I still dream about the day I walked into our home after school and found him with a shoelace tourniquet tied around his bicep and a syringe sticking out of his arm, and every time I wake up in a cold sweat, as if I've been sprinting through my subconscious, away from the sight of it.

When my bag is packed, I make for the door but as I open it I'm confronted by the reality that I'm in the middle of nowhere and it's freezing cold. Where am I going to go? I have barely two hundred dollars in cash to my name. I have no one to turn to either, no friends or family who'd offer me shelter.

I pause for a moment to collect my thoughts. Slowly, I turn around and head back inside. I need to follow the plan and wait it out.

Chapter Twenty

Past

Two Years, Four Months Ago

I lie in the giant king-sized bed after Ryan leaves for work and I stare at the ceiling, thinking about the nail marks raking his back. I have not slept a wink all night. I lay frozen beside him, trying to keep the sobs inside me from bursting out, trying desperately not to picture the woman who had left them there. It was futile of course; I'm still thinking about it now. Is it someone I know? It can't be the nanny – she's in her fifties and happily married. And the same goes for Marie. Is it someone he works with or one of those hyena women who've been circling him for years? Is she younger than me, her skin unmarred by stretch marks? Is she a lawyer like him – able to discuss his career with him in a way that I cannot?

All night I had to fight the urge to shake him awake and confront him, but what point is there in hearing him confirm it or in finding out who it is? It's not as if I can leave him – even if I could work up the courage. What would I do for money if I left? There's the prenup. I wouldn't get a cent and I'm not completely sure that Ryan wouldn't cut me off without a penny. I know Gloria would like to see that happen.

Could I get by on my own? I'd have to go back to waitressing, but can I do that and take care of a baby? And where would I go? I have nowhere to stay. No friends and no family. I have no degree and no work experience either. And even if I did have somewhere to go, or felt capable of living on my own, I know that there's no chance Ryan would ever let me have custody of Sienna.

Before I went to the Sanctuary, I wouldn't have cared if he got full custody but now I'm back home and my depression is under control, the thought of being separated from her kills me.

But it's not just money and Sienna that tie me to Ryan, I admit ruefully to myself. It's also need. I don't know how to live without him. Literally. I am completely dependent on him – financially, emotionally, physically even. He's my drug. And I can't live without a fix.

Plenty of women turn a blind eye to affairs. Maybe I can learn to?

When Sienna wakes, I drag myself up and fetch her. I give her a drink from her sippy cup, and then carry her into the bed with me, wanting to hold her close.

I have dozed off with Sienna next to me, when I hear the doorbell ring and a moment later I'm startled fully awake by the sound of someone shouting. Marie raises her voice in answer, and I stumble out of bed and walk out onto the landing and peer down into the hall below. Marie is arguing with someone at the front door. It sounds like a woman.

Suddenly the door is flung wide open and the visitor storms past Marie and marches into the hallway. 'Rose?' she yells.

It's Daisy. It takes a moment though to recognize her. This skinny, haggard woman in ripped tights and denim cutoffs, with straggly hair and blotchy skin covered in sores, looks nothing like the sister I remember.

She looks up and sees me standing on the landing above her. 'Tell this cow to fucking let me in,' she says, jerking her head at an outraged Marie.

I can see Marie reaching for her phone and know she's about to call security or the police.

'It's fine, Marie,' I call, intervening quickly.

Daisy stalks past Marie and starts climbing the stairs, clutching the bannister. She looks frighteningly thin, almost skeletal, and when she gets close, I am scared by how pale she is – bloodless – her skin like crumpled paper that's been stretched flat, lined way beyond her age. Her eyes are tinged yellow, and her lips are cracked and scabbed in the corners. She has acne on her cheeks and chin.

I don't feel any joy in seeing her. I feel sad beyond belief that I allowed myself to get my hopes up, and tired too – tired in advance of what I know is about to play out and how it will leave me feeling.

I knew she'd likely fallen off the wagon because I'd tried calling her several times and her number was disconnected, which was always the pattern when she fell back into drug use. I even thought there was a possibility she was dead, but the idea of finding that out while I was pregnant wasn't something I could handle so, to my shame, I avoided looking into it. And then when Sienna came, I was dealing with my own issues.

I glance down to where Marie is lingering in the hallway, staring up at us with her phone in her hand, no doubt ready to hit dial.

'Come on,' I say to Daisy, wanting to get away from Marie's prying eyes. I know Marie will definitely call Ryan to inform him of the situation, but there's nothing I can do about that, and I don't want her witnessing whatever is about to occur between Daisy and me.

I lead Daisy into the bedroom. 'Is he at work?' she asks me.

She's talking about Ryan. 'Yes,' I confirm, my nose wrinkling as a sour smell hits me. Judging from the dirt under her fingernails and the stink rising off her clothes she hasn't washed in days, if not longer.

'When I came last time, he wouldn't let me in to see you.'

'What?' I say. 'When?'

'I don't know,' she mumbles. 'Around a year ago.'

I think back. It was around the time I went to the Sanctuary.

'What do you want?' I ask, speaking quietly so as not to disturb Sienna, lying in the bed asleep.

Daisy follows my gaze and notices Sienna and I see the surprise flash across her face. 'You had a kid?' she exclaims.

She walks over to the bed and I find myself torn between wanting to show Sienna off to my sister, and wanting to shield my child.

'Yes,' I say.

Daisy stands over my sleeping toddler, her expression rapt with wonder. But then a bitterness crosses her face, hardening it. 'I can't believe you had a kid,' she says in a mocking tone that hurts me more than I like to admit. Why is that so hard to believe?

'What do you want?' I ask again, struggling to maintain my calm and keep my voice low so as not to wake Sienna.

'I need money.'

I snort. I knew it would be that, but I didn't expect the request to come so fast. Usually, she tries to have at least a five-minute conversation before she hits me up.

'I'm not giving you any money,' I tell her, though it does cross my mind that it might be the easiest way to get rid of her. I could go to the ATM, withdraw five hundred dollars and she'd be gone, but I can't do it. 'I'm not funding your habit.' I refuse to be complicit in her own destruction.

'Who says it's for drugs?' she shoots back.

I roll my eyes.

'I need to get to rehab,' she mutters, gnawing on her lip.

I snort again. Right. Does she think I was born yesterday? I make a mental note not to leave her alone for even five seconds as she'll probably take off with whatever is in reach. She's done that to me countless times in the past and my jewelry box is sitting on the dressing table.

She glowers at me. 'If I wait for a spot to open up, I'm not going to make it,' she continues. 'I need help now. The only places I can get into today are expensive. Private.'

I weigh it up. Is she telling me the truth? 'I can call a place,' I tell her, thinking of the place where I got treated – the Sanctuary. 'Get you in today. I'll pay for it but I'm not giving you money.'

She scowls and I know instantly that she's lying to me. She doesn't want to go to rehab. She's just trying to con me.

'What happened?' I ask, shaking my head, disappointment obvious in my tone. 'You were clean. You were doing so well.'

Daisy snorts at me, her mouth twisting into a grimace. 'Acting like you don't know, just like with Dad.'

I am so taken aback that I gasp in shock. 'I don't get . . . what are you talking about?'

Daisy starts striding around the room, arms waving in agitation. 'You watched Dad do what he was doing to me for years, and you never did anything about it. You didn't try to stop him. You just let him get away with it. It would have gone on forever if he hadn't died.'

I am stunned, speechless. My mouth falls open but nothing comes out. Angry tears glitter in her eyes and hatred radiates off her. I take a step back, almost collapsing down onto the bed.

'You knew,' she spits, stepping toward me. 'You knew what he was doing to me.' Her lower lip trembles, and despite the rage, I see the terrified, broken little girl still living inside of her. 'You could have told someone,' she sobs.

'Daisy,' I stammer, at a loss. 'I didn't know. I swear.' My heart is pounding in the hollow vault of my chest. Everything comes into swift relief: the reason Daisy is the way she is, the root of it all. My father was abusing her. And I didn't know. How could I not have known?

She stares at me in astonishment. 'Bullshit. You were there! You saw. He would come for me in the night.' She hiccups, trying to stifle her sobs, then prods me in the chest with her finger. 'You had to have known.'

I shake my head. 'No. I didn't,' I tell her. I start to cry, fat tears falling down my cheeks. 'I'm so sorry. I'm so sorry.'

'I don't want your fucking apologies,' she spits. 'You bury your head in the sand so you don't have to deal with what's staring you in the face. You did the same with our father. It's easier to just pretend, isn't it? Why bother dealing with reality when you can live a perfect life that's also a perfect lie?' She takes a breath. 'If you had said something back then, if you had told someone what Dad was doing, we would have been put in foster care – that's why you said nothing.'

'No!' I say. 'That's not true.' I desperately need her to know that I had no idea he was doing that to her.

Or did I? Did I have some suspicion? I can recall waking sleepily in the night sometimes and finding Daisy gone from the bed. I can remember her rolling against me and clinging to me at night sometimes too. But I didn't know what was happening. I was a kid. How could I have known what he was doing to her?

Daisy turns away from me and crosses to the dresser, on top of which are several framed photographs of Ryan and me: on our wedding day, on vacation in the Caribbean, with Sienna at her christening. 'Why'd they always pick me?' she asks, her fingers tracing the silver frames. She looks up at me, a plaintive expression on her face. 'Why not you?'

Chapter Twenty-One

Present

It's Tuesday. Two days since Gwen paid me a visit. I've spent those two days on tenterhooks, trying to subdue the urge to flee and to also drown out the voice in my head screaming at me that I'm a fool to trust her. But with each passing hour and no sign of the police showing up to arrest me, the tension ratcheting my spine decreases a notch, and I find myself more able to breathe. I don't think she's ratted me out, which leads me to the conclusion she hasn't any idea who I really am because if she did know who I was there is no way she wouldn't have called the police by now. I guess she either doesn't watch the news, or I look so different from the photos she hasn't recognized me as Rose Reid.

The temperature has dropped even further and it's

now below freezing. Snow is falling thick and fast, but I stick my feet into my boots, pull on my jacket, and go out to check on my alarm system. If the snow has buried the cans, I won't be able to hear them rattle.

Having adjusted their height, I trudge back toward the door. But halfway there I come to a sudden standstill, as though someone has grabbed my insides in their fist. A man has just appeared, walking from behind the cabin. I drop down and scoot behind a bush, praying he didn't see me, and then I peer out and watch him as he continues around the perimeter, stopping to peer through the dirty windows. He's wearing a heavy jacket, a hunter's fur-lined cap and camo pants tucked into military-style boots. Over his shoulder he is carrying a rifle. I can't see his face thanks to the dimming light and the shadows of his cap.

Who is he? What does he want? Is he a local, out hunting and checking up on the place? Or someone living nearby who has seen the candles glowing and the smoke rising from the chimney and come to investigate? I wonder if Gwen has been loose-lipped and mentioned me to someone, someone who might be trying to snag a fifty-thousand-dollar bounty. He certainly looks too well dressed to be a backwoodsman, or anyone living off-grid.

As I watch him prowling around my refuge, it

strikes me that it might be the same person whose footprints I found in the snow alongside the animal ones.

The more terrifying thought is that he's a private investigator. It's occurred to me that Ryan's family will have hired people to hunt me down. They have a contract with a company, Austin Roper Security, who manage the security at their hotels and sometimes provided close protection for the high-profile events Ryan would attend.

The man is now at the front door. I watch him reach for the doorknob and try it, not even bothering to knock. Thankfully, the door is locked, but I'm half-expecting him to kick it open. He doesn't. Instead, he steps back and surveys the place, examining it I guess for signs of inhabitance.

I'm glad I drew all the curtains so he can't see inside. The only thing that gives away the fact someone is living here are the cans I strung between the trees, though given the rusting state of them, he may assume they've been there for a while.

Suddenly, his gaze swings in my direction. I duck lower, covering my head with my hands and praying he can't see me in the dimming dusk and that he doesn't decide to come and investigate.

I wait for at least a minute before I risk another peek, and then I'm startled to find that he's vanished. I scan the clearing in front of the cabin and the trees beyond, with rising panic. Where the hell did he disappear to?

Has he slipped behind a tree? Is he hiding there, waiting for me to appear?

I don't know what to do. I lower my head to my knees and try to think. It's freezing cold and my hands and feet are turning numb.

It's about seventy-five meters from where I am to the front door. I wait, shivering hard and too frightened to move, as the last of the daylight slips away and the snow starts to fall more heavily.

Knowing I can't stay here all night, or else I'll die of hypothermia, I huddle there, knees tucked to my chest, for another thirty minutes or so as darkness cloaks me, arms wrapped around myself and my jaw hurting from clenching my teeth to stop them rattling.

Finally, frozen solid, I stand up, my legs stiff, and hurry through the pitch-black toward the shadowed outline of the cabin up ahead. The whole time I'm terrified that the man will step out in front of me with his rifle, or that he'll surprise me by coming up from behind and grabbing me, but nothing happens. I slip the key into the lock and burst inside, gasping with relief and shaking with cold.

I'm too scared to light a fire. Instead, I strip off my icy layers and throw on whatever clean, dry ones are in the drawer, then I place a chair beneath the door handle and crawl beneath a pile of blankets on the bed. For hours I lie cocooned like that, my teeth still chattering and my body racked with shivers, until finally sleep claims me.

Chapter Twenty-Two

Past

Six Months Ago

The party is in full swing. I am standing on the terrace of the ballroom – the same ballroom where we held our wedding reception – watching as Ryan circulates among the guests. I've always enjoyed watching him in his element like this, drawing people to him like moths to a flame, but not so tonight. Tonight, I'm on edge. Which of these women is the one he's having an affair with?

The room is full of New York's most influential and wealthy inhabitants: a mix of police chiefs and senior officers, politicians, businesspeople, wealthy donors, and Ryan's colleagues from the district attorney's office. There are many women, glowing and resplendent in their gowns. I eye them all, trying to guess who left their markings on my man. It has become a guessing game. Something I indulge in at each of these events.

It has been almost two years since I found out about the affair, but I have never said anything to Ryan. I have smiled and kept going through the motions, playing my role of perfect wife and mother, trying not to give anything away. I decided I didn't want to know the details, and that I would rather live in this state of constant torture than rock the boat and risk losing him. But it is all that occupies my mind, that and what happened with Daisy. Some days, I am able to convince myself I imagined it and he isn't having an affair at all. But that never lasts long.

Grief and anger threaten to overwhelm me at times, but I can't let it. If I fall off the precipice and into depression again, Ryan really will leave me. He might even have me committed again.

Sienna keeps me grounded. And I weigh the good against the bad. It's not as if Ryan is unloving to me or unkind. He buys me flowers. He tells me he loves me. He compliments me. I don't think he is going to leave me for whatever woman he's sleeping with. It would be too much of a scandal and hurt his career.

Every day when Ryan goes to work though, I wonder if he's meeting her. Does he sneak off for lunchtime sex with her at one of his hotels? I find myself freezing at his touch and I have to fake my interest in intimacy, because all I can think of is him in the arms of another woman.

The Police Foundation Gala Dinner is a big event – one that I know is important to Ryan in his quest for the governorship. To which end, I'm wearing the blue Chanel dress Ryan bought for me – his favorite – and I've already received a dozen compliments about it.

'Everyone will endorse me when they see you in that dress,' Ryan joked when I descended the stairs before we left. I smiled at him but my gut writhed. Why is he lying to me? I've started to wonder whether it's not only one woman he's having an affair with. Has there been a long line of lovers that I've been oblivious to? Was I so wrapped up in creating the perfect life that I just didn't notice?

I watch him now as he greets a young woman wearing a low-backed, figure-hugging dress. She's beautiful, olive-skinned, with thick dark hair. My stomach rolls as I watch Ryan lean in toward her, smiling his most charming smile, his hand hovering over the small of her back. The ground rocks beneath my feet and my ears fill with a roaring sound.

It's her. It must be. Ryan can't take his eyes off her. And she is fixated on him. They could be the only two people in the room for all the notice they are giving anyone else. This is the woman whose nails left track marks in my husband's back. I know it.

I want to stride over there and strike her across the face. I want to shove her away from him. I want to tear her limb from limb. But I don't. Instead, I turn my back and stare out over the Manhattan skyline, swallowing back tears and trying to think about what to do. My feet itch to flee. But I can't. I am frozen in place.

It strikes me that after a lifetime of running away, I am now like an animal that's been caged for too long. I've lost my instincts. My grandfather's neighbor had a dog – a vicious animal that bit several people. Instead of giving it up to a kill shelter, they kept it caged in their yard and Daisy and I watched that animal slowly became institutionalized. After a few months of growling at anything that passed by, it stopped. It just lay there, head on paws, ignoring everything and everyone, not even stirring if you poked at it with a stick. One day, a year or so later, they opened the cage door, but the poor beast was by then so used to living in that cage, so broken by it, it refused to come out.

I'm that dog. How the hell did I get so pathetic? I hate myself for it.

'You're Ryan's wife?'

I startle, and whirl around, finding the young woman who Ryan was just talking to, standing in front of me.

Up close she's even more beautiful, in her mid-twenties, with the smooth, flawless skin of someone who hasn't yet had to invest in anti-aging creams.

Out of habit more than anything else, I force my most charming smile, though my jaw is clenched hard. 'Yes,' I stammer, struggling to keep my voice steady.

What does she want? Is she about to confess all on the affair? I don't want to hear it. I'm not brave enough. I'm not ready. I decide I will cut her off if she tries.

'I'm Isabel,' she tells me, in a voice with a trace of a Bronx accent. 'I was hoping I could talk to you, in private.'

Oh God. I don't know what to do. I want to turn and walk away but I am still frozen. Before I have to answer her though, Ryan sweeps in. He puts his arm around my shoulders and leans in to kiss my cheek. 'There you are, my love,' he murmurs. 'Can I steal you away? I need to introduce you to someone.'

He doesn't even glance in Isabel's direction and before he's finished talking, he's already steering me away from her. I let him, my heart racing as fast as my mind is whirring. When I look back over my shoulder, I see Isabel watching us.

'Do you know that woman?' I say to Ryan, my voice shaking.

'Who?' Ryan responds, leading me between the tables.

'That woman I was just talking to.'

'No,' Ryan replies. 'Ahh, here we are.' He turns me to face a phalanx of men, all senior police officials I'm guessing from the uniforms they're wearing, which are bedecked with medals. I smile on autopilot.

'Hi.' Ryan's hand rests on the small of my back. I used to love the comfort of his touch, but now I feel like a puppet that he's controlling. 'Rose,' I offer, introducing myself.

'My lovely wife,' Ryan adds to the men, who shake my hand in turn and tell me how good it is to meet me, what lovely things they've heard about me and what a lucky man Ryan is.

Like a pre-programmed robot, I hear myself asking them how they're enjoying the event, but all the while my brain is throwing up possibilities about Isabel and Ryan: that they've been having an affair for the last five years, that they have had a one-night stand, that he's secretly fathered a child with her, that they're in love and he's leaving me to be with her.

I realize that one of the men in uniform has asked me something, something about where we're spending the rest of the summer, I think. 'Ryan likes to spend it at home,' I respond pleasantly, hoping I'm answering the right question. 'We like to visit his mother in the Hamptons,' I say. 'He's the only child, so it's important to us that we're with family.'

Presenting Ryan as a family man, while also

emphasizing his credentials, is very important for the campaign. This has been drilled into me. Even with my thoughts stuck on Isabel and worrying about what she was about to tell me about my cheating husband, I am still capable of playing the part of the doting wife. No one could guess that inside I'm falling apart.

We take our seats for dinner. I feel like I'm in a dream, looking down on myself from a height as I make polite conversation with those at the table and let Ryan nuzzle my neck and take my hand, all without giving away my dire urge to stand up and run from the room. I could win an Oscar for how composed and at ease I appear. Even Gloria would be impressed.

Perhaps I'm wrong, I tell myself. Perhaps Isabel isn't having an affair with Ryan and I read it wrong. Maybe she didn't want to speak to me about anything of importance, I muse. But why then did Ryan appear at my elbow and whisk me away, pretending he didn't know her?

I can feel him now, watching me out of the corner of his eye. His foot keeps tapping beneath the table in a clear indication that he's anxious. He gets up between courses and weaves between the tables, stopping to gladhand and flatter and charm, but I wonder if he's looking for her. I can't see her. Maybe she's left already. Or she could be waiting for him upstairs in his suite. Sweat breaks out all over my body. I think I am going to be sick. I reach for my glass of water and knock it over.

'Are you OK?' a middle-aged lady sitting beside me asks with concern as I hurry to blot the spill with a napkin.

'Yes, I'm fine,' I reply, smiling. I stand up, on unsteady legs, the room blurring. 'Excuse me,' I say to the table, and hurry off.

I stumble through the doors and toward the nearest bathroom. By the time I make it inside I'm hyperventilating. I lean against the wall, sucking in air, trying not to faint, and swallowing down the nausea rising up my throat.

The door behind me opens. I look up and see Isabel standing there. She takes a step toward me. She has the look of a rat catcher who's cornered her rodent and I look around desperately for an escape.

'I need to talk to you,' Isabel tells me.

I don't say anything in response.

'It's about your husband.'

My gut squeezes. There's a weight on my chest, a sob building, and I bite the inside of my lip to stop it coming out. I promise myself that I will not cry or become hysterical or angry. Whatever she says, I will keep my dignity.

'What about my husband?' I finally manage to respond. I'm trying to come off as indifferent but my voice quivers, giving me away.

She checks the toilet stalls making sure they're empty, then looks back at me. She's truly stunning. I can see exactly what he sees in her. It's not just her flawless skin, or her gorgeous curves. She's got something indefinable about her, a kind of inner fire, a defiance – both in the jut of her chin and the look in her eye – that I'm sure men find attractive. She isn't bland like me. I am a blank wall on which people can project their own ideas; she is a color painting, bold and full of expression. Is that why Ryan fell for her?

'Have you any idea who he is?' she asks.

I blink, startled by the question. What does she mean?

She takes another step toward me, her brown eyes flashing with anger and I reflexively take a step back.

'He's a monster,' she hisses.

Chapter Twenty-Three

Present

I can't shake the notion that the man from yesterday is still out there, prowling around. To which end, I stay cocooned as much as possible under the blankets, rarely surfacing, and when I do, I move quietly, stealthily. I don't light a candle or use the flashlight. I don't open the curtains or start a fire.

By the hush in the air, I can tell it's still snowing and the cabin is cold as an ice box. I lie curled in a ball in bed, trying not to let my thoughts travel to the dark place but there's no place else for them to go. Hope is fading fast that I'm going to make it out of this, and I wonder why I ever thought I could. It's impossible to disappear nowadays, especially when the whole world is looking for you. I wonder if I should have just stayed put at Crosshill and accepted my fate.

My teeth chatter non-stop and I'm shivering uncontrollably, but I can't tell if I have a fever or if it's because the temperature in the cabin is below freezing. The cuts on my arm are burning. I bandaged them back up to stop them from rubbing against the inside of my sweater but when I peel back the dressings I wince and hiss at the sight of the still-oozing scabs, and then at the fiery hot skin around them. Red streaks inch upwards, almost to the elbow. I think I need antibiotics. The antiseptic cream hasn't helped much, if at all, and nor has the iodine. The cuts were too deep. Maybe the blade was dirty. Or I didn't take good enough care of them and that's how they got infected.

I flit between waking and sleeping and dream fitfully.

In the early evening I hear a thud somewhere outside, and I startle awake. I grip the poker and struggle to sit up, feeling dizzy. I hold my breath, feeling my heart thumping, out of rhythm. Is it the man with the rifle from yesterday? Is he trying the doors again? I strain to listen, sitting on the edge of the bed in the gloom, terrified.

Finally, I get up and shuffle my way as quietly as possible to the front door. I stand there for a long time, not sure what to do, but curiosity gets the better of me and I open the door a crack and peer out.

There are footsteps in the snow leading up to the

cabin and my insides clench with terror, but then I look down and see two dead rabbits lying by my feet, right on the doorstep.

I stare at them for several beats, and then I look up and scan the clearing. There's no sign of anyone. I shut the door quickly, leaving the rabbits where they lay, and I stand stock-still, trying to understand what they mean. Is it a warning? A threat? A gift?

Could it be the man from yesterday?

Or is it a neighbor who's simply offering some spoils from hunting?

What if it's a trap?

Nora, the woman at Crosshill who controlled the TV remote, would do that. She would leave the remote lying on a table or a chair and wait for someone to come along, pick it up and change the channel, and then she would launch herself at them and attack them as if they'd tried to steal her baby. What if whoever left the rabbits is doing the same thing? Waiting to see if I take the bait?

I stand there, pondering it. My grandfather and I used to shoot rabbits and he taught me how to prepare and cook them. He had an idea that I should learn useful skills and, never having had a son and having lost his only daughter, I think he enjoyed that he finally had someone to pass his knowledge down to. Daisy certainly wasn't interested.

I was only too eager to play the part, wanting more

than anything to please him so he wouldn't send Daisy and I away, but I hated actually killing animals and even more having to gut them afterwards. I never let my grandfather know though, or see my squeamishness, in case he thought less of me. I just wanted him to love me.

I was already a self-reliant kid before we moved in with him, but he taught me more skills: how to shoot, how to hunt, how to protect myself. Above all he taught me to keep going, even when the going got tough. He was a Vietnam veteran, but he never spoke much about his time in the army, and it was only after he died, when I was going through his things, that I found his purple heart medal and the accompanying letter. While under enemy fire he had saved two of his fellow infantrymen's lives, receiving serious injuries as a result that had led to him being invalided out. They commended him for his selflessness and bravery.

I open the front door again and snatch the rabbits up. Even if it isn't a gift, even if it is a trap, I may as well make the most of them. I haven't eaten fresh meat in weeks and the thought of a good meal makes my mouth water.

I set to work prepping the carcasses, my teeth still chattering, my hands clumsy. The sight of the blood makes memories surge up and I have to swallow down nausea as I remember the blood on the concrete of the garage floor.

The rabbits lie on the kitchen table, staring up at me as I continue skinning them, and a memory flashes to the forefront of my mind. It's my dad, dead, staring at me with glassy eyes.

It was a warm afternoon when I was eleven, and I had returned to the trailer after school. Daisy was outside playing with some other kids. I had a habit of always entering first to gauge the temperature of my dad's mood and to make sure the coast was clear before I let Daisy come in. On good days our dad wouldn't be home, and on bad days he'd be there and in a foul temper because he had no money and needed a fix. On those days, if we weren't fast enough and didn't manage to hide in time, he'd take his frustration out on us.

The day I found him passed out with a needle stuck in his arm was not unusual. I had found him and my mom like that several times before. But this time it was different. He was convulsing. I knew it was a seizure. There was a kid in school who had epilepsy and I'd seen him once fall to the ground, trembling in the same way. The teacher had rolled him onto his side and held him so he didn't hurt himself and put something between his teeth to make sure that he didn't bite his tongue off.

I stared down at my dad as he kept shaking. Vomit started to bubble over his lips. He was making a wheezing sound. He was obviously overdosing. I turned to the door – meaning to run to the neighbor, Jeanie – I knew she had Narcan, because her son was an addict. In fact, most of my neighbors likely had Narcan to hand, as a lot of them were either addicts themselves or had family who were.

But when I reached the door I stopped and stood there, thinking for a moment. It didn't take long – a couple of seconds only – but I made a decision and turned back toward my dad.

I sat down beside him cross-legged, careful not to touch him, and for what felt like a lifetime but was in actuality only several minutes, I watched as the bubbles burst on his lips and the vomit started to dribble down his chin. I kept watching as his skin began to turn a faint green color along his jaw, and his lips turned blue and then, finally, he stopped breathing.

As I remove the head from a rabbit and then slide the knife into the soft skin of its belly, I think about those endless minutes as I watched my father die and how I felt absolutely nothing.

Carefully, I remove the still-warm insides from the rabbit, setting them aside in a bowl, and then, using a dull cleaver taken from the drawer, I separate the hindquarters from the body.

Chapter Twenty-Four

Past

Six Months Ago

'He's a monster,' Isabel says. 'He raped my cousin Angela.'

I fall back against the marble counter behind me. I am stunned. The world has not just tilted on its axis but turned one hundred and eighty degrees. That is not what I expected to hear at all.

'Did you hear me?' she spits. 'Your husband is a rapist.'

My hand flies to my throat. I can't breathe. I try to steady myself, my other hand gripping the edge of the countertop for balance. 'What . . .?' I manage to say.

'He attacked my cousin. She worked here at the

hotel. She was a maid. He raped her one night when she was working. He didn't just rape her, he beat her too,' Isabel goes on, her voice shaking. 'Violently. You should have seen her. She was black and blue.'

I had expected her to tell me they were having an affair, that she loved Ryan, that he was leaving me for her . . . not this. I don't know how to process it.

'He threatened her,' Isabel goes on. 'And she's undocumented, so of course she didn't say a word. She was terrified of losing her job and of being arrested. She couldn't even go to the police.'

It feels as if invisible hands are strangling me. My vision darkens at the edges. I want her to stop but I also want her to go on. I need to hear it all. I need to know.

'We went to the person here in charge of house-keeping at the hotel,' Isabel tells me, a tear falling down her cheek. 'I wanted my cousin to at least make a complaint, let them know what had happened, so they could warn the other maids, and you know what we found out? It wasn't even the first time it had happened. He's done it before.'

I feel my legs buckle and hold tighter to the counter to stay upright.

'A few of them he's paid off. Most of them he hasn't needed to. He just threatened them and that was enough. One person was brave enough to go to the cops and can you guess what they did?' she spits.

'Nothing.' Isabel gestures wildly toward the door, toward the ballroom beyond. 'Go figure! Your husband's friends with all the rich and powerful people in this city. He can get away with anything. Rich men always do.'

'I . . . I . . .' I start to say but then stop, not knowing how to finish the sentence.

'You want to know where Angela is now?' she demands, getting right in my face, her teeth bared. 'She's dead. She killed herself. She jumped in front of the L train two weeks ago. She couldn't cope with the shame of it. What he did to her . . .' She breaks off.

I draw in a breath as sharp as a knife.

'And your husband is out there right now,' she hisses at me, throwing an arm toward the ballroom, 'swanning around, acting like he's untouchable. I just spoke to him and he threatened me too. Told me if I ever said a word to anyone about these "allegations", he'd have me arrested. He accused me of lying to extort money from him.'

I frown. Is that what she and Ryan were talking about earlier when I saw them together? He was smiling at her. I thought they were flirting. Was he really threatening her?

'You think I'm making this up?' Isabel says now, furiously, obviously seeing something shift in my expression. 'You think I'd do that?'

I swallow, steadying myself. 'No,' I tell her, feeling the ground fall away beneath my feet even as I say it. 'I believe you.'

She stares at me, stunned.

Chapter Twenty-Five

Past

Two Years, Four Months Ago

Daisy's fingers trace the silver frame as she stares at the photo of Ryan and I on our wedding day. 'Why'd they always pick me?' she asks plaintively. 'Why not you?'

I frown. *They?* What does she mean by that?

'He raped me,' Daisy says, turning to look at me over her shoulder. 'Your perfect, lovely husband raped me.'

Her words are a slap. I stagger backwards, blinking at my sister in utter amazement. But then anger flares. How dare she make up such lies?

She's done it before, many times: lying to me that my scholarship letters hadn't arrived, lying to me about being clean, about where my money is, about why she couldn't make it to my grandfather's funeral. When she's high or desperate for a fix, nothing she says can be believed. I know she's doing the same now: trying to hurt me, to mess with my life. She's jealous that I have a life, that I have Ryan and Sienna. And I'm sorry that she's turned out the way she has, but I can't keep taking responsibility for that. I tried for years to save her and I can't do it anymore.

'He raped me,' she says again.

'Stop it!' I hiss at her.

The lie she's telling me about Ryan is so absurd I don't even contemplate it might be true. I know Ryan. I know my husband. He'd never hurt anyone, least of all a woman. If anything, Daisy might have tried something on with him. I wouldn't put it past her.

Sex is a weapon for her, a tool, a means to an end. She uses it to get drugs or money, or a ride somewhere, or a bed for the night, or revenge on a sister she resents.

I know for a fact that Ryan wouldn't ever sleep with Daisy. So, I'm confident when I tell her, 'You're lying.'

I say it louder than I mean to and Sienna wakes and starts to cry. I rush over and pick her up, feeling my own upset leaching into her and her cries increasing as a result. It makes me even angrier with Daisy. She's upsetting my baby.

'No,' says Daisy, over Sienna's screams. 'He raped me in my bed in the spare room of this house. I was wearing your blue pajamas.'

'Get out!' I yell. 'Get the hell out of my house.'

Daisy ignores me. 'Afterwards he gave me three hundred bucks and drove me to the bus station. He said if I ever came near you again, he'd have me arrested for stealing and for drug dealing. He said he knew people, people in the police department, and that he'd make sure that if I reported it, I'd go to jail and I'd never get out.'

A shrill laugh erupts out of me at the absurdity. Her lies have always been unbelievable, but she's reaching new heights with this one.

'But I decided, fuck him and his threats. So, I came back. To tell you. I thought he'd be at work. But he was home. And he wouldn't let me in to see you. He called the cops and had me arrested for harassment and stalking.'

'You're lying,' I say again, fury building in me. How dare she come here and say these things?

'What do you see in him?' she says. 'He controls you completely. I don't even know who you are anymore. The way you dress, the way you talk, the way you act . . . it's not you. It's like he's molded you into someone else.'

'If you don't leave right now, I'm calling the police,' I retort, marching to the door.

She lets out a harsh laugh and sets the wedding photograph down on the side. 'I knew you'd never believe me. I don't even know why I bothered coming here.'

'Leave,' I order her, my voice coming out as a bark.

But Daisy walks toward me. 'You know he did the same at your wedding reception?' she tells me. 'He gave me a hundred bucks and told me to fuck off or he'd have me arrested for trespassing and solicitation. Told me that in lockup he'd see to it I came out a lot less pretty.'

I frown, remembering Ryan handing her money in the lobby of the hotel. I remember too the humiliation I felt that night. I hated her then and I despise her now. If I wasn't holding Sienna, I feel like I could strangle my sister.

'Get out!' I shout.

She laughs: a grating, horrible sound. 'There you go, burying your head in the sand again. Not wanting to face facts. You know why you do that?' She smirks. 'Because if you did, your whole world would fall apart. No. It's easier to live in denial, isn't it?' She gets right in my face, paying no attention to Sienna's screams. 'You've always been a coward,' she taunts.

'Get out!' I shout.

Marie is suddenly in the doorway. 'I've called the police,' she says. 'And Ryan. They're on their way.'

Daisy sneers at the housekeeper. 'Don't worry, I'm leaving.' She heads for the door, brushing past Marie. 'See ya,' she says. 'And thanks for everything, big sis.'

It's the last time I ever see her.

Chapter Twenty-Six

Past

Six Months Ago

Isabel does a double take, incredulous. 'You believe me?' she stammers.

I bow my head, clutching the marble counter in the bathroom to stay upright. I'm reeling from the knowledge that what Daisy told me on the day she showed up at my house, strung out and hurling accusations, must have been true. I told her I didn't believe her. A howl struggles up my throat, trying to escape. I want to wrap my arms around myself, sink to the floor and sob but by some miracle I stay standing.

That was the last time I ever saw her. Eighteen months ago, police in Thailand called and let us know that Daisy had overdosed. She died in a cheap motel in Bangkok. I am still processing this news. I haven't yet even grieved for her properly – I've been too angry – and now I'm learning that the last thing she told me was true. And instead of listening, I threw her out of the house.

And now I'll never be able to tell her that I'm sorry.

Oh God.

I stare at Isabel. My world is crumbling, not slowly, but all at once. An avalanche sweeping away my life in one fell swoop. I think about Ryan, in shouting distance of us, moving around the ballroom, charming people as he goes, women staring after him adoringly. None of them have any idea who he is.

But how can they when even I, his wife, had no clue?

It all falls into place. The scratch marks on his back. Those weren't made by a lover in the throes of passion. They were the marks of someone fighting him off. Vomit rockets up my throat like a geyser. I turn just in time and throw up into the sink.

Sweat breaks out on my brow. As I lean over the taps, fighting dizziness, I realize that he has been sleeping with me all this time. He has been professing love for me, acting with tenderness and generosity and kindness. And then he has been carrying out horrific assaults on other women.

He has never once hit me or explored any kind of violent fantasy in the bedroom. How can he do these things to other women? It seems too crazy to be true. But . . . how can I deny the similarity in the stories Isabel is telling me and what Daisy told me?

'I need your help,' Isabel says, the words tumbling out in a rush. 'He can't be allowed to get away with this.'

I stare at her in the mirror. Help? What does she mean she needs my help? I turn on the tap with a shaking hand and splash water over my face.

The bathroom door swings open just then and an older woman in burgundy velvet swans in. She heads into one of the stalls without glancing our way.

'What do you need?' I whisper to Isabel.

A small voice in my head is urging me to walk out, to go back to the party and pretend that I never heard these things or ever had this conversation. It warns me to go back to pretending because pretending is safer than facing up to this reality. If I help Isabel, then my life is over. Sienna's life will be changed forever too. Her father is a rapist! How can I possibly let that come out? Ryan would go to jail. We would be guilty by association.

But as soon as I think it, a wave of disgust hits me. I remember Daisy's words. She was right. I have been in denial. And I can't bury my head in the sand again. I have to learn to confront the truth, even if it's going to cause me pain. There is no choice but to help Isabel. Daisy and all these women deserve that.

The older lady comes out of the stall and crosses to the sinks to wash her hands. She eyes me and Isabel, obviously tuning in to the tension and the arctic silence that has fallen while we wait for her to leave. She smiles at me as she exits, and I recognize her as someone I was introduced to earlier, the wife of one of the police chiefs.

Once she's gone, Isabel starts talking again, in a low, rushed voice. 'The hotel manager gave me the names of a few of the women he assaulted. I spoke to them. The ones I could find. None of them will go on the record. They're terrified. Most of them are undocumented, like my cousin was. And he threatened them and their families. They won't speak up. It's why I had to come to you.'

'I don't know what I can do,' I tell her.

'Find proof,' she says, and she reaches out and takes my hands, squeezing them in her own with an urgent desperation that makes my panic balloon.

'What kind of proof?' I ask, shaking my head in confusion.

'He takes things from them.'

'What?'

'They all told me the same thing. All the women he raped. He took things from them.'

I don't understand. 'What things?'

'Underwear usually. Jewelry too.'

Bile shoots up my throat again but this time I swallow it down.

'He takes their IDs too. He stole my cousin's hotel ID card. And he took another woman's driver's license.'

The room spins out of control. 'Why would he do that?' I murmur, mostly to myself, fighting a wave of dizziness.

'I think he takes them as souvenirs,' Isabel says.

'What?'

'I'm guessing they're like trophies for him,' she says, her top lip curling with disgust. 'And then he takes their IDs so they know that he knows who they are, and where they live. It's to scare them into silence.'

I'm robbed of speech. How can she be talking about Ryan? An image pops into my head of him kissing Sienna goodnight, carrying her to bed, of him kissing me, making love to me. How can that same man be doing such awful things to these other women? My stomach curdles.

Isabel is studying me. What must I look like to her? A stupid, deluded wife, no doubt. Someone who has deliberately buried her head in the sand to avoid messy truths. It wasn't like that, I want to protest, but I know that it was. That was exactly what it was.

'I need your help finding these things,' Isabel goes

on. 'Maybe he's keeping them somewhere at home. In a safe or hidden somewhere. I don't know, I just . . .' Her voice cracks and she looks back up at me again with tears brimming. 'I need to find something that will tie him to all these attacks. If I can do that, there's a chance I can convince these women to come forward. Maybe then he won't get away with it. We can get justice.'

'You really think he's keeping things?' I whisper, still reeling from the thought.

I find it hard to believe, not just because it's so sickening, but because Ryan is an attorney general – a lawyer. He's not stupid. He wouldn't keep evidence of his crimes. But as soon as I think it, I know that he would. Ryan believes that he's smarter than almost everyone. And he's powerful enough and privileged enough to feel untouchable.

Isabel nods. 'Do you have a safe at home?'

'Yes. There's one in his study.'

'Can you get into it?' she asks, eagerly.

I shake my head. 'I don't know the code. He just keeps papers in there. A few family heirlooms, like his dad's watch, some of my jewelry.'

'I know it's a long shot, but can you try?'

'I'm not sure. I . . .' My eyes dart around, unable to settle on anything. Can I do this? Do I have the courage to leave the cage?

But how can I go back out there and pretend like

190

nothing has happened? How can I act like a dutiful wife when I've heard all this? There's no going back now. And that knowledge fills me with terror. Because I don't know how to move forward.

'Please,' Isabel begs me. 'If we let him get away with this, he'll do it again.'

I see the desperation on her face as well as the grief. I think of my dad and Daisy and how I let my sister down. I failed her, and my own feelings of grief rise up and threaten to paralyze me even further.

'You have to help,' Isabel says.

Chapter Twenty-Seven

Present

I am eating leftover rabbit stew in the morning, head bent over the bowl, and I'm thinking about Daisy. I've been thinking about her a lot recently and what she said to me about denial and being a coward. Her words have long haunted me.

I think, as much as it pains me to admit it, deep down I did know that our father was doing something to her, though I'm not sure I understood what exactly.

When I think back on it, I can recall the predatory way he'd look at her sometimes and the way he'd seek her out and pull her onto his lap, holding her there while she squirmed and tried to wriggle free. Though I was only a child, I sensed there was something off about his behavior.

I torment myself, replaying memories over and over.

I could have stopped him. I could have said something. Was I afraid that they would split us up and put us in separate foster homes?

But I did stop him in the end, I remind myself. When I walked into the trailer that day and saw him lying on the floor mid-overdose, I didn't run for help. I let him die.

My only regret is that it didn't happen sooner, because by the time he passed away the damage was done and it was too late to save Daisy. I think about the path my life has taken and I think about the journey yet to come.

I didn't save Daisy. But hopefully if she's looking down from above, she'll see I got justice for her and the others. Or perhaps, a better word would be revenge.

I am taking my last bite of the rabbit stew when Gwen knocks on the door and calls out to me. 'Emma?'

At first, I startle at the unfamiliar name, but then I get up. I'm trembling as I move to the door, a mixture of nerves but also fever. I woke this morning drenched in sweat and shivering. As I open the door I'm anxious that I've been a fool and I'm about to realize it, but Gwen's alone, carrying a bag of groceries. I usher her inside the cabin and quickly close the door behind her before she can let too much cold air inside.

'It's freezing in here,' she says at once, rubbing her arms and stamping her feet. 'Why haven't you got a fire going?'

I shrug.

'Are you out of wood?'

'No.'

She studies me with a frown. 'Well, I've brought you your groceries,' she says, putting the bag down on the table. 'What's that?' she says, gesturing to the bowl of stew. 'Rabbit?'

I nod. 'Someone left a couple on the doorstep yesterday.'

Her eyes flash to mine. 'Who?'

I shrug. 'I don't know. I didn't see.' I hesitate, chewing my lip, not sure whether to bring up the man I saw the day before that – the one prowling around the place – but then deciding there's no harm.

'There was a man,' I blurt out. 'Two days ago . . . I was out and when I came back I saw him checking out the cabin. Looking in the windows. He had a gun, so I hid. I was scared.'

Gwen's expression turns serious. 'What did he look like?'

'It was getting dark so I couldn't really see. He was tall. He looked kind of like he could be military, you know, the way he carried himself. He was wearing military-style boots too and camo pants. He had a scope on his rifle.'

'A hunter,' Gwen says.

'But there are signs all around the property,' I say, 'telling people it's private and to keep out.'

Gwen shrugs ruefully. 'People know this place has been abandoned for years. Locals won't take any notice of those signs. It'll be someone out hunting rabbits or deer,' she says, trying to reassure me. 'Maybe they saw something that made them think the place was inhabited and wanted to make sure no one was squatting or trashing the place.'

I frown. Was I being paranoid, thinking it was a private detective? Am I losing my mind out here all alone? Is the fever jumbling my thoughts? My head does feel like a skein of knotted wool.

'Everyone knows to respect people's privacy around here,' Gwen goes on. 'If he comes again and you don't answer the door, I'm sure he'll know to leave you be.'

I think about the fifty-thousand-dollar reward.

Gwen starts taking things out of the shopping bag: apples, pasta, noodles, milk – all the things I put on the list, but then she also takes out some packets of deli meat, cheese and a loaf of bread. I stare at them hungrily, but also with mounting anxiety. I don't have the money to waste on expensive things like turkey breast and brie.

She dips into the bag once more and pulls out a bar of chocolate with a flourish. 'And some chocolate,' she says with a grin. 'I figured everyone loves chocolate and if they don't there's something wrong with them.'

I swallow away the lump in my throat and smile at her. 'Yeah.'

'Want to make me a coffee?' she says with a smile.

I smile and fill the kettle up. 'How much do I owe you?' I ask, wondering if I can politely decline the extra stuff that I can't afford.

'Oh, don't worry about it.' Gwen grins.

'What?' I say, surprised.

'Think of it as a welcome to the neighborhood gift basket. I'm not much of a cook, so this is in place of muffins.'

'Are you sure?'

'Of course.'

'Thank you,' I say, dumbfounded by this unexpected kindness.

'How have you been?' she asks as I spoon coffee granules into mugs. 'How's the book going?'

'Oh, you know, slowly,' I say. 'I haven't been doing very much on it actually. I'm not feeling very well.'

'You do look a little peaky,' she says now, cocking her head to one side. 'Do you have a fever?'

I shrug. 'I don't know. I do feel warm.'

'You look flushed.' She moves toward me and I flinch involuntarily. It's been so long since anyone touched me without meaning to hurt me but she's only feeling my forehead. 'You're burning up,' she says with a small frown of worry. 'Have you taken anything for it?'

I shake my head. 'I don't have anything.'

'I've got some Advil in my bag, hang on.' She crosses to her handbag, which is hanging on the back of a chair and rummages in it, pulling out a pill bottle. 'Never go anywhere without. I've got terrible back pain.' She offers them to me. 'You keep that. I've got plenty.'

I'm so grateful I could cry. I take three straight-away with a glass of water. 'Thank you,' I say to her again, choking up.

'Do you think you need to see a doctor?' Gwen asks.

I shake my head. 'No, I'll be fine.'

She frowns, like she wonders why I'm being so obstinate, but then she moves on.

'Have you decided how long you're staying for?'

I bite my lip some more. 'No. I don't know.'

'You should stay put, I think,' she says. 'For the moment. Given that you're not feeling well.'

I don't answer her. Staying put might not be an option.

'There's no hurry is there?' she goes on. 'I mean, you don't need to be anywhere, do you?'

I pause, wondering why she wants to know. 'No,' I reply, carefully.

'I can let people know that there's a writer staying here if you like, and that you're looking for privacy so you can work on your book. That way, you'll be left to it.'

I weigh that up. 'Thanks. I'd appreciate that.'

'Of course,' she says, giving me a sympathetic smile. 'And I can keep bringing you groceries by too if you like?'

'You don't need to do that,' I argue, albeit weakly, running a hand through my hair, realizing it's sticking up all over the place and trying to smooth it down. I wonder what I must look like to her – a scarecrow probably. How strange she must think it is for me to be holed up in this freezing cabin without electricity or hot water.

'It's fine,' she reassures me. 'It's not a problem.'

A furrow appears between her eyebrows. My finger is still on the raised scar on my scalp and I hurriedly drop my hand. But too late, she's seen it. I can see her still staring at it, wondering no doubt what caused it. I could blurt a lie – tell her it's from a brain surgery or from falling off a trampoline when I was a kid or from any number of things – but before I can say anything she opens the back door and hurries out into the cold.

'I'll be off,' she says and she's gone, giving me one furtive glance over her shoulder before she disappears among the trees.

Chapter Twenty-Eight

Past

Six Months Ago

The noise from the ballroom follows me as I exit the bathroom and head toward the elevators. I can hear the speeches have begun and I pray that Ryan – who is due to give one of them – is too busy with that to come looking for me, though he must be wondering where I've got to. I reach the bank of elevators and stab the button with my finger. My teeth are chattering, not from cold but from shock. How can this be happening? How can this be real? Nausea churns in my stomach as though I've just stepped off a roller-coaster ride and can't find my balance. I've told Isabel that I will try to help her, but already I'm wondering if I've made a huge mistake.

I'm that dog and I've inched out of the cage but now I'm wondering if I shouldn't just turn around and slink back inside.

I watch as the floor numbers change on the dial, creeping steadily closer. It's taking forever. I glance over my shoulder at the ballroom. There's no way I can go back inside and pretend nothing has happened. I couldn't speak to Ryan, not without giving away that I know something. Things are too out in the open – I can't slink back into denial. I let out a gasp. Ryan has appeared in the doorway to the ballroom. He stops to talks to the old lady in burgundy velvet. She points in the direction of the bathrooms.

Just then the elevator dings and I dart inside, praying that Ryan doesn't turn his head and see me. I jab at the button and wait, terrified, as the doors take an eternity to close.

The ride to the lobby seems to take even longer. I slip out of my high heels and, when we reach the ground floor, I walk as fast as I can in my bare feet without causing suspicion, making straight for the grand entrance. I was planning on taking the town car home, but I worry that the driver might call Ryan and let him know, so instead I burst out into the warm summer night and hail a taxi.

It's a forty-five-minute drive home and the taxi driver isn't too happy about taking me as far as Westchester, but I promise him I'll tip him double and even more if he drives as fast as he can. I wind the window down, hoping a breeze on my face will shock me out of my stupor but it doesn't. The whole way back my mind plays over and over the conversation I just had with Isabel, and the last words I exchanged with Daisy.

I was so blinded by anger that I refused to contemplate that she might have been telling the truth about Ryan assaulting her. The idea was so outlandish. I couldn't believe her. Or was it that I didn't want to? Was it yet another instance of denial?

I replay the memory in my head of Daisy's visit to me, and something else slots into place. She came to see me, she said, and Ryan didn't let her in. I bet it was when I was at the Sanctuary. Did he want me out of the way, in case Daisy came back making more allegations? Did he encourage the doctors to keep me in there all that time – for six long months? The thought makes my head spin.

How could I have overlooked that my husband is a monster? How could I not have seen it? How can you be married to someone for years and not know what kind of a person they are? I was in love with him. I thought he was perfect and the whole time . . . he's a predator. He's the kind of man you read about in the news. I always scoff at the wives and girlfriends in those stories who claim they never knew, but now I find myself in that situation. Am I complicit? Is this my fault? Did I not give him what he needed sexually? The thought makes me sick. No. I can't blame myself. Ryan is a master manipulator. He's most likely a psychopath – how else to explain what he's done and how he's been able to fool so many people?

The thought of that, of what he is and what he's capable of, makes me shudder. How am I going to go up against him?

I hate having to admit this to myself but Ryan has essentially rendered me helpless, fully dependent on him. And I let him. I gave him the power, gave away my independence. I let him cage me. Admittedly, it was a gilded cage, and he was so good at it – at slowly, insidiously taking away my autonomy – that I didn't even realize what he was doing.

I wanted so badly to be taken care of, to get away from my past, that I let him take control. I let him win the argument over me quitting college. I barely tried to fight him on it. I just wanted to make him happy.

I have let him choose everything, down to what I eat – in fact that's where it started, on our very first date with him asking me to let him choose my food. I thought it was romantic. What a fool I've been. I see that now.

The house in Westchester was his doing too, and I didn't argue with him about moving there, even though it further cut me off from any possibility of friends or having a life outside of him. I went along with it because he painted such a picture of domestic bliss. He knew that was my weakness, what I wanted more than anything, and he manipulated me.

I thought I was choosing the décor for the house but now I think about it, those interior designers were ones that he recommended. I wonder if he was briefing them behind my back the whole time, undermining me. The more I think about it the more it makes sense.

He selected my clothes too, from the very beginning, replacing my thrift-store closet piece by piece, but doing it under the guise of spoiling me. He'd often buy me gifts, but really he was creating a model wife. I was a doll that he got to mold to his exact specifications. I even cut and colored my hair in just the style he said he liked, and I did it to please him. You are a fool, I think again.

The more I reflect, the more it all falls into place.

The way he told me not to bother with the women in his social circles, laughing that they were all bitches who were gossiping about us behind our backs. How he subtly encouraged me to keep my distance from them. Now I see it's because he didn't want me to make friends! When I did make acquaintances in Westchester – at yoga and the gym – his response was to buy me a home gym for Christmas and pay for a personal trainer. I thought it was him being thoughtful, but, no, he was just trying to keep me isolated. How did I not see what he was doing?

Sitting in the back of the car, I rack my brains. Have I chosen anything since we've been together? He chose where we got married, he chose my wedding dress, he chose the house, he chose the housekeeper. He chose Sienna's name, not me. He chose the crib and picked out the color scheme for the nursery. He chose the nanny.

He decides what we eat, what we wear, what we watch on TV, where we go on vacation. He never explicitly orders me. He just hints, cajoles with kisses, either withholds compliments or showers them on me, nudging me like I am a stray dog and he the dog catcher with a bag of treats. And I have allowed myself to be snared.

The realization of how thoroughly I've been brainwashed and controlled without knowing it leaves me gasping. It's as if now a spell has been lifted and I can see the truth of our relationship. He must have been laughing at me the whole time we've been together. How easy I was to snare, to control. I never asked any questions. I was just so happy to be his wife.

But why did he choose me? I can't fathom it. And then I realize it's blindingly obvious. I was a stray dog when he met me. I was someone he knew he could easily convince to eat out of his hand. All he needed to do was offer me scraps, show me a little kindness, give me a scratch behind the ear, and I would be as loyal as they come. I would never leave his side or abandon him. I would lie at his feet, I would fetch and carry, I would be dependent on him for my very survival. And he could then get away with everything. He could stick me in a cage, and I would still love him.

That's what he saw that day in the restaurant when we first met. Easy pickings. A poor, naïve waitress from out of town, with no friends and no family. Vulnerable and needy. Attractive enough to look good on his arm, smart enough to hold a conversation but not clever enough to figure him out. Any woman from his world – independent and worldly, and wealthy in their own right – would not have been such easy prey. He couldn't so easily manipulate them. They had money and networks and friends and families to support them. That's why he chose me to be his wife.

He liked my innocence, he said. What he meant was he liked how easy it would be to fool me.

I am going to throw up. I clutch at the door as bile bubbles up my throat.

'You OK?' the taxi driver asks.

I put my hand to my mouth. 'Yes,' I stammer, swallowing down the vomit. 'I'm fine.'

But then I remind myself, I'm not that little girl

from the trailer. And I'm not the waitress Ryan met either. I can do something about it this time.

Shaking, I pull my phone out of my evening bag, noticing that I have a missed call and several texts from Ryan. Oh God. Quickly, I text him back, telling him that I've got a headache and have gone home early. My fingers hover over the keys. Cringing, I paste a heart emoji. I feel sick again doing it, but I need to reassure him that I'm fine. I don't want him coming after me.

As soon as I get home, I throw money at the taxi driver and run inside, surprising the babysitter who assumed we'd be back much later. Foot tapping, I fail to hide my impatience as she gathers her things up and leaves. Once she's gone, I race into Ryan's office and fling open the cabinet where he keeps the safe. It has an electronic lock, and I try Sienna's birthday but that doesn't work. I try our wedding anniversary and that doesn't work either. I try Ryan's birthday, growing increasingly desperate.

What will I do if I can't get inside the safe?

I look around the room in mounting panic, racking my brains for other dates of importance. Just then my gaze lands on a photograph of Ryan with George W Bush, taken many years ago at the White House, when Ryan was at college and spent a summer interning for a senator. A thought occurs to me. Ryan doesn't talk often about his career aspirations – he plays his cards close to his chest – but I know his ultimate ambition has always been 1600 Pennsylvania Avenue.

'2028,' I once overheard him joking with his campaign manager. It's a long shot but I tap in 012028 – the date for the inauguration of the president in the year 2028. To my complete astonishment, it works. I stare at the blinking green light on the safe, incredulous, and then I open it.

Inside there are files of papers, a bound stack of hundred-dollar bills, and his father's Rolex. I take everything out and quickly start going through it all. There are the house deeds and several certificates for stocks and shares. There's even his last will and testa ment, which I didn't even know about, and at the bottom I find a plain black box, like the kind you might get with fancy lingerie. In fact, I think I recognize it as one of mine – perhaps a Christmas present from a few years ago.

I lift the lid off the box and fall back onto my haunches with a gasp. I know then, in that moment, that I didn't want to find proof. I wanted to be able to laugh it off and go back to living in denial, but what lies in front of me leaves no room for that.

I stare down at the dozen or more ID cards. There's also a cheap gold necklace with a cross on it, the chain broken, a pair of ripped red panties, and a black hair tie, with several dark strands of hair attached to it. But the only thing I really notice is the blue silk pajama top. It's mine. It's the one I gave Daisy to wear.

My stomach lurches and I swallow down a mouthful of vomit, gagging hard. Fighting all my instincts, I reach into the box with a shaking hand, and grab hold of all the IDs. I start sorting through them, looking at the photographs. All of the women are young, dark-haired and pretty. There are several driver's licenses, one Soul Cycle gym membership, a library card and a hotel ID. I read the names on all of them: Samantha, Marcella, Amy, Lupe, Diane, Chelsea, Veronica.

Tears fall down my cheeks. It's real. It's all real.

The thin thread I'd been holding on to that this was all a nightmare and that I'd allowed myself to be taken in by Isabel, snaps.

Ryan is indeed a monster.

Chapter Twenty-Nine

Present

I am lying awake in the cabin under a pile of blankets, feverish and unable to sleep. My head keeps spinning with thoughts about Ryan. I'm still trying to untangle years of lies. Every so often a memory will present itself and I'll parse it for clues as to what I might have missed.

After a time I push all of it aside – I'll never know the answers after all – and instead I start thinking of Sienna. The tinkling of the cans makes me startle and leap from the bed.

My first thought is that Gwen has figured out who I am and called the police and I rue my decision to stay put. I should have gone while I had the chance. If I get caught it will mean that everything I've done, all that I've gone through, will have been for nothing.

I hear the creak of the veranda at the front of the house. A footstep.

'Run!' the voice in my head screams at me.

It's already too late, I think. But I can't just let them take me. I stumble out into the hallway. Another creak outside sends adrenaline coursing through me. I dart through into the dark kitchen and slip my feet into my boots. Then, praying no one is on the other side, I yank open the back door and slip out into the frigid night.

I'm half-expecting to be met by a squad of armed cops, pointing guns, but there's no one that I can see. Maybe the person at the front of the cabin is a lone bounty hunter, hired by the Reid family to hunt me down.

Expecting at any moment to hear someone yell at me to stop, or for a gun to crack and my ribs to explode with the force of a bullet, I stumble but keep running, my lungs burning from the effort, my feet clumsy in the snow. My breathing is so loud, my pulse beating so hard in my ears, that I don't hear the growl until it's too late. I skid to a halt three feet from a large animal – a giant cougar, I think – which is crouched in the snow, ready to pounce. It hisses at me.

'Don't turn around!' a male voice sounds.

I jump, fighting the instinct to search out its owner.

'Don't turn your back,' he yells.

I obey, fear twisting my stomach into a knot. The

cougar is about seven feet long, its fur is sticking up on end, and it's baring its teeth at me.

I feel the man suddenly at my back, and the barrel of a shotgun appears over my shoulder. I turn to look at him. It's the man from the store. Not a cop then. And not a bounty hunter.

'Get behind me,' he says quietly but firmly and I do, slowly inching my way around him, not taking my eyes off the cougar, until he is between us.

'Don't shoot it,' I hear myself say.

'I hunted it this far,' he says. 'I'm not letting it go.'

'Please,' I plead.

The man hesitates, then fires. I recoil from the blast. When I open my eyes, I see the cougar bolting off through the trees. He fired wide. He turns to me now and the moonlight illuminates the wry expression on his face. I realize too that he's the man who was prowling around the cabin the other day. I recognize his clothes. And the gun.

I can see him appraising me as well, with a frown. 'What the hell are you doing running through the woods in the middle of the night?' he asks. 'I could have shot you!'

'What are you doing hunting in the middle of the night?' I retort, and then I bend double and press my hands to my knees. The shock, the adrenaline and the effort of running have wiped me out. I feel wobbly, like I'm going to faint.

'I've been tracking that cougar for weeks,' he says. 'Been eating livestock from here to town.'

'You're trespassing,' I tell him, grumpily.

'No one takes notice of those signs.' He grins. 'And besides I thought you were the one trespassing. Saw smoke and came by a few days ago to check on the place. Figured someone was squatting.'

So that's what he was doing.

'Why were you prowling around the cabin just now? I heard you creeping around the veranda.'

'I wanted to check if you were home or if you'd moved on. What are you even doing out here?'

There's suspicion in his voice.

'I'm a friend of the owner,' I explain, eyeing him nervously.

He frowns. 'No one's been out here for years. Thought the owners had forgotten about the place.'

I shake my head.

'My grandfather helped build it.' He jerks his chin at the cabin. 'It's a shame they've let it go.'

'I'm going back inside. It's freezing.' I turn around.

'You get the rabbits?' he asks.

I turn back. 'That was you?' I respond, though of course it had to have been him.

He smiles at me. 'Had extra.'

'Thanks.'

'I figured if you were managing to survive out here

in this weather without heating or electric that you'd know how to prep 'em.'

'My grandfather taught me,' I tell him.

'Outdoors girl,' he says in a newly respectful tone and I catch him reassessing me, his gaze raking me head to foot. My nerves jitter in response. How do I extricate myself? Before I can he holds out his hand. 'I'm Jake,' he says. 'Jake Myerson.' He jerks his head toward the right. 'I have a place couple of miles from here.'

I take his hand. 'Emma,' I say.

'What were you running from?' he asks, his hand still gripping mine.

My heart skips a beat and slams like a freight train into my ribs. 'What?' I stammer.

'Just now. Why did you run?'

I don't know what to say. He lets go of my hand.

'Are you . . . are you in some kind of trouble?' The concern in his voice takes me by surprise. I blink at him in stunned silence.

'Is that what the tin cans are for? Are you afraid of someone?'

It feels as if all my insides are being pulled taut. I study him but he seems genuinely to be concerned. He's waiting on me to answer and before I know what I'm doing, instead of lying and dismissing his notions as silly, I nod.

His lips, which had been parted, purse. 'I guessed as much,' he says quietly. 'I'm sorry.' He pauses, then gives an embarrassed smile, 'I apologize if I've startled you before too, showing up unannounced. And again tonight. I didn't mean to.'

I give a weak smile.

'I'll leave you in peace,' he says, ruefully. 'You ever need me though, I'm a couple miles in that direction, right by the lake.' He points. 'No cell phone coverage out here and I'm guessing you got no landline. But you come find me.'

'Thanks,' I say, feeling choked up.

He smiles at me, touches his hand to his head and starts to walk away. 'Goodnight, Emma,' he says.

I watch him trudge through the snow.

'Jake,' I call after him.

He turns around, his head pricking up.

'Thank you,' I say.

I don't know what I'm thanking him for, and, judging from the bemused look that forms on his face, he doesn't either. I guess I'm thanking him for caring about a stranger, and for seeing the vulnerability in me and not preying on it.

He gives me one last look, then vanishes into the darkness.

Chapter Thirty

Past

Six Months Ago

I am still crouched by the safe, the black box open on my lap, staring in disbelief. My world is crumbling around me.

There's no time for any of this though. I need to get out of here. I need to wake up Sienna and put her in the car and go.

Quickly, I put the lid back on the box and shove everything else back into the safe. Before I shut the door though, I have second thoughts and pull out the will, taking that too.

'Mommy?'

I almost jump out of my skin. Sienna has appeared behind me in the doorway.

'What are you doing up?' I ask, forcing brightness into my voice.

She's yawning and half-asleep, still wearing her *Frozen* costume and clutching her rabbit toy in one hand. She must have refused to take the costume off when she went to bed.

'What's in the box?' she asks, pointing. 'Is it a present?'

Suddenly, I hear the sound of a car tearing up the driveway and my stomach drops to my feet. It's Ryan.

He knows. He must. Or at least he must suspect that Isabel spoke to me. Why else would he abandon the gala and race back here?

I sweep Sienna up into my arms and, hefting her on my hip, while still clutching the box in my other hand, I look around in desperation. What do I do? Should I confront him? But the thought is terrifying. I'm suddenly afraid of him. I don't know what he's capable of anymore. I don't know him at all. This box in my hand tells me that.

Should I hide? No. I can't hide. Should I put the box back and act like everything is normal? But I know I'm not that good an actress.

I hurry toward the French doors before I can think twice. I slide them open and step out onto the terrace overlooking the backyard and pool. 'Where are we going?' Sienna asks.

'Do you want to play a game?' I whisper.

The car pulls up on the other side of the house. I hear the door slam.

'Daddy?' Sienna asks loudly.

'Shh,' I say, hushing her. 'We're playing hide-and-seek.'

I scoot along the side of the house, toward the garage, managing to trip one of the exterior security lights so the whole backyard illuminates like a football pitch under floodlights.

I hear Ryan yell my name in the house.

'Hide-and-seek!' Sienna whispers loudly, then giggles.

'Shh,' I hush again. 'We're going to hide in the car.' I hope the side door to the garage is open. It is thankfully, and I slip inside. My Porsche SUV – a gift from Ryan – is parked in here, alongside Ryan's Range Rover. I open the door of the Porsche and throw the black box onto the passenger seat before putting Sienna in her car seat, fumbling with the straps until they click into place.

'Mommy?' Sienna asks, confused.

I shut the door and run around to the driver's side. I get in and then my stomach sinks when I realize that I don't have the car keys with me. Oh God, what a stupid mistake. They're in the bowl by the front door.

I glance in the mirror at Sienna. Her bottom lip is trembling. She's scared. I'm making her scared. 'It's

OK, darling,' I say, smiling at her in reassurance even though I feel anything but. 'We're just playing a game.'

She starts to cry. 'I don't want to play.'

Panic grips me. 'I need you to close your eyes,' I tell her.

'Why?' she sobs.

'Because I'm going to get you a present.' It's the only thing I can think of saying that might stop her from screaming and crying if I leave her in the car alone. 'But you need to shut your eyes,' I remind her. 'And wait for me to tell you to open them.'

Enticed by the idea of a present, she does as she's told.

I ease open the door.

'Mommy?'

I glance over my shoulder and find Sienna has cracked one eye open and is staring at me in alarm. Damn it.

'Mommy has to get the present. I left it in the house.'

'No!' she whimpers.

It's dark in the garage and in the car. 'I have to, baby,' I say, my own voice breaking. 'I'll only be a minute. I promise I'll be right back.'

'No!' she sobs.

I leave the car to the sound of her crying and I hate myself, but what choice do I have?

My whole body quivering with adrenaline and fear,

I slip out of the garage, hoping that Sienna's screams won't be heard outside, and thankfully they're not. I dart in my bare feet back toward the house, driven on by terror.

Creeping toward the French doors to Ryan's study, I spy into the room. He's standing in the middle of the doorway, looking around the room.

He walks toward the safe and I notice that I didn't shut the cabinet door properly. It's slightly ajar. He's spotted it. He pulls it open. I watch him tap the code in. As it opens, he checks inside and then curses, before dashing out of the room, heading for the stairs.

This is the only chance I'll get. I slide open the door, then sneak through the study and peer out into the hallway. Ryan has reached the top of the stairs and is tearing along the landing toward our bedroom. As soon as he disappears out of view, I dart across the hall and snatch my handbag and the keys from the table by the front door.

The keys clink loudly against the bowl. I wince, and then I run, back the way I came, through the study and outside, sliding the doors shut behind me.

I'm outside, sprinting for the garage, when I hear the phone in my bag start ringing. Oh shit. It's him. I know it's him. I don't have time to silence it but now I can hear the doors to the study sliding open behind me. He's following the sound of the ringtone.

I dart inside the garage, throw myself into the car

and find Sienna, sobbing loudly, her face red and wet with tears and snot. 'Mommy!' she hiccups with relief when I jump in the car, locking the doors behind me.

'I'm sorry, I'm sorry,' I cry, hitting the car's power button at the same time as I reach for the remote to get out of the garage. I rev the engine impatiently. The side door flies open and Ryan rushes inside. We lock eyes through the car window and his face is that of a stranger – the mask has dropped and I see the monster beneath.

I hit the gas and take off, scraping the roof of the car against the garage doors, which are still rising.

Ryan jumps out of the way just in time and I glance back in my rearview mirror and see him running toward his own car.

Sienna is still screaming in the back seat and I don't have time to calm her down. I'm terrified. What will he do? I speed down the drive and through the gates, seeing Ryan's headlights bearing down on me. I turn right out of the drive. I don't know where I'm going. Away from here – that's all I can think of. Somewhere safe where I can stop and think and tend to Sienna and try to figure out what next.

If I keep going straight, I'll hit town and stoplight after stoplight, so at the last moment I swing a right, deciding to take the longer route to the freeway – a backcountry lane with no stoplights. With any luck Ryan will assume I'll take the shorter road through town. But that hope quickly fades as he roars up behind me, so close he's almost touching my bumper. He honks his horn. Terrified, I put my foot to the floor. It's pitch-black out here. Too dark to see anything beyond what's illuminated by the car's beams.

Sienna is sobbing and I twist briefly to look at her, to reassure her, and I see that her straps are undone. She's wriggling out of her car seat.

'Stop!' I shout. 'Sienna, don't!' But she doesn't listen. She's reaching for her rabbit, which has fallen on the floor. 'No, Sienna!' I shout again but she ignores me. I swerve across the road, struggling to right the car.

I look in the rearview mirror. Ryan is gaining on me. I can't pull over. Sienna grabs her bunny from the floor and then struggles back into the car seat. 'Mommy!' she yells. 'I want to go home. No like this.'

But I can't. 'Do up your straps, baby!' I shout.

She fumbles with them: they're too big and clunky for her little hands to work. Ryan's Range Rover rams the back of my SUV. He's driving like a maniac. Doesn't he know I've got Sienna in the car? No. I realize just then that he has no idea. Why would he assume that I've got Sienna in the car? He thinks she's home asleep in bed.

I glance in the rearview mirror and Ryan's headlight beams fill my vision, blinding me. Dazzled, I squint through the window trying to see the road, but it's disappeared. All of a sudden a tree springs into relief. I'm heading right for it.

Time slows. In that awful moment before impact, memories flash before me in a long stream; the pink sheets stained yellow on the bed in the trailer, the vomit bubbling on my dad's lips, my grandfather showing me how to work the bolt on a shotgun, me handing Ryan a menu, hearing him call my name on the sidewalk, Ryan sliding a ring onto my wedding finger on a beach, Daisy dancing at our wedding reception. Sienna sitting on my lap earlier today as I read her a story. The IDs of a dozen women lying scattered in a box.

BANG!

Chapter Thirty-One

Present

The axe thwacks the ice. I heave the blade out, hissing through my teeth as fire shoots up my arm in response. My fever isn't going away. This morning I woke up with my jaw aching from how hard my teeth had been chattering in the night.

The Advil that Gwen gave me are taking the edge off but not enough and I know I need to get antibiotics to treat the infection before it gets any worse. Gwen won't be back for another two days and I don't think I can wait. But the lake is frozen over so I can't travel by kayak and I don't have the energy to walk around the edge. It would take a whole day, trudging through snow. My only option is to walk across the ice, but I need to determine whether it is thick enough to hold my weight.

I don't have a tape measure, but I poke a stick through the hole I've made with the axe trying to guess how deep the layer of ice is. By my estimation it's around four inches thick. The problem is that four inches is the minimum it needs to be to walk on. I know all this because my grandfather taught me. He sometimes took me ice fishing on a friend's pond. Any less than four inches and he warned me to never step foot on it. What if I'm overestimating and it's more like three and a half inches thick? And this is just one measurement, taken right by the jetty. What if there are places where it's thinner? Snow blankets the lake, so I won't be able to see what color the ice is – another helpful indicator of whether it's safe to walk on or not.

I sit back on my haunches and survey the expanse of frozen water. Shit. I look back at the cabin, trying to decide whether to stay put or whether to risk it. It's a choice between dying of sepsis or dying from drowning. I decide to at least give it a go. Carefully, I ease myself off the jetty and put my weight slowly onto the ice, keeping a grip on the wood in case the ice starts to crack beneath me.

I am right by the jetty so if I did fall through I could drag myself out, but if I fall through in the middle of the lake, I'm definitely dead.

The ice creaks but feels solid enough beneath my boots. I let go of the jetty and stand there, terrified, waiting for a shearing sound and to fall through into the icy water below, but it holds and so I take a tentative step. And then another. OK, I think to myself. Ice is always thinnest closest to shore so if it's thick enough here, it should be strong enough to cross.

I glance back at the shore and the cabin one last time, before I head out across the lake. I gain confidence as I go and by the time I reach the middle, it's solid enough that it feels like walking on concrete.

The last lot of Advil I took is beginning to wear off and I'm shivering again, though it could be because of the sub-zero temperatures. I touch my forehead and find it's coated in sweat.

Feeling tired and dizzy I force myself to keep going for another twenty minutes and as I approach the other side of the lake the ice begins to creak and moan. I move slowly, more deliberately, testing my weight before each step.

An inner voice warns me to be careful and so I stop, kneel and paw at the snow, clearing away a patch so I can see what color the ice beneath is. It's gray – the danger zone. I don't know how big the patch is or how far I need to move to circumvent it. I step backwards, retracing my steps slowly onto more solid surface and then I go sideways, stopping every twenty feet to check the color of the ice beneath the snow. Eventually I find a more solid patch and inch forwards again, but toward the shore the ice once more starts to thin and every step I take is met with a resounding moan.

I'm so close – about five feet from the tree-lined edge of the lake – when my foot plunges right through, cracking it like an eggshell. My leg sinks straight down into the freezing water, and I gasp in shock, but manage to scramble backwards before I completely fall in, dragging my soaking boot out of the hole. I'm wet to the knee, my foot sopping and already numb. Beneath me the ice moves and a tremendous cracking sound, like the earth splitting in two, shoots terror into me.

Chapter Thirty-Two

Past

Six Months Ago

The black hole is infinite. I sink down into its depths as though I'm chasing after fast-fading fragments of star. Finally though, when the darkness becomes so absolute I don't know where it ends and I begin, I stop and I let myself float, hanging suspended for a time that feels immeasurable. It could be minutes. It could be years.

But then, suddenly and without warning, light floods in. It is as jarring and harrowing as being born; an assault of faces, colors and sounds jumbling in front of me. I struggle, wanting to burrow back into the dark, to reach for the receding edges of it and delve back under. But I am not allowed. Someone is poking at me, prodding at me. A voice is saying a name loudly and insistently.

Pain knocks gently at first, but then more insistently. I cry out and a nurse pats my arm, says something to me that I don't catch, and I drift off, the dull ache ever present, like an animal scratching at a door to be let in.

When I wake up again I see that I'm in a hospital room. I try to turn my head, but it hurts too much, throbs as though an axe is buried in my skull. I squint down at my body. My right leg is in traction. What happened? How did I get here?

I was in a car. I remember that much. I was driving. It was nighttime. How long have I been in the hospital for? Something presses at my consciousness, a memory trying to hand me a piece of the puzzle, but I'm unable to turn toward it or take it.

'Oh, you're awake.'

I blink. An unsmiling nurse, around forty years old, stands over me.

'What happened?' I ask. My lips are cracked and my throat raw so the words come out as a croak.

'You had an accident,' she tells me.

I frown and it makes my head throb.

'How . . .?' I start, wanting to know how long I've been here.

'You crashed your car into a tree,' the nurse answers.

I draw a stabbing breath, the image of a tree silhouetted against headlights popping into my head. I brace myself and hear the tinkle of glass and the screech of metal ripping apart. But there is nothing beyond that. No memory whatsoever. I feel like there's something there, something nudging at me, trying to force its way into the light, but I can't quite grab hold of it.

'You had a subdural hematoma. A blood clot on the brain,' the nurse tells me. 'The doctors had to operate to relieve the pressure.'

I lift a heavy arm, spaghetti-junctioned with IV tubes, and touch my head, feeling the gauze bandage wrapped around it. That explains the feeling of an axe embedded in my skull.

'You're lucky to be alive,' she adds. I close my eyes and drift off again into the dark.

An hour later, or it could be a day – I'm losing track of time – I hear my name being called: 'Rose?'

I force myself to open my eyes. The room is startlingly bright, and I squint. I turn my head and there he is. Ryan. I reach for him, mumbling: 'Ryan.' My fingers brush his. He presses his hand over mine and grips it tightly.

There are dark new worry lines etched across his forehead. I notice gray at his temples too, which I don't think was there before. 'You had an accident,' he says.

I nod. 'I crashed,' I say.

'What do you remember?' he says.

I shake my head. 'Nothing.'

'You don't remember anything?' he presses.

I frown. My memories are still fragments and the sedation and painkillers are fogging my mind. 'Not really,' I rasp. My throat feels like it's been stripped with acid. 'What happened?' I press.

He sighs. 'I don't know.' He looks down at his hands, clasped in his lap, and I get a sudden sense of foreboding. He looks up. 'Sienna was in the car with you.'

I stare at him without blinking. It's as if the world has stamped on the brakes. I have been flung forward into a new reality and right now I'm spinning through the air, knowing that when I land the impact is going to kill me.

Ryan saying Sienna's name aloud lifts the spell that had been cast, and now I can see clearly the thing that has been nagging at me, the thing I couldn't grab hold of – it was the knowledge that Sienna was in the car. How could I have forgotten my daughter? How could I have forgotten she was there?

I must have blocked the memory on purpose, knowing that once I remembered, it would destroy me.

Another memory shoves its way to the forefront of my mind. It is shortly after the crash. My eyes are fluttering open, and I am trying to lift my head off the steering wheel. My body is made of pain, and I fight off the encroaching darkness that is dragging me down because I need to make sure that Sienna is OK. She was in the back seat. Blood trickles down my head, but through a red haze and the broken windshield I can see the headlights illuminating a shape, lying in the ditch to the side of the tree.

I can't make out Sienna's features, but I know it's her from the pink cape she's wearing – her *Frozen* costume.

'She's dead,' Ryan says to me, shattering the memory and bringing me back into the present moment.

A howl is trapped somewhere deep inside me, as though it's an animal caught in a cave. I fear letting it out; that if I do, I will be ripped to shreds. That the pain will be never-ending. So instead, I force numbness into every cell. I block everything. I don't know how long I can manage to hold it all inside, but I know I have to try because there is no other alternative.

'Why wasn't she strapped in?' Ryan asks, and his face crumples. I've never seen him cry before and my instinct is to reach for him and comfort him, but he lets go of my hand and then jerks away, staring at me with such hatred I feel eviscerated.

'Why?' he spits, his voice shaking with rage.

'I don't know,' I stammer, looking around the room for something to cling to because it feels as if the world has started moving again, like a carousel ride, but much too fast. The room is spinning. I strapped her in, didn't I? I desperately try to recall. Why were we even in the car? Where were we going? Why can't I remember?

How did it even happen? I must have swerved out the way of another car or an animal in the road. I'm a good driver. I'm careful. I've never even had a ticket. 'What caused it?' I manage to stammer.

Ryan stares at me, his expression full of disgust. 'You were off your head on Ambien,' he tells me.

The news hits me like a punch to the stomach and for a moment I stop breathing. I stare at Ryan, hoping he's going to tell me he's lying but he doesn't. 'You took enough to tranquilize a horse, then you got in the car with our daughter and you drove.'

'No,' I say, shaking my head. 'No.'

There's no way. I wouldn't. I didn't.

'They ran blood tests. You had enough in your system to tranquilize a horse.'

I shake my head, the horror of what he's telling me makes me want to block my ears. It can't be true. It isn't true. Is it? I don't remember. I don't remember anything about the accident or what happened before it. I try to force my way through

234

the fog to find something to grip on to, some shard of memory from the night of the accident, but there's only blankness. I push back further – trying to remember any details about the last month, but I can't remember a single thing. What's going on? I seem to only be able to recall things in my long-term memory, nothing recent.

I stare at Ryan who is still glowering at me with disgust and hatred.

Oh God. What if he's right? What if I did take Ambien?

An unearthly, ear-shattering scream fills my ears, deafening me. It's me, I realize. I'm the one screaming. I couldn't hold it back any longer. The animal has been let loose from the cave.

I tug at the tubes running into my arms and yank them out, tumbling from the bed onto the unforgiving floor. I claw at my skin like it's on fire, tear at my hair, and I hear voices shouting and then hands pinning me down, as nurses and doctors intervene.

I scream and howl, trying to displace this wild, rabid animal clawing at my insides, because I don't know how I can occupy the same space as it and not be torn to pieces.

There is a sting in my arm and the animal retreats back into its cave. A dullness comes over me and my limbs become heavy. I stop fighting. My thoughts turn to Sienna. My baby. My love. I can see her gap-toothed smile, can feel her sticky, hot hand in mine. I can hear her giggling laugh as I tickle her soft belly. I can even smell the baby shampoo in her dark curls.

How can she be gone? How is it possible?

Because you killed her, the voice in my head answers harshly.

I look up and notice, through the sea of white coats pinning me to the ground, Ryan, walking out the door, tears streaming down his face.

'Ativan. Two milligrams,' I hear the doctor say.

'Ryan,' I whisper but he's gone.

The young nurse kneels beside me and pushes a syringe into the IV tube running into my arm. My eyelids droop shut and I am sucked down into the empty place.

For the next few days, whenever I resurface for long enough, only one image is clear: the one of Sienna lying on the road, her broken body illuminated by the car's headlights. I try to picture other things, strive to recall the details of her face, her fingers, her feet. I want to imprint every inch of her body into my mind, carve it into my flesh. I am so afraid that I will start to forget, but the only thing my mind keeps offering up from the shadows is the image of her lying in the ditch.

Tears slip silently down my face.

The young nurse enters the room, just then. Her name is Sandra, and she is the only one of the medical staff to show me any kindness.

'There's someone here to see you,' she tells me.

For a moment I think it will be Ryan and my stomach curls into a tight ball. I haven't wanted to ask about him. He made it clear enough how he feels and I don't blame him for being angry or for hating me. I just wish I could explain.

I turn my head with trepidation toward the door and see that it isn't Ryan. Instead, there are two men waiting in the hallway outside my room. Sandra beckons to them and they enter.

'She's sedated,' Sandra tells them. 'So you might not get much response.'

I know they are police, even though they are in plain clothes. I know it from the guns holstered on their waists and from the fact they look like every cop from every movie I've ever seen. One is older, probably late forties, with a rash of salt-and-pepper stubble. The other is around my age, Asian-American, clean-shaven and athletic.

'Rose Reid?' the older guy says, though it's a rhetorical question. 'I'm Detective Adams.' He points his thumb at his partner. 'This is Detective Lim.'

I don't answer. I look between them, waiting, aware of my heart rate increasing thanks to the machine announcing it loudly beside the bed.

Detective Adams steps closer. Lim stands where he is, blocking the door.

I swallow, my throat still raw from the intubation and all the screaming.

'We're here to talk to you about the accident,' Adams says, taking out a notebook and pencil.

'I don't remember anything,' I croak before turning my head away from them both.

'Actually, I'm here to inform you that you're being charged with homicide.'

The words take a while to penetrate and then I realize that I am being charged with killing my own child. Surprisingly, I don't feel any response to the news. It's meaningless. I don't care if I go to jail. I don't care if I am locked up for the rest of my life. I don't care if I live or die. What does it matter?

'Your husband has given a statement that you and he fought on the night of the accident.'

I stir at that, puzzled. Did we?

'He says that you threatened to kill both yourself and your daughter.'

I blink at him and then shake my head vigorously. 'No . . . I would never . . .'

'He's given the statement under oath.'

'He's lying,' I stammer. There's no way that can be true.

'The housekeeper has confirmed it.'

My mouth falls open, but no words come out.

'Your husband had asked for a divorce.'

It's Lim speaking. I turn to look at him, my head foggy with all the drugs they're pumping into me.

'He'd told you he wanted a divorce,' he repeats as if I'm slow in the head. 'And you took it badly. You'd been drinking. Had taken a sleeping aid. And you threatened to kill yourself and your daughter. Before he could stop you, you got behind the wheel.'

'No,' I stammer again, feeling the walls closing in on me and my chest constricting with panic. 'He didn't. I didn't.'

'You didn't get behind the wheel and drive?' Adams asks, his voice dripping with scorn.

'No. I drove . . . but . . . I didn't say that. I didn't want to kill myself. Or Sienna,' I wail.

He ignores me. 'We're here to officially charge you. You'll have a court-appointed lawyer come and see you to discuss how you want to plead. Guilty or not guilty.'

'I'm not guilty,' I say, my pulse still racing in alarm despite the sedation I'm under.

'If you plead not guilty and it goes to trial, you're likely going to get life and then some,' he adds. 'You'll be locked up for thirty years, possibly more.'

Lim speaks up. 'If you plead guilty,' he offers, with a hint of empathy in his voice, 'you can cut a deal. Fifteen years. In a psychiatric hospital – Crosshill. It's better than prison.'

'But . . .' I start to argue. My mind is a forest fire of confusion. I'm sure Ryan didn't ask for a divorce. But then what did we fight about?

'Given your recent history of mental illness, your psychotic break that led to you being institutionalized, you're not going to win a trial.'

It wasn't a psychotic break, I want to argue. It was postnatal depression, but then I remember that it was postnatal psychosis. They think I'm crazy.

'Fifteen years is a good deal,' Lim says. 'Take it.'

Fifteen years? In a mental hospital? I cannot fathom. I cannot even respond.

He stands, shaking his head at his partner.

'Someone from the DA's office will be here later today with the paperwork for you to sign,' he tells me.

Chapter Thirty-Three

Present

I can feel the ice starting to give way beneath me, and so I leap, throwing myself forward onto the narrow, snow-covered shore. I glance up at the six feet of sheer bank in front of me and then I look back across the lake. It's too far to return and even if I didn't have a soaking wet and frozen stiff leg I'd need to find a place where I could safely get back onto the ice. There's no choice. I need to climb up the bank somehow and make my way to the store. I need Gwen's help.

'You OK?'

I almost topple backwards into the water. Looking up, I see a couple standing above me on the ridge. They're in their twenties, wearing expensive-looking winter wear: North Face jackets and Patagonia beanies. The girl is pretty and fresh-faced. She has the kind of lustrous blonde locks of someone who regularly showers and shampoos, unlike me. The boy is handsome and preppy.

'Yes,' I say, keeping my head down and examining my soaking boot. 'I'm fine.'

'We saw you fall through the ice,' the girl says.

'I'm fine,' I mumble.

I look at the bank again searching for a way up but there's no obvious one.

'Here,' the guy says. 'Take my hand.'

I take hold of a tree trunk and haul myself a couple of feet up until I reach his outstretched hand. It's hard with a numb leg dragging behind me and my arms throbbing beneath their gauze bandages but I manage. He heaves me up, grunting. I almost collapse at the top, panting and sweating and shivering, but also grateful. I don't think I would have made it on my own.

'Ae you sure you're OK?' the woman asks, concerned.

I keep my head lowered as much as I can, pretending to be examining my wet boot. 'Yeah, I . . . it was stupid. I wanted to see how solid the ice was.'

'Not that solid.' The guy laughs.

'Are you staying around here?' the girl questions.

'Yeah,' I mumble.

'We didn't think anyone else was at the campsite.' She frowns. 'Thought it was just us.'

'Oh,' I say. 'No, I'm staying in a cabin.' I wave vaguely toward the town. 'I better get back and get dry.'

'You sure you don't want to come back to our RV? I can lend you some dry socks.'

'No. Thanks,' I say. 'It's not far. I better get going.' I make to move off. 'Thanks again,' I mumble.

'OK, bye,' they say and I catch the slight bewilderment in their voices. How odd I must look to them. A strange, unkempt woman in mismatched clothing falling through the ice and now refusing their help and hurrying off into the woods with a sopping wet leg. I don't dare look back to see if they're watching me.

The walk to the store takes even longer than normal. I'm shivering hard, limping, and seeing double by the time I reach the road. My legs are so weak I don't think I can make it the final few meters.

I force myself to focus on putting one foot in front of the other until finally I push open the door and hear the ding of the bell. Relief washes over me that I made it.

Gwen is sitting behind the counter. She sees me and a look of alarm crosses her face. She bustles out from behind the counter toward me.

'Help,' I whisper, collapsing to my knees.

Chapter Thirty-Four

Past

Five Months Ago

Crosshill is not like the Sanctuary. There's no swimming - pool, no five-star restaurant and no equine therapy.

Crosshill is more like the mental hospital in *One Flew Over the Cuckoo's Nest*. But it is also a prison. Everyone here is a convicted criminal. Most are violent offenders.

My room is a cell in which there is only a single bed, screwed to the floor, where I lie for up to eighteen hours a day, either sleeping fitfully or staring at the stains on the walls and the rips in the linoleum floor. There's a rusting metal toilet bowl attached to the wall.

The only communal spaces are the recreation room with a television that's controlled by a bullying inmate called Nora, and a dingy room used for the group therapy sessions. We are supposed to be allowed outside into a yard that's surrounded by twenty-foot-tall fences and razor wire, but I have not yet been permitted. It is apparently a treat to be earned.

There's a cafeteria too, where the noise of chairs scraping and people shoveling food with plastic spoons is deafening. At lunch and dinner, I join the other patient-cum-prisoners, shuffling in lines with beige trays to receive an inedible dollop of whatever is on the menu that day – usually mashed potato or rice with some questionable form of protein, not that I have any appetite anyway.

Most everyone is a zombie, heavily medicated into dribbling submission. I trudge through the days, my mind a thick sludge, unable to grip on to more than one thought at a time and that thought is usually of Sienna.

I signed the deal the DA offered me. My public defender told me I had no choice. The cops were right, he said. Any prosecutor would dredge up my recent depression and my stay in rehab. Ryan's witness statement would be enough to sink me. It was his word against mine and I had amnesia.

I still have amnesia. Though I don't know how much is down to the sedatives they are giving me. I take them though without complaint because the fog keeps the grief at bay, hidden just beyond the horizon. And I would rather have the numbness than know the truth of what happened that night. There's a part of me that wonders if Ryan is telling the truth. What if I did try to kill myself and Sienna?

I think I have been here three weeks so far, but it might be longer. I've stopped counting. The days run into each other anyway. I shuffle to the rec room. I am only passing through on the way to my cell but I hear someone call my name and so I stop and look around, confused, before my gaze lands on the TV.

Fox news is playing. A woman with blonde hair sprayed into a helmet shape is talking to camera. Behind her there's a large picture of me and Ryan and Sienna – the one we took at Christmas to go on the front of our cards. I step closer to the TV, drawn to the picture of my baby. Tears slide down my face at the sight of her, and I can feel my body starting to tremble convulsively.

'. . . we really have to ask ourselves whether it's punishment enough. If you ask me fifteen years really isn't . . .'

The host is talking but I only catch snippets, my focus trained on my little girl. Now I try to switch my attention to what the woman is saying, in case she can offer me a clue to what happened on the night of the accident.

'. . . she was high out of her mind . . . and she killed her daughter. Should she be let off with fifteen years?' the woman says. 'The debate continues to rage hotly over whether Rose Reid's wealth and connections have helped her get a more lenient sentence.'

I blink in surprise at the television. *I'm not being let off!* I want to shout at the woman. *I've lost my daughter!*

'. . . some people say it's time to be compassionate, but I don't know . . .' The host continues, 'Let's take another look at video footage from the scene of the accident, or should I say, crime . . .'

Aerial footage of the crash appears on screen. The words "HORROR CRASH" flash up along the bottom. My breathing becomes rapid as I stare at the smoking wreckage of my car wrapped around a tree. Everything around me starts to fall away, the noise of people arguing behind me in the rec room becomes indistinct as the blood roaring in my ears drowns it out. I step closer to the TV, desperate for any scraps of information I can gather.

The footage was shot at dawn by the looks of things. In the background I can make out police investigators examining the car – my black Porsche SUV – but no paramedics or ambulances, which makes me think this must have been filmed hours after we were initially discovered in the wrecked vehicle and I was taken away in an ambulance, hours too after Sienna's body had been taken away by the coroner.

It's a country lane. On either side are trees burning with bright autumn colors. It looks familiar to me and then I recognize it as a road not a mile from our house. It's the road I'd take to circumvent traffic in town and get to the freeway.

What would I be doing out there in the middle of the night with Sienna? From the direction the car is facing it looks like I am coming from the direction of the house, but I suppose the vehicle could have spun on the road.

The image on-screen returns to the studio where the host is still sounding off about me. 'Earlier that evening we know she and her husband Ryan Reid were at a gala dinner for the Police Foundation.'

Another photo appears in the corner of the screen. It's a photo of Ryan and I at the event. I'm wearing a long, dark blue dress. Chanel. It comes back to me all at once, like a closet door has been opened and the memory has tumbled out into the light.

I took Sienna to the library for story-time in the afternoon. Then I got her ready for bed at the usual time of seven and started reading her a story. Her babysitter came and took over, as I needed to meet Ryan in town for the gala.

My attention is drawn back to the TV.

'. . . and witnesses have said she was definitely

drinking at the event, which fits with what the police are saying about how she was three times over the legal limit for alcohol . . .'

How is that possible? I rarely drink. But how can the reports be wrong? The police wouldn't lie. The doctors wouldn't lie. Would they?

Once again, I wish I could get my hands on the police report. Why would I wake Sienna up in the middle of the night and drive off with her? What was I running from?

Ryan. That's the only thing that makes sense. I must have been running from him. The thought has been brushing at the edges of my consciousness, but I've not wanted to examine it closely or had the mental clarity to think it through. I know that I would never have gotten behind the wheel under the influence with Sienna in the car. So Ryan must be lying to the police. But why does he want to keep me locked up in here under sedation? The truth lies out there on the periphery of my mind, but I'm too sluggish and tired to fight my way to it.

Shouting erupts around me in the rec room. I'm pushed hard in the back and stumble into the ping-pong table. A fight has broken out. A skinny woman called Lina has tried to snatch the remote from Nora, the woman who controls it, and she's attacked her. Nora's a big woman – and I heard she's in Crosshill for bludgeoning her parents to death with a fire extinguisher. She lunges like a dervish, all meaty fists and kicking over chairs, but Lina is agile on her feet and Nora's swing goes wide and lands on another woman instead. This woman comes at Nora like a hellcat, in a fit of irate rage, scratching and yanking at her hair and booting her shins.

It takes five orderlies to pry them apart and I watch them sedate Nora until she stops resisting, her eyes roll back in her head and she drops to the floor like a sack of grain. She's hefted off to one of the cooldown cells – a padded room that patients who misbehave are dragged off to and sometimes kept in for days.

Lina, now happily in control of the remote, turns the channel to *The Voice*. No one argues with her. She might be skinny, but I overheard someone say that she smothered eight old people to death in their beds at the home where she worked as a nurse's aide.

I return to my cell, sifting through the information that I've just learned and trying to match it to any shards of memory. Now things have started to resurface I can't ignore them. Later, when an orderly arrives with my sedative, I refuse it. I don't want to be foggy and tired anymore. I want to figure out what happened on that night, and if that means shaking off the numbness and facing the pain and grief that I've been happy to suppress, I will. Because even though I'm afraid to face the truth, my daughter deserves it.

My new resolution is short-lived, however. I am

told I have to take the sedative and when I continue to refuse he calls in backup in the shape of another attendant. The two of them pin me to the bed. I struggle against them like Nora did earlier, begging them not to do it, but they stick me with a needle and seconds later I drift away.

A couple of days later, when I'm just about conscious enough and alert enough to communicate, I tell them I want to see the doctor. I want him to reduce my sedation. I need to be able to think straight. But the staff merely laugh at me. 'Pill or prick?' they smirk, showing me a syringe filled with sedative.

I take the pill and they check my mouth to make sure I've swallowed it before leaving and locking me in my cell.

In the brief interludes where I'm lucid, I beg to speak to the doctor again, but I get nowhere. The sedation is making my thoughts increasingly slow. My tongue is thick as a brick in my mouth and I'm slurring my words. I wonder if they've upped the dose.

I am frustrated that no one is listening to me and that I can't make myself understood. And then I'm increasingly paranoid that I am being held here and kept sedated on purpose. The orderlies are spying on me, I decide. They must be in Ryan's pay. His old office – the DA's office – must be in on it too. I wonder if the doctors are as well. I glance at the cameras –

are they watching me right now? Is Ryan watching me? I feel like I am going mad. Is that what they want? Am I mad? Did I kill my daughter?

Eventually I become like one of the zombie women in the rec room, my eyelids drooping, my head hanging on my neck like a crushed flower on a broken stem.

I watch the world from behind a heavy veil, drool hanging from my dried lips, knowing that the answers to my predicament – and to Sienna's death – lie just beyond, but completely out of reach.

Chapter Thirty-Five

Present

I wake in a pink floral bedroom with sunlight streaming weakly through a crack in the curtains and, at first, I don't know where I am. I have no recollection of how I got here. It's not the cabin and it's not Crosshill. Then I remember it's Gwen's house. She brought me here, half-carried me from the store, her arm anchored beneath my shoulders to keep me upright.

Her house is down a rutted lane behind the store. I don't remember much else, except for her making me take some pills and then putting me to bed. I look down and see I'm wearing a white cotton nightgown that's much too big for me. One of Gwen's no doubt.

I touch my forehead. My fever has broken. I still feel hot, but I'm not burning up anymore. My head is woozy, filled with cotton, and a dull ache sits behind my temples. How long have I been asleep? I look around for clues but there's no clock and I can't see my backpack so I can't check my phone for the time.

The room is cozy with a farmhouse feel to it. The furniture is all wood in the Shaker style, and a patchwork quilt covers the bed. There's an antique dresser with a mirror and a pink velvet stool sitting in front of it.

I swing my legs out from under the duvet and notice how wobbly I am when I get to my feet. For a second I think I might faint, and I wonder how long it's been since I ate anything. On the bedside table I notice a prescription bottle and I remember Gwen twisting off the cap and telling me something about them, though the words didn't really sink in at the time. I read the label now. Penicillin. Prescribed for John Willis. That must be Gwen's late husband. They're three years out of date, and there's only a couple of pills left in the bottle.

I have a vague memory of Gwen explaining all this to me and insisting that I really needed to see a doctor. I remember freaking out at her and trying to leave, and Gwen ushering me back into the bedroom, reassuring me that she wouldn't call anyone.

I suppose that the penicillin, even if it's lost some of its potency, is still working because I do feel better, not great but definitely not as bad as I was. I wonder though whether the couple of pills that are left in the bottle will be enough to fight off the infection. Won't I need a whole course? My arms still feel sore beneath the fresh bandages Gwen put on, but yesterday they felt like they were on fire.

Shame floods over me as I remember sitting on the bed as Gwen unpeeled the dirty dressings and took in the two oozing knife wounds on my inner arms. She winced and then looked at me but I couldn't meet her gaze and so she went silently on, not asking me what happened but just cleaning me up as gently as she could with warm water and cotton balls. She smeared antibiotic cream on the cuts and then redressed them, but when she was done, I noticed her frowning in consternation. Did it look like a suicide attempt? Or defensive injuries? I wondered what I should say to her. Lying seemed futile, so I decided to say nothing and leave her to draw her own conclusions.

I shuffle to the bedroom door and ease it open. I can hear voices from somewhere downstairs. It's Gwen. She's talking to someone and I creep out into the hallway and cock my ear to listen, on edge and afraid. Has she told someone about me?

'I don't know. Maybe a day or so,' I hear her say. There's no reply.

'No, I'm fine. I'm sure I'll be OK . . .'

A pause.

'Thanks so much. Yes. See you then.'

She's on the phone. But who to and what is she telling them? My paranoia cranks up a notch. I hurry back into the bedroom. Now my head is clearer and my fever has broken I realize the magnitude of the risk I took by coming here and throwing myself on Gwen's mercy.

Footsteps in the hallway make me look up just as Gwen enters the room. 'Oh,' she says, seeing me awake. 'I thought I heard you up and moving around.' She looks genuinely relieved. 'How are you feeling?' she inquires, coming toward me.

I feel myself reddening with embarrassment. 'Better,' I mumble, making to stand. 'I'm sorry. I shouldn't have come here. I'll get out of your way.'

She puts a hand on my shoulder to stop me getting up. 'Oh no,' she says, shaking her head. 'You're staying right here in bed. You've still got a fever,' she adds, putting her hand to my forehead. 'And you're weak as a day-old puppy.'

I try to stand again, protesting. 'I don't want to be any trouble.'

'You aren't,' she answers firmly. 'I'm here alone. You're fine to stay.'

I bite my lip, thinking of the effort it would take to get dressed, let alone walk back to the cabin feeling the way I do. 'OK,' I finally sigh, resigning myself to the fact I'm not strong enough to go anywhere right now. The lure of the plush bed and the warm comforter and the gas heating is also a deciding factor. The idea of the freezing cold cabin makes me shudder. 'Thank you,' I say to Gwen, this time raising my gaze to meet hers.

'You're welcome,' she says, patting my arm. She nods at the bottle of penicillin. 'They seem to be working.'

'Yeah,' I say, grateful.

'Why don't you take a cool bath or a shower?' Gwen says to me now. 'It'll make you feel better. And I can fix us something to eat.'

'What time is it?' I ask.

'It's three in the afternoon,' she answers.

I frown. Have I only been asleep then for a few hours?

'You got here yesterday,' she says, seeing my expression. 'You've been asleep for nearly twenty hours.'

I take that in, shocked to my core and disorientated by the loss of a whole day.

'Go and have a wash,' she urges. 'The bathroom's along the hall. There are fresh towels in there and I washed and dried all your things too. You'll find them on the side.'

'Thank you,' I say again, a lump rising up my throat at her kindness.

She smiles and crosses to the door. As she walks out of the room I almost stop and ask her why she's helping me. I still don't understand. Regardless of whether she's recognized me or not, this is a long way to go for a stranger, but she's already bustling off to make us something to eat.

I take a long bath, taking care to keep my clean bandages dry, and it is the best bath I've ever had in my life, despite the fact I keep the temperature tepid. My knotted muscles start to come undone, and I dunk my head beneath the water and then use shampoo to lift the layers of dirt and sweat from my hair.

As I lie in the rapidly cooling bath, I let my mind drift to Ryan and to what I have done. I think about the pool of blood, slick and glossy, and the weight of the knife in my hand, shockingly light for something so deadly. I think about how there was no regret, only relief when it came to it – when I sliced that blade through flesh and made him pay.

I wonder if the police have found the crime scene yet. Did I clean it up well enough? All that blood. There must be traces they could find. The knife I disposed of, along with all my blood-stained clothes. I made sure not to leave fingerprints. I was careful. And they won't find the body, so it will be hard to prove there has been a murder.

Chapter Thirty-Six

Past

One Month Ago

I don't know how long I have been at Crosshill – it feels like years but it must only have been months – when one day I'm prodded along to a room to meet someone. I am pushed down into a chair. My head weighs a hundred pounds, and my eyes won't stay open, but flicker instead, giving me a strobing view of the pea green walls and cracked lino world.

I squint long enough for me to also notice a woman in a gray suit sitting in the chair opposite me.

'Hi,' she says. 'I'm Ms. Rodriguez. I work for Anderson Tait. It's a law firm. I'm here with divorce papers for you to sign.'

Her words penetrate through the gloom. I force

261

my eyes wider and take her in. She's younger than me; twenty-five or so, pretty. Her hair is dark and soft, like Sienna's, and I want to reach out and stroke it. She looks vaguely familiar somehow, but I don't know why.

'Can you understand me?' she asks, sounding irritated. 'Your husband, Ryan, is filing for divorce.'

She pulls a black box file stuffed with papers out of her briefcase and suddenly I am reminded of a black box on the passenger seat of the car. The image appears with startling clarity as though it was there all along and someone has whipped away the blackout curtain covering it.

I remember the box. I took it from the safe in Ryan's study. I can see myself doing it. That's why I was in the car. I stole the box and was running from Ryan!

Now the floodgates have cracked open, another breakthrough memory pushes its way through: the minutes after the crash. I can feel my neck stiff as a pole, my vision curtained by blood, I can't lift my head from the wheel, but I stir when I hear the passenger door open. Ryan stands there, silhouetted against his own car headlights. He reaches across me and takes the black box from the passenger seat. He doesn't even check to see if I'm alive.

He doesn't check to see if Sienna is OK. He shuts the door on me and leaves.

He left us there to die.

But no. No. That's wrong. He didn't know Sienna was in the car with me. He didn't see her lying in the ditch.

'Rose?' the woman says.

I blink and refocus back on her. Who is she? Why is she here?

'I'm so sorry about Sienna,' she says.

Hearing my daughter's name spoken out loud is like being stabbed by a million knives at once. The pain of it sharpens my thoughts, making the fog I'm floating in dissipate a little.

'I'm here to have you sign the papers,' she says.

But what was in the box?

'Do you remember the night of the accident?' the lawyer asks me.

I frown at her. I definitely know her. How do I know this woman?

'Do you remember me?' she says.

I frown. I do and I don't. Everything is so confused. I can barely hold on to these new thoughts about Ryan and the box, though I know I have to. I can't let those go. They're the key to unlocking this whole mystery. What was in the box?

'My name is Isabel,' the woman says to me. 'We met on the night of the accident. At the police gala dinner.' She searches my face for any sign of recognition. 'We spoke in the bathroom.'

I reel back in my seat. *Monster. Your husband is a monster.*

Oh God. It's all there, all the memories that have been buried – they're right there. Everything. The whole conversation that we had in the bathroom. The box I stole from Ryan's safe. The contents of it. The escape. The car chase. I remember it all. The floodgates are now fully opened.

'He raped your cousin,' I stammer.

She nods, then glances up at the camera on the wall before looking back at me. 'They're recording us, but not with audio, as I told them I was a lawyer and it was a privileged conversation, but they're probably watching us, and we don't have much time.' She leans across the table. 'I'm sorry,' she says to me, her eyes glinting with tears. 'I feel like it's all my fault. If I hadn't told you about him . . . If you hadn't gone back to the house . . .' She breaks off.

I shake my head at her. My throat is constricted and it's hard to swallow the lump. 'It's not your fault,' I tell her.

She gives me a tremulous smile, not accepting it.

I notice her briefcase then. Didn't she just introduce herself as Ryan's lawyer? Didn't she say something about a divorce?

'What are you doing here?' I ask. 'I don't understand.'

'The day after the accident I was watching the news,' she replies. 'And I knew . . . I knew he must have followed you home after the gala. That you must have found something: proof of some kind. And I knew that it was my fault. I tried to come and see you at the hospital, but they wouldn't let anyone in besides family.'

So how is she here?

'I'm studying for the bar exam,' she explains, leaning across the table and lowering her voice even further. 'So I managed to get myself an internship at the firm that represents Ryan. I was hoping I could get access to some non-disclosures that he might have made women sign, something that might give us the evidence we needed. I don't know whether there are non-disclosures, but I was all out of ideas. I thought if I could find something, anything to tie him to these women, I might be able to out him. And I thought, if I did that, I might convince someone that you didn't deserve to be in jail, but so far . . . nothing.' She sighs with disappointment. 'I can't get access to the files. I'll keep trying.'

I sigh. For a moment I felt my hopes rise, thought that this nightmare could be over, that Isabel had a way to get me out of here.

'When I heard Ryan was filing for divorce,' she goes on, 'I arranged it so that I could be the one to deliver the papers to you. None of the junior partners wanted to trek all the way out here to see you so it was easy.'

I take that in, still struggling to put all the pieces together but impressed by her ingenuity.

'Do you remember what happened that night?' She squeezes my hand. 'Did you find something in the safe?'

I breathe out slowly, needing to excavate the memories. 'Yes. It was there, where you said it would be. In the safe. He had a box full of . . . souvenirs.'

I remember now all those IDs, all those women. The jewelry. The blue pajama top. Daisy! I gasp. I betrayed her. I didn't believe her. I threw her out of the house. Guilt and sorrow rush over me and I find tears running down my cheeks. How could I have forgotten it all? Was it the accident, the drugs or was I just in denial? Probably all three.

'Do you know what happened to the box?' Isabel presses, jolting me out of my memories. 'The evidence that you found – was it in the car with you when you had the accident?'

'Ryan came home,' I say in a hoarse voice. 'He chased me. He didn't know Sienna was in the car. I crashed.'

Isabel looks stricken as I talk.

'I remember him . . .' I break off, squeezing my eyes shut as the memory assaults me. 'Ryan. He opened the car door . . . I think he thought I was dead. He didn't see Sienna. He thought she was at home in bed. He took the box with all the proof in it. And he just left me there.'

I open my eyes and find Isabel staring at me in horror. 'It's his fault,' she says. 'He killed Sienna. Not you.'

'I wasn't drunk,' I slur. 'I didn't take any Ambien.'

'I know,' she says. 'I believe you.'

Hearing her say that makes a dam break inside me and weeks and weeks of pent-up despair and grief and confusion all come gushing out. I have been feeling so alone. And now here's someone believing me and wanting to help me. I cry, my shoulders heaving with emotion. Tears falling down my cheeks.

Isabel squeezes my hand. 'They're framing you,' she whispers. 'Ryan is. With help from the doctors and I'm guessing the police too.'

More sobs erupt out of me. I'm not paranoid. I'm not misremembering things!

'It's why you're here,' she says, without moving her lips. 'Ryan must have done a deal with the DA's office. He must have faked your blood tests. It all makes sense. He wants to keep you quiet. It's why they're keeping you sedated too, so you don't remember anything, and so you don't cause him any problems.'

My breathing is coming so fast that I feel faint. I clutch her hand, scared that if I let her go and she leaves, I might never see her again. I might never find

267

anyone else who believes me. It's proof that I'm not paranoid. Proof that I am sane.

'You need to stop taking whatever they're giving you,' Isabel whispers to me. 'Can you do that?' She speaks louder and I realize I've zoned out, thinking about Ryan. 'Rose,' she says, louder. 'It's important. You need to be more alert.'

I frown at her, my tears slowing. 'Why?'

'Because,' she says once again lowering her voice so I have to strain to catch the words, 'we need to get you out of here.'

'What?' I splutter. 'How?' It's useless. If Ryan has worked this hard to get me locked up in here it's going to be impossible to get me out.

Isabel gets up and walks around to the other side of the table. She sits down, chewing her lip and frowning, deep in thought. 'I've thought about speaking to your defense lawyer, but you've already signed the plea deal, so they won't hear an appeal. And the problem with you telling people what happened – your lawyer or your doctor or the police – is that Ryan will find out.'

We lock eyes. We both know what that might mean. If I make allegations, I won't be safe. Not even in here. *Especially* not in here. We need a watertight case before we can accuse him, and I need to be somewhere he can't reach me.

Chapter Thirty-Seven

Present

On weak legs, I finally haul myself out of the bath and wrap myself in a warm towel. It's amazing how luxurious the simple pleasures feel after so long without them. For a moment I am reminded of lifting Sienna out of the bath and wrapping her up in her robe, feeling her body snuggled warm and damp against mine, and I think I might fold over and sob right where I am on the bathroom floor, but I take a deep breath and refuse to submit to the wave of grief.

I get dressed and towel-dry my hair in front of the mirror. I am even thinner than before, and so tired and pale. In a way it's a relief as I look so unlike the person in the photographs in the paper and on the news, but it's also like a stranger is staring back at me.

Gwen has left out a hairbrush and a new toothbrush

and I brush my teeth and hair, get dressed and then head downstairs, holding tight to the bannister because I still feel wobbly.

I follow the smell of cooking toward the kitchen and find Gwen serving up two bowls of chicken soup. 'It's store-bought,' she tells me. 'I'm not much of a cook. But I figure chicken soup is exactly what you need.'

I sit down at the table and she hands me a spoon. At first, I don't feel much appetite and have to force myself to eat, but after a few mouthfuls my hunger stirs like a bear coming out of hibernation – I haven't eaten anything this good in months – and I manage to finish two whole bowls and four slices of buttered toast before I have to lean back in my chair, full to bursting.

Gwen watches me, smiling ear to ear. 'That's a good sign, getting your appetite back,' she says happily.

I smile back at her. 'Who's looking after the store?'

'I have someone who works part-time. She's covering for me. I told her that I was sick.'

'I'm sorry,' I say, embarrassed at the trouble I'm causing.

She smiles, dismissing my concern, then pushes up from the table, removes my plate and carries it over to the side.

'Why are you helping me?' I ask suddenly, unable to hold it in any longer.

Gwen leans against the side and gazes at me for a long moment. 'Well . . .' she starts with a thoughtful sigh, 'I guess I like helping people. And I think you need help.' She pauses, weighing her next words, then says: 'I got a fair idea that you're running from something bad.'

I swallow hard.

'And I'm not prying,' she hurries to add. 'Whatever it is, it's your business. I had a granddaughter,' she goes on. 'Bella. Something happened to her too. She had an abusive boyfriend. She tried to get away from him. And . . . well, he killed her.'

'I'm so sorry,' I say, startled by this admission. But it all makes sense now. That's why she's helping me.

'He couldn't stand the thought of her leaving. He came after her. Beat her.' She grimaces. 'It damn near killed me when the police came to tell me.'

I nod, tears welling.

'I tried so hard to get her away from him. But she wouldn't listen. He was charming at first. Good-looking. Then he started acting jealous. He wouldn't even let her call me or visit. She was such a beautiful girl. Inside and out. And only twenty-three years old. She had her whole life ahead of her.' She takes a moment to gather herself. I watch her, feeling her pain echo inside my own chest.

'To be honest, you remind me of her,' Gwen says, smiling sadly at me. 'You had the same look when I first saw you, that I saw in Bella. A haunted look. That's when I knew I wasn't getting the whole story.'

My throat seizes up with unspent sobs.

Gwen's gaze drifts off to someplace else, somewhere in her memory, before snapping back to me after a few moments. 'Was a few years ago now,' she says, 'but the pain doesn't go away. I think about her every day . . .' She tails off, her gaze falling to the dregs of her coffee.

'I know how that feels,' I find myself saying. 'I lost my daughter.' A dam breaks. A wail erupts out of me and my shoulders heave. Gwen moves around the table in an instant and puts her arm around me. I lean into her and she hugs me tight, stroking my hair. 'It's OK,' she says. 'You cry.'

'I'm sorry,' I say, tears streaming down my face. 'I'm so sorry.' I can barely speak.

'You've got nothing to be sorry for,' Gwen says soothingly.

As I cling to Gwen, crying into her side, I wonder at how wrong she is. I've got plenty I should be sorry for. But I'm not sorry for any of it.

Chapter Thirty-Eight

Past

One Month Ago

I give Lina, the skinny woman who's rumored to have killed eight people at the nursing home where she worked, my butterscotch pudding for three days in a row. In exchange she steals the remote from Nora.

The judges are just about to announce the winner on *The Voice* and the TV room is full of about thirty patients all placing bets and getting as excited as their sedation will allow. When I give my co-conspirator the signal, she lunges for the control and changes the channel. She then sticks the remote down her pants. All hell breaks loose as Nora bellows her outrage and comes after Lina, who does her quick-footed dance out of the way, laughing as Nora, clumsy from the drugs she's on, lumbers toward her, knocking over chairs.

The other inmates, half excited by the fracas and half mad because they're missing *The Voice*, start screaming and clapping, and some join in, so that within minutes a riot is kicking off.

The orderly in the room is outnumbered and hits an alarm on the wall to call for backup. It starts to blare but the screams and the cheers are so loud they threaten to drown it out. Another three orderlies come running – instantly recognizable by their mint green scrub shirts. I am positioned by the door as they pelt in and though my mind is not yet fully clear from all the sedatives and my hands feel clumsy, the movement is surprisingly familiar to me from the very many times I shoplifted as a kid. I am reaching for the security pass hanging on the nearest orderly's waist before I can think twice.

In the rush and chaos, he doesn't notice it being yanked off his belt, and I am out the room in the next second, walking full steam toward the security doors that lead out of the ward, the stolen pass gripped tightly in my hand.

I may be rusty, but I still have skills and that knowledge, and this first little victory gives me a spike of hope to go along with the rush of adrenaline.

As the drama continues in the rec room and the alarm blares, the door I'm heading toward flies open.

274

Four more staff come running, holding syringes in hand, headed for the TV room.

I flatten myself against the wall as they run past and then I keep walking. My heart is pounding. I am fully prepared to be stopped at any moment. But I know this is my one chance, my only shot at freedom, and I will do whatever it takes to seize it.

I swipe the pass against the card reader and shoulder open the double doors and I am out, into a hallway beyond the ward, where only staff are allowed. I duck into the first alcove I find and throw on the green scrub shirt that Isabel sneaked to me when she came to see me for a second time, yesterday. She came on the pretext I'd forgotten to sign one of the documents and brought with her an escape plan, including a hand-drawn map of the hospital's exits and the place where she'd be waiting for me, beyond the fence.

The plan was hastily pulled together. We didn't have much time. With my skills as a shoplifter, I told Isabel that I could probably manage to steal a pass from one of the guards. We decided to act within a week, enough time for me to try to shake off the sedation by throwing up the pills they were giving me and for her to work out where to hide me on the outside. We chose the night of the *The Voice* final, knowing this would create the best cover for my escape.

Wearing the green scrub shirt, I blend in somewhat, though my joggers and soft-soled shoes still betray my true identity as an inmate rather than an orderly.

I resist the urge to run and instead walk purposefully as though I belong here among the white coats and the staff.

There's a locker room and a break room and up ahead I can see the double doors leading outside to freedom. It's so close. But then two security guards exit a room in front of me and turn in my direction, heading my way. Luckily, they're deep in conversation and so I grab for the nearest door handle and slip inside a room before they can spot me.

I find myself in another corridor with several rooms coming off it – they look like administrative offices and I up my pace, aware that the alarm has stopped. I don't have long. They'll do a roll call straight after the riot is contained and everyone is locked up in their cells. I have minutes or less before they discover that I'm missing.

One of the office doors is open and a woman is sitting behind a desk, typing. She's wearing a white coat. One of the doctors I presume. She looks up as I pass the door and I see her frown at me, but I keep moving, wishing that I wasn't wearing the soft gray cotton slip-on shoes and sweatpants that every inmate is forced to wear. They are such a giveaway.

I hear her shout something – she's recognized me,

or at least my shoes – and I break into a sprint, racing for the end of the corridor. I bash into an exit door at full speed, but it doesn't open. Fumbling for the pass that I stole, I look desperately for the reader and catch sight of the camera on the wall pointed right at me. Above my head, another alarm kicks off. It's much more urgent-sounding and louder than the one that went off in the rec room. A red light starts flashing too.

'You! Stop!'

I glance back and see the doctor has chased me out into the corridor. The door behind her opens just then, and the two security guards from earlier appear. They spot me and come running.

I swipe the security pass in desperation over the reader. The door opens with a click. I am through in a second and then hurry outside, into the darkness. The cold air blasts me, making me gasp in shock. I have not been outside or felt fresh air in so long, and I want to stop and turn my face to the sky and the stars shining above, but I can't. I have to keep going.

My legs are unused to exercise and I'm panting already, but I dart across the parking lot and down a slope, aiming for a bunch of trees up ahead. The moon is only a sliver and that helps.

I hear shouting behind me. They've followed me into the woods. Flashlights strobe through the branches. I can hear someone thrashing through the undergrowth.

I stumble on, panting, desperate, until I spot a wire fence, which Isabel told me I would reach after about three hundred feet.

I look over my shoulder now as I go and see flashlights poking through the darkness. There are voices yelling. They're spreading out through the woods, trying to hem me in.

I reach the fence and fall to my knees, panting hard, and shaking. Where is she? Where's Isabel?

I look left and right. The fence is impossible to climb. Too tall, no footholds. The voices are getting louder. Then I hear Isabel's voice calling my name and a flashlight beam in the distance, around fifty meters to my left.

'Over here!'

I run toward the beam. Isabel is on the other side of the fence. She's kneeling in the dirt in front of a hole she's made in the fence with some wire cutters. She holds the peeled-back wire up so I can crawl through.

Isabel takes my hand and hauls me to my feet. We run down an embankment and toward a waiting car. She races around to the driver's side and I jump in the passenger seat. Isabel starts the engine.

'Get down!' she says, and I slide into the footwell as she drives off. A few minutes later I dare to peek my head up.

'We did it,' Isabel says, looking at me in disbelief. I smile shakily at her.

'Stay down though,' she warns. 'Just in case. The police will be looking for you.'

We drive in heavy silence for another thirty minutes before we deem it safe enough for me to sit up. We have cleared the first hurdle, but it is only the first, and perhaps the easiest. Isabel tosses me a black hooded sweatshirt and I put it on over the scrubs.

She checks on me as we approach Westchester three hours later. 'Are you sure you want to do this?' she asks.

'Yes,' I say. I'm not backing out now. There's only one way forward. I take a deep breath. 'He did it to my sister,' I whisper.

Isabel does a double take, looking away from the road and at me. 'What?'

I stare out the window at the road ahead, unable to look at her. 'My sister, Daisy. Ryan raped her. I didn't believe her when she told me. But it's how I knew you were telling the truth when you told me about your cousin. He did the same to my sister.'

Isabel exhales slowly. 'I'm sorry.'

'I didn't believe her when she told me. And she died before I got to apologize to her,' I say, fighting back emotion. 'This is how I make it up to her. And all the others.'

Isabel nods. 'What if you get caught?'

'No one knows we're connected,' I point out, trying to reassure her that at least if I am discovered, only I will get in trouble. But then I remember that Ryan saw Isabel talking to me at the gala. He must have guessed it was Isabel who told me the truth about him.

'Did Ryan ever try to find you? After the gala?' I ask.

'No. He doesn't know who I am. I never told him that Angela was my cousin,' Isabel says. 'He doesn't know anything about me.'

'He knows your face,' I say.

Isabel shrugs, but I see the worry line etched across her forehead deepen. There's no way Ryan would let her get away with upending his life like she's done. She's a threat to him. A big one. He would try to find her. And he would try to silence her. But how far would he go? Does he just threaten women, or does he go further? Isabel said he beat her cousin. And I think about how he left me in the car, not even checking if I was alive. My earlier guess that he's a psychopath returns to me.

I glance again at Isabel. Her hands are white-knuckled on the wheel and I feel a sickening sense of guilt at what I'm dragging her into.

'OK,' Isabel says, pulling over and putting the car in park. 'We're here.'

I look out the window. We're in a church parking lot. It's the church Ryan likes to attend at Easter and

Christmas, for appearance's sake only, because he doesn't believe in God. I wonder if Sienna's funeral was held here and a bolt of pain rips through me at the thought.

Isabel hands me a small backpack. I unzip it and see that it contains a roll of trash bags, a bottle of bleach, plastic gloves, a white forensic suit, and some cleaning cloths – all things she bought in preparation for this, things that I asked her to buy.

'Thanks,' I say to her. Then I hesitate.

'Are you really sure you want to do this?' she questions.

'He needs to pay for what he's done,' I say, locking eyes with her.

Isabel holds my gaze. 'I'll wait here.' She checks her watch. 'It's just after midnight,' she says to me. 'You've got one hour. Be back by then.'

I get out the car.

There's a treehouse in the backyard that Ryan had built for Sienna's third birthday. From the raised platform there's a view straight into the living room and Ryan's study. I huddle in the pitch-dark inside the treehouse, watching the house for any signs of life. I have been careful to avoid the security cameras, crossing through the conservancy land behind the house and climbing over the back wall before circumnavigating the sensors embedded in the lawn that trigger the lights.

There are cameras covering the whole exterior but none inside. I don't have my phone so I can't access the alarm system to shut them off. Ryan goes to bed around eleven normally and the house is dark, including in the master bedroom. I wonder if the cops will have called him to let him know about my escape. I decide to wait a few minutes, observing things, until I'm as sure as I can be that he's sleeping before I break in.

The temperature is around freezing but I ignore it, too focused on my goal to care about the cold. And being outside is such a relief after being locked up for so long that I don't care that I'm shivering. Lights twinkle through the trees off to my left and after a long, confused moment I realize that it's Christmas tree lights in our neighbor's yard. They always string them around the trees at this time of year.

Is it Christmas already? I have completely lost track of time. There are no Christmas decorations at my house and I figure that's because there's nothing to celebrate this year.

Last year we took a trip to the Christmas tree farm with Sienna to choose the tree. Ryan carried it to the car and tied it to the roof. We spent the afternoon as a family decorating it, Ryan picking Sienna up so she could hang the star on the top. I smile sadly and a clawing pain makes me clutch my stomach. I honestly don't know how you're meant to keep going after something like this. How do other people do it? I start to wonder why I bothered fleeing from Crosshill. What was the point? But just as quickly, I remind myself that Ryan is the reason my daughter is dead. And I'm not letting him get away with that.

A light comes on upstairs, startling me. I freeze, gripping the edge of the treehouse. A second later a glow emits from downstairs and I gasp as I see Ryan, dressed in sweatpants and a T-shirt, walking into his study along with two men – detectives Lim and Adams.

They must be here to let Ryan know that I'm missing from Crosshill. I wonder if they'll search the grounds for me? Even if they don't, I suspect they'll put a patrol car out front, and I'm glad I thought to climb over the back wall. I watch the three of them chat. Ryan has his back to me, so I can't read his expression on hearing the news of my escape, and I wonder what he's thinking or saying to them. Is he shocked? Is he concerned? He should be.

The men chat for ten minutes and I watch Lim walk toward the window and look out across the dark lawn. It seems like he's staring right at me, although I reassure myself that he can't see me, not in the pitch-dark. Still, my pulse races.

After they finish talking, Ryan walks them out of the study. I can't see the front of the house, but I assume he's showing them to the door.

Chewing nervously on my lip I watch and wait. Ryan returns to his office. He slumps down in the chair behind his desk and stares off into space for a couple of minutes. Finally, he turns on the TV and flicks through to CNN. I wonder if the news is already covering my escape, or whether they're hushing it up. I can't see the screen so there's no way to know. I wish he'd hurry up and return to bed. What if he doesn't? Isabel is waiting.

My dog, Toby, pads over to the window and stares out. Can he see me, or sense me out here? I hadn't thought about Toby. That could be a problem. If Ryan lets him out for a pee, he'll come right for me. He's a good guard dog. Even getting in the house with him there is going to be a challenge. The only good thing is that Toby is my dog, and hopefully despite how long I've been gone, I can still make him behave for me.

After what feels like forever, Toby slouches away from the window and goes to lie by Ryan's feet. He always used to follow me around like a shadow and it feels like a mini betrayal to add to all the others, watching him treat Ryan as his master.

Five minutes or so later, Ryan turns off the TV and vanishes from the study. The lights go out in the hall and then, after a few more minutes, so does the one upstairs in the master bedroom. I make myself wait a few more minutes before I slip down from the treehouse, silent as a wraith, and pad across the lawn, taking care to avoid the sensors.

Not caring if the cameras capture me now, knowing that this will all end soon, I move to the kitchen door. I find it locked, which is unsurprising, but there's a key I long ago hid in a hollowed-out stone beside it, just in case I ever found myself without my house keys, and I dig it up now and slip it into the lock. Entering the kitchen, I'm on edge. If he has changed the alarm code, then the whole plan will fail. As soon as I've opened the door a rapid beeping lets me know that the alarm system is primed. I quickly program the code. Thankfully, it works: the alarm switches to green and the beeping stops. I say a silent prayer of gratitude.

I'm moving through the kitchen on silent feet when the kitchen door bursts open startling me. But it's just Toby. He doesn't bark, like he would with a stranger, instead he races toward me, skidding across the tiles in his excitement, his tail wagging furiously. I kneel down and gather him up in my arms. 'Hi,' I whisper to him. 'I missed you.' I want to bury my head in his fur and sob. I've missed him more than I realized.

I don't have time for a reunion though, so I hurry over to the pantry and quickly hunt around for a bag of dog treats. They're exactly where I left them six months ago. I drop a handful on the floor and Toby loses interest in me and starts vacuuming them up. Making the most of the opportunity, I steal a carving knife from the wooden block on the side and then slip out into the hallway.

Gripping the knife, I tiptoe up the stairs. At the top, on the landing, I turn toward the master bedroom. The light is out. The whole house is dark and still as the grave. I crane to listen. Is he asleep?

I take a step toward the bedroom, my feet sinking silently into the carpet. The knife is heavy in my hand and I weigh it, wondering how much force it takes to stab a man – as much as it takes to cut into a deer hide when you're dressing it? I've done that before. My grandfather taught me. I remember the brute strength it takes to break through the layer of skin and wedge of fat and muscle, how careful you have to be not to plunge the tip of the knife into a bone and snap it off, or to pierce the entrails and poison the meat.

I don't have to do this, I think to myself. I could walk away and disappear.

But that, I tell myself, wouldn't be justice.

Chapter Thirty-Nine

Present

When I wake the next morning in Gwen's spare room, it is bright and sunny and the clock on the side says it's almost twelve in the afternoon. Gwen is standing in the doorway, holding a cup of coffee.

'Did you sleep well?' she asks as I sit up.

'Yes, thanks,' I say. Though I'm not sure I did sleep well. I tossed and turned all night. My dreams were bathed in blood. Nightmares about Ryan and a pool of spreading crimson.

'How are you feeling?'

My head is aching from all the crying I did yesterday. My cuts still sting and one arm still burns, but when I check my forehead, I find my fever is almost gone so I smile and tell Gwen that I'm fine. I've finished the last of the penicillin pills. I'm still worried that it won't be enough to stave off the infection for long – normally you need to take a seven-day course – but there's no point in dwelling on that for now. There's nothing I can do about it. And if I tell Gwen that I'm still feeling unwell she may insist I stay with her and see a doctor, and I know that I have to leave. I would never forgive myself if I got her in trouble after all she's done to help me.

'Come downstairs,' she tells me, patting my leg. 'I've made breakfast.'

I get dressed and follow the smell of bacon and eggs into the kitchen where I find Gwen standing with her back to me, spatula in hand, staring at something I can't see.

The bacon is burning and I hurry to turn the heat down. As I do, I see what it is that has captured Gwen's attention. She's watching the news on a small television on the countertop.

It's a local station and the newsreader is talking while a photo of Ryan and me on our wedding day fills the screen behind him along with the word 'MURDER'.

A sense of dread washes over me, as well as relief that the inevitable has finally occurred. They've finally discovered what I've done.

I become aware of Gwen standing stock-still beside me, staring at the TV. The spatula in her hand dangles at her side. Oh God. I want to explain but it's too late for that and the newsreader keeps on talking.

'Breaking news,' he says. 'Police have arrested Ryan Reid for the murder of his wife, Rose Reid, who went missing several weeks ago now.'

I hear Gwen make a low gasping sound behind me but I don't turn around. I am glued to the screen.

'Police have not found a body but have said that there is incontrovertible evidence that a crime was committed at the family's home in Westchester. The police are refusing to give details but a source has told us that a trash bag containing Rose's blood-stained clothes was found not far from the property a few weeks ago, and that they have now found evidence of a crime having taken place on the property.'

The footage cuts away to a bird's eye view of my house, shot from a helicopter. The garden is full of activity. A white tent has been erected beside the garage and parts of the lawn and treehouse, and people in white forensic suits are swarming all over the place like ants.

'As you can see from this aerial footage of the house where the Reids have lived for seven years, the police look to be focusing their attention on the garage area. And we're seeing now a police truck towing away what looks to be an SUV.'

I watch as Ryan's black Range Rover is towed down the drive.

The image jumps to a middle-aged woman who I instantly recognize. It's Marie, our housekeeper. She's wiping away a tear as a reporter on the ground holds a microphone to her mouth.

'It's just too much to believe. I've worked for the family for years,' she cries. 'I've known Ryan since he was a boy. There's no way he's guilty of this.'

We cut back to the studio.

'Well,' says the newsreader, 'it seems like Westchester police feel that there's enough evidence against Ryan Reid to charge him, despite there being no body. Let's cross now to the courthouse where we understand Ryan Reid was taken earlier this morning to be officially charged. Once again, for those just switching on, Ryan Reid, the New York attorney general who is currently running for the governorship, and who has long been touted as a future presidential candidate, has been charged with the murder of his wife.'

The camera once more cuts away, this time to a reporter outside the county courthouse. She's teetering on heels and wearing a silk shirt tucked into a short skirt. 'Thank you, Peter,' she says, smiling to camera. 'We're here at Westchester county court, waiting for a statement from the chief of police and . . . oh . . . wait . . .'

There's a commotion behind her and the camera pans and zooms in on Ryan, exiting the police station with two men flanking him either side – one of whom

I recognize as his lawyer. At the sight of Ryan, I put my hand on the chair back to steady myself.

The female reporter looks gleeful as she talks to camera; 'It looks like Ryan Reid has been released, probably on bail. We'll find out more about that as soon as we can but for the moment . . . Oh . . . it looks like he's stopping. He might be about to speak.'

Behind her there are another two dozen reporters and cameras, and they all swarm toward Ryan, shoving microphones in his direction. Ryan stops on the steps of the police station and surveys them all like an emperor who's been dethroned. He looks shell-shocked and yet, he's still Ryan. He knows how to play to the camera. He clears his throat.

'I will make a proper statement later today,' he announces to the assembled reporters, 'but for now I just want to say, I did not kill my wife. I'm innocent. I believe my wife, actually my ex-wife, Rose, is still alive.'

His jaw clenches and I see his lawyer try to tug him away, but Ryan digs in. His voice cracks. He's playing for sympathy and I have to grit my teeth to not scream. The pretense of it is what gets me. Can't they tell he's acting? But how can they? I was married to him for years and never guessed.

'Rose is a consummate liar,' he says. 'She's mentally ill and, according to the doctors at Crosshill, she's also suffering from paranoid delusions. I will do everything in my power to find her and prove to the world that I am innocent of this ridiculous charge. To which end I am doubling the reward for information on her whereabouts to one hundred thousand dollars.'

The lawyer tugs at his sleeve again but Ryan isn't done. He looks straight into camera. 'Before I go, I have a message for you, Rose.'

My body goes rigid.

'I know you're out there, and I know you're trying to frame me,' he says, talking directly to the camera, directly to me. 'But I will not let you get away with either this or with killing our daughter. You will pay for your crimes. I will make sure of it.'

The ground tips beneath my feet and I sink down into one of Gwen's kitchen chairs. On TV, I watch the lawyer and Ryan duck into a car and roar away, as the reporters yell and scream questions to him. I turn my head slowly toward Gwen, terrified of what her reaction will be.

She's staring at me, holding the spatula. Her eyes are wide with shock. 'You set him up?' she exclaims.

I swallow, and then I nod. 'He set me up first.'

Chapter Forty

Past

One Month Ago

A few steps from the door I stop and take a deep breath. If I kill Ryan, they will hunt me to the ends of the earth, and I will be entombed in Crosshill for the rest of my life. If I kill him, I will regret it. I am not a murderer. It's not who I am. I would no sooner be able to plunge this knife into Ryan's sleeping body, than I would be able to plunge it into my daughter – if she was still alive that is. I don't have it in me. I might have been able to stand and watch my father die, but it was at his own hand. I could never have plunged that syringe into him myself.

I turn in the other direction – toward Sienna's room – and tiptoe along to it, slipping inside. The room is dark, and I switch on the mermaid night-light.

Seeing Sienna's empty bed, with her princess duvet cover, makes me almost fall to my knees. I take in the circle of stuffed toys sitting on the floor with a plastic tea set arranged in front of them. Ryan hasn't moved a thing. Nothing has changed since the night our daughter died. There's a book lying on the floor – a library book, the pages splayed – and I remember leaving it there, interrupted part way through the story by the arrival of the babysitter.

I shove my hand against my mouth to stifle a sob, and my gaze lands on her pajamas, lying folded where I left them on the top of the dresser. I press my fist even harder against my teeth to stop the tears from coming and collapse down on the bed.

My attention is stolen at once by a photo on the nightstand. I reach for it with a trembling hand. It's a picture of Sienna and me, taken last summer at the beach. Her dark hair is a tangled mess and she's laughing because I'm tickling her.

I trace Sienna's image with my fingertips, my chest heaving. I thought there was nothing left of my heart to break, but it turns out there is.

I want to take the photograph with me, so I can keep the image of Sienna sharp and never let it fade, but then I realize I can't. I can't leave any clues behind.

Putting it back on the nightstand takes a monumental effort. I rest my hand on the pillow, caressing the indentation left by her head, and then I lay my own head down in the same place, and try to breathe in the last traces of my daughter.

Fighting the urge to curl into a ball, I force myself up and cross toward Sienna's closet. Ignoring the neatly folded clothes and the row of tiny shoes, I reach up to the top shelf and fumble my way around until I feel a shoebox.

It contains a few of my memories from my past life – the life before Ryan. I kept it in Sienna's room as I knew he wouldn't find it here, and it was up too high for Sienna to discover. There's nothing in it that I needed to hide, but I never wanted to mix my old life with this life and keeping it in our bedroom meant I would have seen it every day.

Inside the box are a few photographs; a wooden owl my grandpa carved me; my birth certificate; a photograph of Daisy and me as toddlers playing in the dirt outside the trailer on a broken scooter; my grandpa's Vietnam War medals; and Daisy's passport wrapped up in the letter the US embassy sent when they mailed it back to me from Thailand.

I contemplate taking the whole box with me, but it's too big and bulky, so I take the wooden owl, the photograph of Daisy and me, as well as the passport, and stick them in my pocket, then I put the box back on the shelf, pick up the knife, switch off the light and tiptoe to the door.

I listen for a while before I slip back out onto the landing and down the stairs into Ryan's study. I need to check the safe, just in case, to see if he's arrogant enough to have replaced the box of souvenirs in it.

I kneel down and open the cabinet but when I input the old code it beeps loudly at me and flashes red. I shut the cabinet door, hoping the noise hasn't woken Ryan, and quickly head for the kitchen. I need to let the dog out and reset the alarm, but just as I step out into the hallway, I hear the bedroom door upstairs open, followed quickly by footsteps on the landing above. I dart across to the kitchen and ease open the door, slipping inside and hurrying over to the back door, even as the dog jumps at me in excitement.

With a shaking hand I tap the code into the alarm system to re-arm it and disappear outside just as the kitchen door opens and Ryan steps inside.

I duck down beneath the kitchen window, praying that Ryan doesn't notice Toby, who I can hear whining at the back door. Terrified he might let the dog out, I scoot along the side of the house, heading for the garage. Once I make it, I duck around the corner and peek out. I wonder what Ryan is doing. Did he wake to get a glass of water? Did he hear the noise from the safe and come to investigate? I wait on tenterhooks and after what feels like an eternity, I see the light in the kitchen go off and then a moment later I see the one in the upstairs bedroom turn off also. He must have gone back to bed. I wait another minute and then I let myself into the garage and switch on my flashlight.

'Rose.'

I spin around, letting out a muffled cry. It's Isabel. She's wearing a white forensic suit with a hood covering her hair, and black rubber gloves. My hand pressed to my galloping heart, I stare at her in shock. 'What are you doing here?' I whisper.

'You can't do it on your own.'

The plan was for her to wait in the car. I can't believe she's doing this. It's too dangerous.

'You should go,' I tell her. 'You can't be here. What if he finds you?'

'I'm staying,' she tells me. 'So, let's get on with it.'

Seeing she's not to be dissuaded, I sigh. 'OK.'

'Still want to do this?' she asks me, taking a step closer.

I nod. I told her from the beginning that I wasn't interested in escaping but in bringing Ryan to justice. But without evidence I know it won't be possible. And because we don't have proof of what he's done, the only way of getting justice is to frame Ryan for murder, the same way that he framed me.

I will set him up just as he has set me up, and if

all goes to plan, they will arrest him for my murder and the evidence will be so damning that he will have no defense.

Of course, he will claim innocence. He will tell the world he is being framed by me. But who will believe him when the evidence stacks up? He will go to jail – at least, that's what I hope for. Not for a crime that he committed, but that's a moot point. He will go to jail; that's all I care about. He will finally pay for what he has done.

Isabel holds out her hand. 'Give me the knife,' she says.

Reluctant, I hesitate and so she takes it from me.

'Take off the sweater,' she orders.

I follow her instructions, and then stand there like a lamb to the slaughter, shaking as she brings the knife up and rests the blade against the pale skin of my arms.

'I'm sorry,' she says, looking at me anxiously. 'This is going to hurt.'

I grit my teeth. 'Just don't hit a major artery,' I joke.

She grips my wrist tight and then slices the knife quickly along the inside of my arm. I gasp out loud, startled by the searing hot pain. Crimson blood gushes from the wound and I feel instantly light-headed at the sight of it.

Isabel brings the knife up over her head, as though

she's about to plunge it down and the blood left behind on the blade sprays against the wall above the workbench. She then takes my injured arm and lifts it up in the air. More blood splatters the floor from the open wound.

'Here,' she says, turning my wrist over. Blood drips all over my shoes and clothes.

She takes my now bloody palm and presses it to the bumper of Ryan's car, leaving a handprint that's all but invisible against the matte black plastic.

'Give me your other arm,' she says now, grimacing.

I grit my teeth as she slashes that one too and I try not to cry out. I can feel the blood dripping thick and fast onto the ground but don't look down as I don't want to faint. We need to make a mess though. We need to make it look like a believable crime scene.

Isabel orders me now to take off my clothes. I can't lift my arms because of the pain so she helps me undress. Blood soaks my green scrub shirt as I pull it over my head and it splashes my sweatpants. When I'm standing in my underwear, Isabel orders me to take that off too and so I do. I'm naked and shivering, and she makes me lie on the floor of the garage, my limbs coating the floor in blood. 'We need as much of your DNA here as possible,' she tells me, before she heaves me to my feet.

Next, she helps me into the trunk of Ryan's car. I bleed into the carpet, leaving dark stains, and Isabel runs my fingers through my hair and yanks out several strands, which she scatters there as well.

After she's done, I stagger out and she shuts the trunk. I'm starting to feel dizzy from the toxic mix of blood loss and spurting adrenaline. Isabel quickly wraps my arms in the bandages she brought, winding them so tight that they act like tourniquets.

'Are you OK?' she whispers anxiously as she works.

I nod, ignoring the blinding pain and the fact that the bandages are soaked red before she has even finished tying them. I look around. My blood is everywhere. My clothes are drenched with it. Fat red drops mark a path to the door and there is a spreading pool of crimson, marking the spot where I lay.

The blood will soon be washed away. The clothes disposed of. Hands will be scrubbed clean of any trace. No one will find a body so there will be no proof that anyone is dead.

Perhaps no one will ever be charged with my murder or be punished for it. Perhaps he will get away with it.

Or maybe not.

I hope not.

As the pain begins to ebb, I think of the women he hurt, and Sienna and Daisy – lying buried in the frozen ground, and I wonder what will happen now.

Chapter Forty-One

Present

Gwen drops heavily into a seat at the kitchen table opposite me. I digest the fact she knows who I am. How long has she known?

'I can explain,' I tell her, praying she gives me the chance to.

'Go on then. Why did you set him up?' she demands, eyeing me with a new wariness and suspicion.

I take a deep breath. I have to convince her of my side of the story, which might be difficult now thanks to Ryan's little speech to camera. I have to make her understand why I've done what I've done though. I inhale again and then I begin.

'My husband is a monster,' I say.

It takes over an hour to tell the story from beginning to end and dredging up the memories feels like

excavating my soul, but at the same time it's liberating. I am able to finally put my side of the story
across to someone. I am finally being listened to and
I so want her to believe me. I keep glancing at her,
trying to read her expression as though she's a one-
woman jury that I'm trying to convince, but Gwen
keeps up a stony front and I can't tell what she's
thinking.

I avoid giving her Isabel's name. I tell her though
about the party where I met her and what she told
me about my husband, and how I ran back to the
house and searched through Ryan's safe looking for
evidence. I tell her about the souvenirs I found, and
I see Gwen's face slacken with shock. I cry when I
tell her about Daisy and how I didn't believe her and
what it felt like to find the blue silk pajama top in
that box – the sorrow and the shame that overwhelmed me and still does.

I tell her about Sienna waking up and appearing
in the study clutching her stuffed rabbit, and about
Ryan returning home, the gravel spitting under his
car tires, how I scooped my daughter into my arms
and ran. I choke up as I tell her how I fled and that
Ryan followed me. I explain the terror of those
moments: losing control of the car and slamming into
a tree and coming to in a world where everything
was shrouded in fog.

'I wasn't drunk and I wasn't on drugs,' I say to

Gwen, my voice cracking. 'I would never have tried to kill myself or Sienna. Ryan has so many people in his pocket. I think he probably bribed someone to falsify the bloodwork.'

I pray she believes me, but she's shaking her head.

'I always thought it sounded strange the way they were saying you tried to kill yourself and your child,' she says. 'Why would you drive into a tree? Plenty of other ways to do it that are far more certain. It never added up in my mind.'

I stare at her, feeling a rush of relief. She does believe me! But then I realize what she just said.

'How long have you known who I am?' I ask.

Gwen smiles widely. 'From the minute you walked into the store looking for candles.'

My mouth falls open.

'You're fairly easy to recognize. Even with that haircut.'

I blink at her in astonishment. 'You've known this whole time? Why didn't you turn me in? I mean, if you knew who I was and what they were saying I did, why didn't you call the police on me?'

She shrugs. 'I didn't think it was fair what happened to you. Punishing you when you'd already lost a child. It seemed so cruel.'

My throat squeezes tight. Having someone believe me is such a relief.

'They would have kept me at Crosshill for the rest

of my life,' I tell Gwen. 'Kept me sedated so I could never speak up. And Ryan would have gotten away with everything.'

'So that's why you framed him,' she says, almost to herself.

'It was the only thing I could think of doing to get those women justice. To get Sienna and Daisy justice.'

Gwen takes that in for a moment, then abruptly gets to her feet. 'You can't stay here,' she tells me.

I stare up at her, my stomach clenching tight. What?

'You have to leave.'

I stand on shaking legs. My shoulders sag. I haven't managed to convince her. For a moment it sounded like I might have, but I'm a fool. Of course, she doesn't want to help me now. Not after I've admitted what I did to Ryan. I have made her an accomplice too, in my crime.

'I'm not going to tell the police,' Gwen says, surprising me. 'You can trust me. But if you stay here much longer someone is going to discover you. My friends will keep coming around to see if I'm OK and someone will spot you, sooner or later. You're safer out in the woods.'

Exhaling with yet more relief, I nod at her. 'I don't want to put you in any danger,' I tell her. 'You've done so much already to help me. I'm so grateful.'

She steps toward me and squeezes my hand. 'Thank me when you get away with it.'

Chapter Forty-Two

Past

One Month Ago

I am dead.

I look around the garage at the crime scene I've just staged. Without a body it will be harder to prove Ryan has killed me, but not impossible, especially with the evidence we will plant. The only thing that could ruin it is if they find me, alive. And Isabel has a plan for that: a cabin belonging to her boyfriend's family. Hidden away in upstate New York, I should be able to lie low there and avoid detection. And then, if we can get Daisy's out-of-date passport renewed, I have a shot at making it out of the country. Because Daisy died in Thailand her death was never officially recorded in the US. I am hoping that means renewing her passport won't be difficult.

Isabel helps me into a pair of clean, black sweat-pants and the hoodie and then drapes an old winter jacket over my shoulders. I can't fit my arms through the holes as my arms are hurting too much to lift them.

'I'm sorry about the clothes,' she apologizes in a whisper. 'I got them from Goodwill.'

I suppress a smile. 'It's fine. Thank you,' I say. I still can't believe she agreed to this plan, but she did, straightaway. It's not perfect justice for Ryan's crimes, but it's better than nothing. And we both knew that there was no other way Ryan would ever face trial or anything amounting to punishment for what he's done. We're both committed, regardless of the outcome, to making him pay.

Now that we're so close, my eyes dart to the door in terror. We could be caught at any moment. Ryan could walk in and all this would be for nothing. We need to hurry and get out of here.

Isabel helps me slip into some clean sneakers next, and then she quickly gathers up my bloody clothes, stuffing them into a trash bag, which she tosses to one side.

I look around the garage again and spot the toolbox on the workbench. Using the plastic gloves to cover my fingerprints, I pick up the bloody knife and drop it inside the toolbox, burying it beneath hammers and a wrench.

Isabel has moved on to dousing the garage floor with bleach. She scrubs at the bloodstains on the concrete with a rag. As I watch her, I wonder if we've gone too far. Staging a crime scene seemed easy when I suggested it, but now I see how messy it is, and I wonder if we have enough time to clear it up well enough that Ryan won't notice and have a chance to fix it, but not so well that the police won't find it when they start looking.

I try to help Isabel but she can see that I'm struggling and tells me she'll manage. I'm grateful now that she didn't wait in the car as we'd arranged but came to help me, as I don't think I could have done this on my own.

She has a gallon jug of water with her, and she uncaps it and sloshes it over the floor, then mops up the remaining blood with several old towels, including one of Ryan's that I find in his gym bag on the back seat of his car.

Isabel leaves a few spots of blood on the wall and then rinses the floor down again with the remaining water. When she's done, she stuffs all the bloody towels, the plastic water containers and the bleach into another trash bag.

I check the time. Almost one twenty. 'We need to go,' I say.

Isabel takes my bloody bra from the trash bag and shoves it down beneath the front seat of the Range Rover. She then puts the rest of the unused trash bags in a drawer in the workbench.

We take one last look around at the crime scene before we leave.

Outside the garage, Isabel unzips the white suit and takes it off, though she keeps the gloves on. She pushes the white suit inside the backpack and then, picking up the trash bags, we set off, skirting the backyard to avoid the sensors, until we make it to the far wall where Isabel helps boost me over.

We are back at the church at one thirty, and it's with relief that we jump in the car, cranking the heating to the max, both of us shivering from the cold and what we've just done. We drive five miles to a wooded area, and Isabel pulls into a parking spot and jumps out of the car with the trash bags containing my bloody clothes and stained towels. I watch her jog toward the woods and come back a few minutes later without the bags.

'Do you think we should have thrown them into the trash?' I ask when she gets back in the car. I know that if Ryan had really committed a murder he'd never be so stupid to leave behind evidence, and he wouldn't dump bloody clothes in a trash bag in the woods. He's a lawyer. He knows how to dispose of evidence.

308

'No,' Isabel says, finally removing the plastic gloves. 'If we threw them in the trash, we'd have no control over if or even when they would be found. This way I'll call it in anonymously in a couple of days' time.'

She's thought this through – she's thought everything through – and I'm grateful. We didn't have long together to work through the details and most of it she's figured out alone, because I was stuck in Crosshill. I hope to God the police don't work any of this out, or that she's involved, because it's enough that my own life is ruined, without hers being destroyed too.

I rest my head against the window and close my eyes. We drive in silence, Isabel concentrating on the directions, me resting my head against the cool of the glass. My arms are burning as though they've been plunged in acid. The bandages feel hot and sticky beneath my sweater. I cradle them against my body.

'Are you OK?' Isabel asks, noticing. 'Your arms? Are they still bleeding?'

I shake my head. I don't want to worry her. She turns up the heat in the car even higher, because I'm still shivering, and soon I find my eyelids growing heavy.

When I startle awake some time later, I see we've left the freeway and are driving down quiet country roads. There are no road signs or houses, just darkness stretching in every direction. We could be driving through space.

'We're nearly there,' Isabel says to me.

It's almost five in the morning, but there's no sign yet of the dawn.

'The cabin belongs to my boyfriend,' Isabel says, frowning as she peers through the windscreen at the vanishing road ahead. 'It's been in the family for years. But they never visit. It's just sitting there, empty, so I don't know what state it will be in. My boyfriend said they always planned on getting around to fixing it up, but they haven't yet.'

'What did you tell him?' I ask. 'Your boyfriend?'

She shrugs. 'That I had an undocumented friend who needed a place to lie low for a while. I told him you'd lost a daughter and were grieving and needed some space.'

'He doesn't know who I am?'

'Of course not. But we can trust him. He won't tell anyone you're staying here. Not even his family. You'll be safe.'

Ten minutes later, Isabel pulls to one side and kills the engine. Silence drums in my ears. The darkness engulfs us as soon as we step out of the car. I can't even see Isabel until she turns on a flashlight.

'There should be a track somewhere around here,' she says, taking out a map from her bag and opening it up. She studies it while I gaze around at the forest on either side of us, and the stark tree shapes outlined against the silken black of the sky. The stars are dazzling, the moon a sickle of silver. But I feel no sense of awe or wonder. I know right then that even if I manage to succeed, if I get through this and am able to start a new life, I will never again see the world in the same way. It will always be through a veil, with me stranded on the dark side and the rest of the world in the light.

'Come on,' Isabel says, setting off into the woods. 'I think it's this way.'

The sky is hot pink, the dawn breaking, by the time we stumble exhausted upon the cabin. We stop and stare at the log exterior. The windows are all intact and though it looks abandoned, and the wood is rotten in places, it feels to me like a refuge, a cave that I can burrow into and hide inside.

Isabel smiles at me in relief. 'Come on.' She trudges to the door and inserts the key into the rusting lock.

Inside, it smells of damp and mildew and dust but we throw open a few windows to air the place and walk through the rooms, trying the lights, which don't work. The taps in the bathroom and kitchen are set to a slow trickle, a way for them not to freeze in the cold winters, I suppose, and for that I'm grateful too. At least I will have water. And food. Isabel has brought supplies to last me a few weeks.

'It's not much,' Isabel says, looking at me anxiously.

'It's great,' I say, sitting down gingerly on the musty sofa. I feel woozy and exhausted. 'It's better than Crosshill.'

Isabel notices I'm shaking. 'I'm sorry there's no heating. There's a fireplace though. Maybe there's some wood outside. I'll take a look.'

'It's fine. I'll manage,' I tell her. She's done enough. She should leave, get herself as far away from me as possible.

Isabel takes off the large backpack she's wearing and sets it down on the floor in front of me. 'OK, I've packed clothes and food for a few weeks – noodles mostly, I'm afraid. And a camp stove with fuel. Should last. There's also a first aid kit in the bag. And some more clothes: underwear, socks, that kind of thing. I hope you'll be warm enough.'

'I'll be fine,' I say, thinking of the winters I spent in Missouri in an unheated trailer.

'And here,' she says, handing me an envelope. 'It's not much, I'm sorry. It's all I could get right now.'

I peek inside and see there's several hundred dollars in notes.

'You didn't need to . . .' I start to say, pushing the envelope back at her, but she cuts me off.

'You might need money. If there's an emergency. I've only packed enough food for a few weeks. I hope that's enough but . . .'

'When will you be back?' I ask, suddenly realizing

how alone I'm going to be out here in the woods. I haven't been alone or had to live by myself for years. I'm not sure I know how.

Isabel shakes her head. 'Hopefully, between three and four weeks. It depends how long the paperwork takes to come through. Which reminds me, do you have the passport?'

I remove Daisy's passport from my pocket. 'Is that how long it takes to renew it?' I ask, handing it to her.

'I don't know for sure,' Isabel answers. 'Two to three weeks minimum it said on the website, but it can take longer. And it's probably best we have no contact, just in case they figure out that I helped you. So if I'm not back here within four weeks, you should go. Assume that I've been arrested.'

My stomach knots at the thought of Isabel getting into trouble after everything she's done for me and then again at the thought of where I'll go if in four weeks she doesn't return.

She rummages in the backpack for a pair of scissors and a box of platinum blonde hair dye. 'OK,' she says, looking up at me. 'Last step. Ready?'

I'm not – all I want to do is lie down and sleep – but I follow her into the bathroom and she positions me on the toilet seat. I sit there drowsily, as she hacks off my hair, watching the strands drift to the floor at our feet.

Her fingers brush the ridged scar on the side of my head. 'Does it hurt?'

'I get headaches,' I tell her. 'And I find it hard to remember things. Sometimes I don't even remember who I am.'

'Head injuries can do that,' she says.

They can alter your personality too. One of the doctors mentioned it – telling me that it was common to experience intense mood swings, personality changes, confusion, sleeplessness and slurred speech after a traumatic head injury. I do feel like I'm a different person. But I don't know how much of that is down to the head injury.

'Tell me about your cousin,' I say as she cuts my hair.

She pauses, then keeps cutting. 'She was more like a sister to me,' she says quietly. 'She came to the US a few years ago. From El Salvador. She made the trip all by herself. It took her five months.' Her voice quavers and for a moment her hands still in my hair. 'She didn't have a choice. Back home it's . . .' She breaks off. 'There's a lot of gang violence. This guy, a gang member, decided he wanted her to be his girlfriend. You have to understand, you don't get a choice in that. So she had to go along with it, but then her brother – my other cousin – found out. He attacked the guy. Stabbed him. He didn't kill him though. So the guy took revenge. He killed my uncle and my aunt and Angela's brother. So she fled, with nothing but the clothes on her back.'

I've been holding my breath the whole time she's been talking and now I let it out.

'I'm sorry,' I whisper. 'That's awful.'

'She came here,' Isabel continues, 'to New York. To me. I paid a coyote to get her over the border. When she got here, I helped get her a job at the hotel. It's not easy when you're undocumented to find work. But she was so grateful for any job, for a chance to pay me back, and to have a life, you know?' Her voice chokes up. The scissors fall to her side. 'She was just starting to get her life back on track. After everything she'd been through and then . . . Ryan attacked her.'

I stand up and put my arms awkwardly around her, and she cries against my shoulder. I hug her, stroking her hair and making soothing sounds, like I used to do for Sienna. It feels strange to hold someone. It's been so long. In fact, I think Sienna was the last person I held like this.

Isabel wraps her arms around me and hugs me back and I feel my own grief well up to meet hers. After a moment she draws back and looks at me.

'Oh dear,' she says, pulling a face. 'It's not the best haircut.'

I stand up and look in the bathroom mirror. The woman I see staring back at me is a stranger. She looks terrifying – hollowed out, her eyes, swollen and red, are empty wells that have no bottom.

'No one is going to see me,' I reply, with a wan smile, taking in the hack job approximation of a pixie crop.

Isabel opens the box of bleach and, after wrapping a towel around my shoulders, applies it to my hair.

My scalp burns but we leave it on until what's left of my hair has turned white blonde, then we wash it out using freezing cold water from the tap.

When we're done Isabel leads me through into the living room. She dives into the backpack again and brings out a digital camera. 'OK, we need a photo,' she says, looking around. 'And we need a white background.'

As it's a log cabin, there are no white walls, so Isabel hangs a sheet from the bedroom over the bathroom door and I stand against it. She snaps a dozen photos as I stare into the camera.

'You really do look like her,' she says, flicking to the photo of Daisy in the passport.

I look at it too. It must have been taken shortly after the penultimate time I saw her, when she was sober. She fell off the wagon because of what Ryan did to her. I think about the trauma she suffered as a little girl and then at the hands of my husband, and rage flows in me like lava. My sister is dead because of Ryan. He didn't kill her directly but he may as well have.

I wish I could turn back time. I've got so much to make amends for. I know that setting up Ryan is as much about that as it is about making him face justice. But even if they do arrest him and send him to jail for life, I will still have to live with myself.

Isabel pockets the passport, then touches my arm. 'I should go,' she says, checking her watch. 'I have to get back. But let me make you up a bed first. I saw a pile of blankets in the closet and I bought you a sleeping bag too, so you should be warm enough.'

After she leaves, giving me one final hug goodbye, I crawl into the sleeping bag beneath the nest of blankets she's made up for me and I close my eyes, but despite how exhausted I am, sleep refuses to come.

Chapter Forty-Three

Present

After Gwen drops me back at the cabin with a bag full of food and a pile of clean clothes, including her husband's expensive down jacket and a fleece-lined hat, I curl up in my bed and fall into a fitful sleep. I lied to Gwen about feeling better. I feel like death. My fever has returned, and I sleep for the best part of the afternoon and late into the night, dreaming of Sienna. She visits me in my dreams often, but most times I see her lying dead in the ditch and I cannot reach her. This time she is in the bedroom with me, standing by the bed. I'm asleep but also aware of her there. She is calling my name, calling me 'mommy'.

I wake with a startle. Someone is in the room. I can feel it. I sit bolt upright. 'Sienna?' I say.

Moonlight slices across the room, illuminating

someone standing in the doorway. Not Sienna. Not a ghost. A person.

'Jesus,' I say, hand to my chest, adrenaline coursing violently through my body. 'You scared me.' Then I stumble out of the bed and run toward Isabel.

'I let myself in,' she says, holding up a spare key. 'I'm sorry. You didn't hear me knock.'

I throw myself into her arms, relief bursting out of me. 'You're here. I was so worried.' I have been trying desperately not to think about Isabel, to keep my mind from wandering to the what-ifs, because I knew it would drive me mad to wonder, but I know that deep down in my subconscious I was playing out all the different versions of things that could have happened to her: that Ryan had figured out who she was and got to her, that someone had linked together her visit to me at Crosshill with my escape, that the police might have brought her in for questioning or even arrested her . . . God knows what. I have been counting down the days, wondering what I will do if a month passes and she doesn't return. But all those thoughts that have been plaguing me now evaporate. She's here.

'Are you OK?' she asks, searching my face.

'Yes,' I say. 'I haven't been very well,' I admit, though that's an understatement. That short burst of movement, jumping out of bed and running over to her has left me dizzy but I don't want to worry her.

'Yeah, you don't look good,' she remarks. 'I'm sorry it's taken so long.'

'It's OK, it's OK,' I say, feeling my anxiety rising. 'Did you get it?'

She grins and whips something out of her pocket. It's a passport. She hands it to me. 'It came yesterday. I found out in the morning that I passed the bar, and then your passport arrived. It was a double banner day!'

'Congratulations!' I say.

I take the passport from her, my hands shaking, and open it up to the ID page. There's the photo she took of me with my platinum blonde shorn hair and gaunt face. And there's my new name, or rather, my borrowed name: Daisy Elizabeth Lewis.

I examine the page closely. I can't believe it worked. This is my way out. We might just pull this off after all.

'I'm going to drive you north across the border into Canada,' Isabel says to me now. 'We'll go east to Niagara Falls. From there you can catch a bus to Toronto. And then a flight. I think you're safest heading to South America. Ecuador.'

I sink down onto the bed, holding the passport. Until this moment I hadn't dared to dream about a future – I've just been living day to day, sometimes minute to minute – but now it's within reach. I should feel a spark of something – relief or excitement – but

I don't. I feel numb. What will I do in Ecuador? How will I survive? I don't even speak Spanish.

'We can talk about it more in the car,' Isabel says.

'We're leaving now?' I say, looking up at her, surprised.

She nods.

Now the moment is here I feel all at sea. This cabin has become my safehouse. And there's Gwen. If I disappear, she'll worry. I need to thank her for everything she's done. But there's no time. I could leave her a note I suppose. Or one day hopefully I can send her an unsigned postcard so she knows I made it. *If* I make it, that is. We're not out of the woods yet, literally or figuratively.

'Here,' Isabel says shoving something else across the table at me. 'It's all I could get together. It's a few thousand dollars.'

I look down at an envelope of cash. 'I can't take that,' I tell her, handing it back.

She sits down beside me. 'You've got no choice. You have to take it.'

I chew the inside of my lip. I know she's right as I have no other money and how will I get to Ecuador without a cent to my name? So I nod my thanks. 'I don't know how I can ever repay you,' I mumble. I am so grateful to so many people, most of whom are strangers. No matter what happens to me, these last few weeks have made me believe for the first time ever in the goodness of people. I've been so suspicious for so long and so untrusting. I feel like I've made friends for the first time in my life, which given the circumstances is quite remarkable.

'You don't need to thank me,' Isabel says. 'I didn't just do this for you, you know.'

I nod, remembering her cousin, Angela, and all the other women we did this for.

'It's going to be OK,' Isabel says to me now, seeing something shift in my expression. 'He's going to go to prison.'

'Is he?' I question. 'What's happening? I haven't seen the news for a day or so. I saw that Ryan got arrested but they let him go, didn't they?'

'Yeah. He put up three million dollars' bail. But the case is pretty strong against him.'

'Is it?'

'Yes. I called the police anonymously – told them I'd found a trash bag in the woods containing blood-stained clothing. They linked it to you straightaway because of the Crosshill labels on the clothes, and Ryan came under immediate suspicion. I think though there was some kind of delay in getting a search warrant on him and the house – maybe because of his links to the police and the DA's office, but when they finally did get it—' she gives a sly smile '—what do you know? They found traces of your blood in the garage and all over his car.'

I smile back. 'It worked.'

'It worked,' she agrees, grinning. 'I have to admit, I wasn't sure it would.'

'Me either.' I'm still stunned, given her fears, that she agreed to go along with the plan.

'You think he'll go to jail?' I ask. 'For certain?'

'I don't see why not. There's enough evidence for a jury to convict. He has a motive,' she goes on. 'And you were seen on his security tapes entering the house, just as we wanted. I'm sure they found the knife too, as well as the trash bags. There's so much evidence against him. I'm not sure how he can get out of it, even though they don't have a body.'

'And you're safe?' I ask. 'He doesn't know who you are? They haven't wondered how the hell I escaped from Crosshill without help?'

She shrugs. 'No. No one's come knocking at my door. I've been really careful. I quit my internship at Anderson Tait, telling them I was focusing on my exams, and I've been lying low. We should get going,' she says, standing up. 'I want to be on the road before there's too much traffic.'

'OK. Let me get my stuff.'

When I'm packed, I pull on my jacket and my boots, slipping the envelope of cash into my pocket. I pick up my bag and turn to look around the room. It's so cold my breath puffs in front of me in clouds. It feels strange to admit it, but I'm going to miss this place.

'Ready?' Isabel asks.

'Yeah,' I start to say but I'm cut off by a familiar hollow rattling sound.

'What was that?' Isabel whispers, seeing the alarm on my face as my head snaps toward the window.

It was the cans tinkling. 'Someone's out there,' I say, adrenaline firing through me.

Isabel's eyes widen in fear.

I've been here before though. I order myself to stay calm. It was an animal last time, setting them off. And Jake the second time. But what if Ryan has figured out Isabel's connection to me at Crosshill and tracked her down? What if he has followed her here? He might have been watching her this whole time, waiting for her to lead him to me. I surprise myself by moving past Isabel and crossing to the back door. I peel back the curtain to look out, but of course it's too dark to see anything outside.

'What is it?' Isabel whispers, coming up behind me.

'I don't know,' I whisper back, dread shuddering up my spine. 'Someone or something's out there.'

If it's the police, they can't find Isabel here and if it's Ryan or his people then it's best one of us gets out. I grab the flashlight that Isabel left on the table and turn to her. 'You have to go.' I put my hand on the door handle.

Isabel grabs my arm and stops me. 'What are you doing?' she asks, confused.

'Going out there,' I tell her.

'Why?!' she asks in a panic.

'If it is the police, I'll lead them away from here. They'll come after me. You can get away.'

She grips my arm tighter. 'No! Are you crazy?'

I wrench my arm free from her grip. 'It's better this way, if only I get caught. Get out of here; go out the back way!' And with that, I yank open the door before she can stop me and run outside. I take off running for the trees, shining the flashlight beam ahead of me, trying to lead whoever it is away from the cabin and away from Isabel.

I make it about a hundred feet before I hear a man yell. 'Stop! Or we'll shoot!'

I freeze instantly, throwing my hands up in the air. I play statue but I'm shaking.

Lights scour my face, blinding me. I squint, making out dark shapes in the darkness moving toward me. When they get closer I catch glimpses of police SWAT vests, helmets and guns.

I look around for an escape, but I know it's too late. It's over, I think to myself. It's all over. I've failed.

Chapter Forty-Four

Present

They call it the ice box but to me it is no colder than the cabin. If not for my fever, which is back with a vengeance, I would be OK. As it is, I'm shivering hard enough to crack my teeth. They stripped me, searched me and put me on suicide watch. I'm not suicidal but this allows them to keep me away from general population.

It also means I can't speak to anyone, which is what Ryan is afraid of. I wonder whose ear he spoke into to make that happen. But as I look at the slat in the door and the thick stone walls, I also realize that it makes me vulnerable, and I wonder if that's the real reason I'm in here.

Ryan must want me dead. He knows the risk I am

to him alive. And it's easier to get to a prisoner on suicide watch, as there aren't any witnesses, plus you have an in-built modus operandi. He would just need to pay off one of the guards who checks on me every fifteen minutes with enough money to make them look the other way or even to do the job themselves. They could make it look like a suicide and no one would investigate.

I sit on the bed, knees drawn to my chest, staring at the far wall, determined not to fall asleep so I'm not taken by surprise. Although, what does it matter? It's over anyway. I heard them talking about transferring me to Crosshill once they've processed me. They'll drag me back there, drug me, and forget about me. Death might be a better option.

I pray that Isabel managed to get away. She had enough time to, surely? The guards won't tell me anything though and, of course, I can't ask about her. I hope the cops don't expect me to explain how I got to the house in Westchester from Crosshill, and from there to the cabin. And I hope they don't link the cabin to Isabel through her boyfriend. I will tell them that I hitched a ride north and that I found the place and broke in, thinking it was abandoned. They should buy that.

Who turned me in?, I wonder. Did Ryan figure out who Isabel was and have her followed? Or was it Gwen, finally deciding that one hundred thousand dollars was too much to pass up? If it was her, I hope she makes good use of the money.

It crosses my mind that it could also have been Jake. He might have put two and two together finally.

The window in the cell door clangs open. 'Hands,' calls a rough voice.

I want to resist, terror gripping me. What if this is it? What if they're here to kill me?

'Move!'

I have no choice. I stand and shuffle to the door, turn around, and stick my hands through the window so they can cuff me.

'Step away from the door.'

I follow the order and the door swings open and two police officers enter. I flinch as they rush me, grabbing my arms, but they're not here to harm me. Instead, they haul me out of the cell and drag me along a grim corridor.

I am brought to an interrogation room – the same room they locked me in when I first arrived. They tried to interview me then, but I refused to speak to them until there was a lawyer present.

Now I find a tired-looking man in a rumpled suit sitting at the table with a briefcase and a Starbucks cup of coffee in front of him. He stands up and introduces himself to me as Miles Underwood, my public defender. The cops sit me down and leave the room, making it clear that they'll be waiting just outside. Underwood sighs as he sits down opposite me and starts to pull papers out of his briefcase.

'You had quite a search party looking for you,' he says as he sets his briefcase to one side and starts to look through the paperwork.

'How did they find me?' I inquire. 'Do you know?'

'Someone made a call.'

'Who?'

Underwood scans the papers in his hands. 'It says here that a couple who were camping by the lake called it in for the reward. Said they saw a woman on the lake. And they thought it was you. It led to a massive search of the area.'

I sink back in my chair in surprise. That couple who helped me when I fell through the ice? It was them?! I curse inwardly at my bad luck. Damn it. But at the same time I'm relieved because it means Isabel wasn't followed. I'm also relieved that it didn't turn out to be Gwen. That's something of a silver lining I suppose.

'The state is going to press for the maximum charges,' Underwood tells me next. 'They'll tack on wasting police time too. And frankly,' he says, giving me a stern look, 'you've got no case. Your best bet is . . .'

I interrupt. 'I'm not taking a plea deal.'

He's about to say something but I lean across the table reaching toward him. He glances down

330

nervously at my handcuffed wrists. 'I didn't kill my daughter.'

He frowns at me, confused. 'I thought you'd accepted the plea deal on that charge already?'

'I wasn't capable of making any decisions. I was in the hospital. I don't even remember discussing it.'

He rummages through the papers and after a minute looks back up at me, his frown deepening. 'They said you're mentally incompetent to stand trial. They put in a request to hold you indefinitely until you're found competent. I didn't know about this.'

'Me neither,' I say, reeling. 'I'm not mentally incompetent.' I lean across the table, shooting a look at the camera on the wall. They're not meant to be recording this conversation due to attorney-client privilege, but I wouldn't put it past them. Still, I need to tell him. He's my lawyer. It's my only chance of getting out of here.

'My husband is trying to frame me. He's a DA. He has connections. He knows people. He has friends everywhere. You have no idea what he's capable of . . .'

Underwood leans back, away from me, eyeing me skeptically. I realize I must sound like a lunatic.

'Well,' he says. 'I can request a second opinion on your mental state. They shouldn't refuse that.'

'How long is that going to take?' I query, frustrated.

'There is a backlog,' he says with a shrug. 'It could take a while.'

Panic surges in my chest. 'No! No. I don't have that time. If he doesn't try to kill me, they'll move me back to Crosshill. I can't go back there,' I say, pleading with him.

Underwood's expression tells me that he really does think I'm crazy. The frustration of not being able to convince him makes me want to scream. He shrugs at me, indifferent. 'I can't stop that from happening, I'm afraid.'

My voice becomes shrill. 'No, you don't understand,' I say, trying to keep hold of my temper and the hysteria rising up in me. 'If they send me back there, they'll pump me full of drugs. I'll never get out. They'll never find me mentally competent. They'll keep me there until I die.'

Underwood is inching back in his seat as far as he can, watching me like he thinks I'm about to lunge at him.

'This is useless,' I mutter, through gritted teeth.

'What is it that you are accusing your husband of?' Underwood asks, seemingly deciding to at least try acting like my defense attorney.

I look up at the camera in the corner of the room again. 'He's a rapist,' I say, lowering my voice.

Underwood stares at me in open disbelief.

'He's raped a lot of women,' I go on. 'I found out.

That's why he was chasing me in the car. He's trying to silence me.'

There's a long pause as Underwood appraises me. 'And you have evidence of this?' he finally asks.

My shoulders drop. I rest my head in my hands. 'I did. But not anymore.'

'So, it's your word against his.'

I nod.

'And you just tried to frame him for your murder,' Underwood says, talking to me like I'm an idiot.

'I had to,' I spit back, banging my fists on the table.

He winces. 'Don't say that to the police. Or anyone, in fact. It's not a good defense. All I can advise is that you plead the fifth.'

That's his advice? I shake my head in disbelief. Desperation and panic whirlwind inside my mind.

'I thought you were supposed to help me?' I cry, angrily.

'I can only advise you on the best course of action.'

There's that word again: 'advise'. 'Your advice is shit,' I yell, trying to stand up but restrained by the cuffs chaining me to a metal hoop in the ground. 'You don't even believe me.'

'I don't need to believe you. That's not what I'm here for.'

'Great,' I mutter, slumping back down in my chair. My eyes land on the papers in front of him. 'Is that my case file?'

'Yes.'

'Is the original report about the accident in there?'

He flicks through and finds it. 'Yes, it's here.'

'Who filed it?' I demand.

He checks the name on the bottom. 'Detective Adams.'

'Can I read it?'

He hands it to me, warily, his patience growing thin. I scan the typed report, skipping over the parts about Sienna.

Suspect was transferred to Community Memorial Hospital in Westchester at 3.43 a.m. on the morning of June 21st.

Suspect. How was I already a suspect then? That doesn't even make sense. At the time I was the victim of a car accident. Why would the officer who arrived first on the scene put me down in his report as a suspect? The murder charge came days later.

'Is there a copy of my medical records? From the night of the accident?' I ask Underwood.

Annoyed and increasingly impatient, Underwood roots through the folder. 'No. But there's this.' He takes out a sheet of paper. 'It's the bloodwork they did on you after the accident.'

I tear it from his hands, startling him, and read the results: 'Blood alcohol level 0.32%. Ambien 12.5mg.' There's a signature at the bottom of the page: Doctor Thatcher.

'This has been forged,' I tell Underwood, shoving the report under his nose to read.

He glances briefly at it then gives me a long, hard stare, as though he's finally had enough of my paranoid delusions. 'Right,' he says.

I ignore his tone. 'Why don't you find out if there's really a Doctor Thatcher at Community Memorial and then check if they signed this off?'

I pick up the accident report and compare Detective Adams's signature to the one for Doctor Thatcher. They look similar. 'What if Detective Adams faked the signature?'

'Why would he do that?' Underwood replies, rubbing the bridge of his nose as though he has a terrible headache.

'Because he's in Ryan's pay,' I hiss.

I sound completely delusional. I know I do, but I can't stop myself. This is my only chance. I need to convince Underwood or I'm done.

'I need to go,' he says, his patience having clearly worn out.

I stare at him in disbelief. That's it? I'm completely screwed. There is no way out of this.

I watch Underwood start to pack up the papers and case file.

'Wait!' I say, reaching across the table with my bound hands clasped together.

He stops and looks at me.

'Do you have a card?' I ask.

He rummages in his pocket for his wallet. In the few seconds that he's distracted I slip the paperclip from the case file into my palm.

He hands me one of his business cards.

'Thank you,' I say.

Chapter Forty-Five

Present

'Shit . . .'

Keys rattle in the cell door. An alarm starts to blare. Someone lifts my head off the floor. Faces and shapes waver in front of me.

The paperclip lies bloody in my palm.

'Where did she get this?' someone growls angrily, prying it from my hand.

'Oh God,' someone else exclaims.

I have ripped through the barely healed scabs on my inner arms, and torn open the existing knife wounds using the paperclip. Hands lift me onto the metal slat of a bed, jostling my arms. Stars burst on the backs of my eyelids.

Someone is wrapping something around my arms.

They're rough with me and I cry out but that makes them even less gentle.

'We need to get her to the hospital,' comes then, but the words feel very far away.

I don't open my eyes again until I'm wheeled out of an ambulance and into the ER. I feel faint and floaty and I think the paramedics must have given me Valium or something because it's a fight to keep awake.

I am lying on a gurney and I look up at the fluorescent lights rushing by on the ceiling as I'm sped into a triage room. There's an IV in my arm – bags of clear fluid and blood are being pumped into me. Two cops in uniform are stationed by the door and then I notice Detective Lim is with them. What's he doing here? A chill runs up my spine. I wonder if he's the one in Ryan's pay. Lim might be here to report back, or even to carry out a hit job for Ryan. Am I in even more danger here than I was at the jail?

A doctor in a white coat – a young Indian-American woman – walks in. She looks askance at the two uniformed officers stationed on one side of me and Detective Lim on the other, then she looks at me.

'Why the hell is she handcuffed to the bed?' she demands of Lim, angrily.

The patrol cops look at each other and then at Lim.

'She's a fugitive risk,' he explains.

'In this state?' she snorts. 'She's going nowhere. And I need to examine her arms.'

Lim pauses then addresses one of the officers: 'Undo the cuffs. Fasten her by the ankle instead.'

The cop obeys and the doctor approaches me. She takes my left arm and carefully unbandages it. Her name badge reads 'Dr. Karthi Karuna.' And underneath her name it says Community Memorial Hospital. I smile to myself.

'What did she use?' Karuna asks.

I'm right here, I want to say, but my tongue is useless, and I can't find the words.

'A paperclip,' Lim responds.

'It looks like she opened up old knife wounds that hadn't properly healed.'

'Yeah,' he says. 'We think the first ones were from when she tried to frame her husband for her murder.'

I see the doctor do a double take and recognition lights her face. She knows who I am.

'It looks like she's got an infection,' she says now. 'We'll need to run tests. And get these stitched up. I'm going to need you to leave the room,' she informs the police officers.

Lim crosses his arms over his chest. 'We're not going anywhere.'

'You can stand just outside, but I need to examine her for further injuries, and I'm not doing that with you here.'

I like this doctor. She's no-nonsense. Direct. Maybe I can talk to her, get her to listen.

Reluctantly, Lim leaves the room along with the other two cops.

'Right,' the doctor turns to me, her tone softening. 'Let's get you fixed up.'

I grimace as she touches my arm gently.

'Were you trying to kill yourself?' she asks.

I shake my head, my eyelids unbearably heavy, my mind clouding. I didn't even cut deep. I didn't want to die, just to make it look that way. 'No,' I say, forcing myself to stay conscious. 'I need your help,' I slur.

She smiles at me. 'That's why I'm here. I'm going to help you, Rose.'

'No . . .' I start to say. 'I need . . .' but I can't finish. The drugs they gave me in the ambulance are finally overcoming me, and before I can tell her about Ryan and beg her to protect me, my eyelids flutter closed and I sink into the dark.

When I wake I'm in a different room. My arms are throbbing as if the skin is being stretched like a hide on a frame. The pain is muted though and indistinct, like background noise in another room. I look down and see I'm attached to wires and machines and an IV bag of fluid. Through half-closed eyelids, I spot a police officer sitting in an armchair in the corner of the room, playing with his phone. My hands aren't cuffed but when I move my ankle, I realize my foot is still chained to the bed. How am I going to get out of here?

Doctor Karuna pays me a visit before too long. She checks my chart and asks me how I'm feeling. The wooziness from whatever they gave me is wearing off. 'Better,' I say to her, casting a sideways look at the cop. I wish Karuna would send him outside again so I could talk to her.

'You had a very bad infection,' she tells me, sitting down on the edge of the bed. 'Sepsis had set in. You're lucky. If you'd left it any longer to get treatment you might have lost an arm, or worse, gone into septic shock. We're treating you with antibiotics intravenously. You've responded well. Your fever's coming down.'

I frown. 'How long have I been here?' There's no window in the room or clock.

'A few hours,' she says.

I take that in, wondering how long I'll be kept here before they return me to that prison cell, or worse. I shoot another look at the cop in the armchair. He's still occupied with his phone. I look back at Karuna. 'Doctor Thatcher,' I say to her, in a whisper.

Karuna frowns at me, confused.

'Do you know a Doctor Thatcher?' I press.

'Yes,' she says. 'He works in the ER. Why?'

'I was brought here, after my car accident.'

Karuna nods at me. 'Yes. I know. I read your chart.'

'They took my blood,' I whisper to Karuna. 'Can you help me? I need to find the original bloodwork report. I need to see it.'

The cop stands up. 'What are you talking about?' he demands, stepping toward the bed.

I stare at Karuna beseechingly. Her brow is still puckered, and she's obviously unsure why I'm asking. But then she looks over her shoulder at the cop. 'She's wondering if she can get more painkillers,' she tells him.

The cop scowls at us both, suspicious, but he goes and sits back in his chair and resumes looking at his phone – though I can tell he has one ear cocked to our conversation.

'They want to transfer you to Crosshill,' Karuna tells me now.

I jerk upright in the bed and she startles back. 'No!' I beg her. 'Please!'

The cop stands up again, this time resting his hand on his gun. I ignore him and focus on Karuna. 'Please,' I say to Karuna, pleadingly. 'You can't let them send me there.'

I wish to God the cop wasn't there and I could tell her what I need to tell her. But then I wonder if it's a good idea. If I do, she might be like the attorney, Underwood, and dismiss me as crazy. She already thinks I tried to kill myself. And that I tried to frame my husband for my murder. My best bet is to stick to this one task, convince her to do this one thing for me.

Karuna purses her lips. 'It's not up to me, I'm afraid. But I won't be releasing you until I'm sure you're on the mend. That'll be at least three days.'

I can tell from the look on her face that she's doing the best she can to help me. But three days? My foot flexes against the cuff and I lie back in the bed, struggling to hold back tears. I don't have a plan and now I have just three days to come up with one. Escaping for a second time is going to be impossible. All I've done is postpone the inevitable, I realize. And who knows if I'm safe from Ryan?

Doctor Karuna leaves the room and I desperately try to stifle the screams rising in my chest, and to force some kind of order to my churning thoughts. I remind myself of the positives: at least I'm not yet sedated, which I would be if they'd taken me to Crosshill, and I have seventy-two hours of clear thinking to find a way out of this. There is a chance, a small chance, that Doctor Karuna will look into it and find my original bloodwork. Maybe it will still be on file – though I admit it's a long shot – but if it is, it might reveal the truth: that I wasn't drunk or high when I got behind the wheel. That gives me some hope to cling to – not much – but a flicker.

Somewhere in the distance I can hear a TV and I wonder what the news channels are saying about me.

I wish I could get my side of the story out. I wish Daisy and Angela were still alive and could speak up. If only there was one woman who was willing to corroborate the story, besides me and Isabel, then we could have a chance of proving Ryan is the bad guy, not me. But then I remind myself that fifty women telling the same story will still struggle to be believed over the word of one man. That's the bullshit world we live in.

If I still had the IDs from the box then there's a possibility we could cast doubt on Ryan, but it's hopeless. I don't have them and I don't remember their names. Plus there's the fact that even if I did miraculously manage to escape and find the box and contact the women that he attacked, they likely wouldn't agree to come forward. What's happened to me would be a warning to them to stay silent and I couldn't blame them.

At some point during the afternoon, I am brought food on a tray, but I can't lift my arms to use the plastic knife and fork provided, and the patrol cop isn't interested in helping, so I go hungry.

The cop switches out with another officer in the evening and shortly after the door opens and a nurse's aide enters with a plastic bowl and a towel slung over one arm.

'Time for a bath,' she says brightly.

I look up and my jaw drops. It's Isabel – wearing a pink hospital uniform. She gives me a look, warning me not to say anything in front of prying eyes. 'Can we get some privacy?' she asks the cop with a smile. He sighs and leaves the room, stationing himself in the corridor outside with his back to the door.

As soon as he's gone, I turn to Isabel. 'Oh my God,' I whisper. 'What are you doing here?'

Isabel yanks the curtain around my bed. 'I saw on the news that you'd tried to kill yourself and they'd transferred you here,' she says in a hurried whisper.

'I didn't try to kill myself,' I tell her. 'I was trying to stop them from taking me to Crosshill.' I stare at her in amazement and overwhelming relief. 'I'm so glad you got away. I was so worried that they'd caught you.'

She smiles. 'No. Those tin cans gave us enough warning. I slipped out the back door of the cabin while they were arresting you. They were so focused on you, they didn't see me.'

'I don't know what to do,' I say, rattling the cuff chaining my foot to the bed.

Isabel frowns, staring at the chains, and I realize that she doesn't have a plan either. She didn't come here to break me out. My heart sinks.

'There are cops all over the place,' she whispers. 'Not just the one outside the door here. There are two more by the front entrance as well – and probably others that I haven't seen too.'

She doesn't implicitly say it, but I know what she's

trying to convey: it's hopeless to think about escaping. The look of sorrow and desperation on her face clearly indicates that she thinks I'm screwed.

'I was thinking about those women,' she says to me. 'The other women he raped. I went back to all of the ones I knew about. None of them will come forward. They're all terrified.'

Whatever latent hope remained in me is dashed.

'But what about the IDs you found in the box?' she asks. 'Do you remember any of the names?'

I shake my head, as a wave of despair crushes me, making me sink back onto the pillow. All I remember is that they were all young, dark-haired, and attractive. There were drivers' licenses, a hotel ID, and a library card. And a Soul Cycle card too. I pause and sit back up.

'What?' Isabel frowns, seeing something in my expression shift.

'I just remembered something. It's probably nothing, but there was a Soul Cycle membership card in the box. I didn't think about it at the time, but it seems odd to me now. We thought Ryan was targeting maids at the hotel. Or people like my sister. Vulnerable people – those who would be too afraid to go to the police. But Soul Cycle . . . I mean, *I* had a membership there. It's only rich people who can afford it. So,' I say to her, 'what if it's not just hotel maids he's assaulted?'

346

Isabel absorbs that.

I think of all the women in Ryan's orbit, all the young women who work on the campaign trail with him and at the DA's office, all the women who attend the same functions as him. Could he have targeted someone in those circles?

'Do you remember the name on the card?' Isabel presses.

'Everything's so blurry.' I frown, trying to conjure up the memory, like rooting through an old photo album. I picture the box filled with IDs, try to play through the scene in my mind, focusing on the moment I sifted through them. Squeezing my eyes shut I try to zoom in on the ID cards.

'Diane?' I whisper. 'Maybe? I can't be sure.'

I open my eyes. Isabel rubs her temples, frustrated. How are we going to find someone called Diane who has a Soul Cycle membership?

I inhale with a gasp as another image floats tantalizingly close. It's an image of a woman with dark hair in a black dress, glaring at me.

'Everyone's shooting me daggers,' I whisper under my breath.

'What?' Isabel asks.

I turn to her, excitement buzzing through me. 'My wedding reception.'

Isabel looks at me, puzzled.

The evening that Daisy showed up high and made

a scene. Everyone was giving me looks. Ryan told me ignore the haters. *Ignore Di,* he said. *She's just jealous. They're all just jealous.*

'Di,' I say to Isabel now. 'There's a woman who Ryan knows. She was at our wedding party. I've only seen her a few times over the years since at different social events. Ryan warned me away from her, saying she was a horrific gossip and not to be trusted. And, truth be told, after my run-in with her, I was only too happy to give her a wide berth.

'I thought she was always giving me the evil eye,' I tell Isabel, 'because she thought Ryan was too good for me and that she was jealous. But what if she was throwing dirty looks at Ryan?'

Watch yourself. That's what she said to me when I bumped into her. I thought she was telling me to mind where I was going, but what if it was actually a warning – from one woman to another? What if she was telling me to be careful of Ryan? Only, I was too focused on the drama with Daisy, too humiliated by what had just happened on the dance floor, to take it in.

'You've no idea what her last name is?' Isabel presses.

I chew my lip in thought. 'No, but she'd be late thirties by now. Slightly older. Tall. Striking. Dark hair. There are probably photos online of the party – it was in a few magazines. The guest list must be somewhere too. And she clearly knows Ryan's family. She should be easy enough to track down.'

Isabel nods. 'OK. Let me see if I can find out who she is.'

'Thank you,' I say, clutching her hand, gratefully. It's a lead, finally.

'I have to go,' she says, standing up and picking up the bowl and towel. 'Stay safe,' she tells me, squeezing my hand.

'You too.'

Chapter Forty-Six

Present

Doctor Karuna comes to check on me the next morning. I am antsy, not having slept well, and keen to know if she's looked into my bloodwork or talked to the doctor who signed off the report. 'How are you feeling?' she asks me.

'Fine,' I mumble, glancing at the cop in the corner as she undoes the dressings on my arms to check how the injuries are healing. I look down and almost gag at the Frankenstein-like stitches running up the insides of my arms.

'There will be scars, I'm afraid,' she says as she inspects the wounds for signs of infection.

I snort. As if I care about any of that.

'But the antibiotics are working,' she goes on. 'You're healing nicely.'

I wish I wasn't. If there was still an infection, they might keep me here longer. I sneak a look at the cop in the corner of the room – my armed guard – and then back at Karuna. I am running out of time and anxiety spurts adrenaline into my bloodstream. 'Did you find the blood test report?' I ask her in a harried whisper.

She opens her mouth to answer but before she can say a word the door opens. I stop breathing. It's Ryan. Seeing him again is like being struck by a bullet. My stomach clenches into a knot. I feel a desperate urge to scramble out of the bed and grab a weapon to attack him with, my flight response giving way to my fight response. But in the end, I don't move, mainly because I can't. I'm still cuffed to the bed.

Ryan stands in the doorway for a long moment, taking me in – and I see the faintest flicker of rage ripple across his otherwise blank face – before he turns to the cop.

'Can I have a moment alone with her?' he asks.

The cop opens and shuts his mouth like a fish. He knows who Ryan is – that he might soon be the Governor of New York – and I can tell he doesn't know if he has the authority to argue with him – what it might mean for him if he does. Will his bosses be angrier if he doesn't obey or angrier if he does? He weighs it, eyeing my ankle shackled to the bed as though to reassure himself, and then scurries from the room.

'I'll be just outside if you need me,' he mumbles to Ryan as he goes.

'Would you mind leaving too?' Ryan says to the doctor. It's not a request.

Doctor Karuna looks Ryan up and down. 'I'm sorry, this is my patient and she's not allowed visitors,' she tells him, visibly affronted.

Ryan cocks his head and offers her one of his most charming smiles. For the first time I see him for what he is: a sociopath pulling on a mask. The blinkers have fallen away and I am stunned I was ever fooled by him. 'I'm her husband,' he says to Karuna. 'I just want to see her. Speak to her. Make sure she's OK.'

His words and charisma deflect off Karuna like she's made of Teflon. She crosses her arms over her chest. 'Ex-husband, isn't it?' she remarks snidely.

Ryan narrows his eyes at her, the smile fading.

I'm amazed by this interaction. Most women crumble before him but she's impervious to his charm. Can she tell it's just an act? Or is it that lots of people can see through Ryan but I, for some reason, have never been able to?

'It's OK.' I swallow, switching my gaze back to Ryan. 'I'll talk to him.'

Karuna turns to face me. 'Are you sure? You don't have to. I can call security and have him removed.'

I shake my head, even though I'd very much like to see that. 'No,' I say. 'I want to talk to him.'

Karuna purses her lips, giving me a confused look, but I plaster on a broad smile to reassure her, and she leaves the room. 'You've got five minutes,' she says to him before she shuts the door.

After she's gone, Ryan walks over to the bed and looks down on me. My pulse leaps in response. His gaze flicks to my bandaged arms. He's curious, I can tell, as to whether it was a genuine suicide attempt. I wait for him to speak first because I'm afraid that my voice might wobble, and I don't want to give away my fear.

'You look terrible,' he says to me.

'So do you,' I retort, surprised that my voice comes out strong and sure. He does look like hell. There are deep pouches beneath his eyes and fresh gray in his hair. It feels like a small triumph to know that my attempt to frame him for murder has obviously taken a toll. I wonder what was worse for him: knowing that he might go to jail for a crime he didn't commit or losing his perfectly crafted life.

'You thought you'd get away with it,' he says to me now with an amused but bitter smile.

'So did you,' I point out, struggling to sit up.

He steps even closer to the bed, his expression hard as nails. All I see now is the monster, not the man I loved. 'I *have* gotten away with it.' He smirks.

'You make me sick,' I spit back. 'How can you do this?'

He shrugs. 'Do what exactly?'

'All of it. Rape those women. Beat them. Threaten them. Lie to everyone.'

'I don't know what you're talking about. You're crazy.'

My blood boils. I want to lash my fingernails across his face and draw blood but I manage to keep control of my temper. 'You raped my sister.'

A furrow appears across his forehead and a spark of surprise crosses his face.

'Careful now,' he warns in a quiet voice. 'Those are some terrible accusations.'

'And they're all true. Admit it.'

He smirks again. 'So what if they are? No one will believe you.'

I gasp. He's finally admitted it.

'How could you do it?' I ask, holding back tears. 'She was getting better. She was clean. Then you did what you did, and it sent her spiraling backwards. She'd be alive now if it wasn't for you.'

'Would she?' Ryan leers. 'It's not likely. She was always going to overdose sooner or later.'

'No. She was sober. And then you sent her off the rails again,' I argue. 'You've destroyed my life,' I tell him, my lip trembling and tears welling up even though I will them not to. 'You've taken everything that was good away from me. My education. My daughter. My sister. You had me committed when you know I'm innocent,' I say, my voice finally breaking. 'You faked my blood tests. I don't know how, but I know you did. You pulled strings to have me admitted to Crosshill too. You wanted me silenced. Just like you silenced all the women you raped.'

He studies me. 'I wouldn't have had to do what I did if you hadn't stuck your nose into things. If you'd just kept on playing the role of the dutiful wife.'

Heat rises up my chest. 'How much money did you pay the doctors to falsify my records?' I spit. 'Which cops are in your pay? I wasn't drunk and I wasn't on drugs. You set me up. You convinced the world I was mentally ill because you wanted me out of the way. Everyone thinks I'm mad, delusional, thanks to you, so no one will believe me.'

'Sorry about that.'

'Are you?' I snort.

'I am, actually. I'm sorry for all of this. You were a good wife.'

My stomach clenches. My jaw too. 'A good wife?' I growl through gritted teeth.

'Yes,' he says. 'Until you got too curious for your own good.'

'Did you ever love me?' I hate myself for asking it, the moment the question comes out of my mouth.

He pauses, clearly enjoying my discomfort. 'What is love?' he replies stonily.

Even though I hate him, even though he repulses

me, the thought that my whole adult life was a lie – that he never loved me, only pretended to – makes me want to cry. But then the pain of it is wiped out by white-hot rage. 'How could you do that? How could you marry me? Lie to me all those years?'

'You made it so easy.' He laughs. 'You never asked for anything. You were always so desperate to please.'

Something hits me then – the knowledge that I'm no different to Daisy or any of the women he chose as victims. 'That's why you chose all those women isn't it? Including me.'

'What do you mean?'

'All the women you've raped – you choose women that you think are weaker than you, women you think you can manipulate.'

'Ha, you sound like my therapist. All women are weaker than me. Most men too.'

Incensed, I go for the jugular. 'Do you at least feel bad for what happened to Sienna?'

His expression darkens. 'Don't talk about her.'

'Why?' I bark. 'You killed her.'

Fury flashes across his face. Sienna is his weakness. She's probably the only person besides himself that he's ever loved. 'She wasn't strapped in,' he says.

'If you hadn't been chasing me at speed, I wouldn't have crashed.'

'I didn't know she was in the car,' he shouts.

'You left her in a ditch,' I say, hurling the words

at him like bullets. I feel a small spurt of triumph when I see him flinch and his normally ramrod-straight back curves in on itself. I press my advantage. 'You left me to die,' I say. 'You opened the door. I remember. You took the evidence I'd stolen from your safe. All those women's ID cards. Mementos from all the rapes you committed. What were they? Souvenirs? You sick fuck!'

I have the satisfaction of seeing Ryan shocked. He rears back from me, regarding me like a stranger. He's never heard me curse before or raise my voice. I've never once stood up to him in all our time together.

'You shouldn't have broken into the safe and stolen my belongings. If you hadn't, we wouldn't be in this situation.'

I snort. 'So, it's *my* fault? I guess you'd probably say the same about the women you assaulted. That they deserved it too?' I continue.

'Wow,' Ryan says, regaining his composure and smiling toothily. 'I like it. I like this new Rose. Who would have thought? You actually have a backbone – and a brain. You're finally seeing the full picture. You're finally seeing me.'

A shudder runs through me. He touches my cheek and I flinch back.

'I like being seen,' he whispers. 'A therapist might tell me that's why I do it. I spend every waking minute . . .' he gestures to his face, 'playing a part. It's exhausting to keep it up.

'It's so wonderful to be able to stop the act occasionally, to let people see me for who I really am.' He gazes at my face, studying me. My whole body is shaking. He puts his hand on my thigh and his touch is a cockroach scuttling over my skin. I want to scream at him to get his hands off me, to kick my leg and throw his hand off but it's the leg that's cuffed to the bed so I can't. 'There,' he says, smiling. 'You're afraid.' He has a look on his face that I know well – desire.

'Get the fuck away from me, you sick bastard,' I hiss.

His smile widens. He sighs and stands up. 'It's almost a shame.'

'What?'

'That they're taking you away. I'll miss you. I'm not sure wife number two will be as good.'

Wife number two? What is he talking about?

'I might go back to that restaurant where we first met,' he muses. 'Find another hopeful young girl from some Podunk town, someone who'll do anything to be with a man like me, who I can mold without her even knowing it.'

A lump rises in my throat, rage mingled with sorrow.

'You were like clay,' he adds. 'So pliable.' He checks

his watch. 'I must be off. I have a press conference to attend.' He moves to the door. 'All this free publicity has been great by the way. I should thank you for that. My stock is rising. I'm the favorite for the governorship thanks to you and all this drama you caused. So goodbye, Rose. Thanks for the memories. Enjoy your time at Crosshill.'

He walks out and I catch a glimpse of four men waiting outside my room. Ryan stops to talk to them.

'No!' I shout, realizing who the men are.

They enter the room. 'No!' I scream again, registering the green of their orderly shirts. 'What are you doing? Help!' I cry as they come toward me, though I already know the answer: they're from Crosshill and they're here to take me back. I thought I had more time, but of course Ryan must have found a way to speed that up.

The cop has followed them into the room, and I try to make eye contact. 'Help me!' I beg.

The officer pushes between the orderlies and me, and I think he's going to stop them but he's only undoing the handcuff linking me to the bed. He snaps it off and the Crosshill lackeys grab me. Gathering all my strength, I fight but one of them is doing something with my IV, starting to inject something into it.

I scream and rip my hand free, tearing the canula out of my arm. Pain rockets through me, and I throw myself off the bed, but there are four of them and they easily pin me down.

'What the hell is going on in here?' I hear someone shout.

It's Doctor Karuna. She's standing in the doorway with a hospital security guard behind her. 'What are you doing?' she demands of the orderlies.

One hands her a piece of paper. 'We're transferring her. It's court-ordered.'

Karuna snatches the piece of paper, reads it and then holds her arms out to block the doorway. 'You're not leaving here with my patient. I haven't discharged her.'

'We have an ambulance waiting and a specialist psychiatric nurse on hand to deal with her. She'll be fine in our care.'

Karuna stares coolly at the two men still gripping hold of me. I am panting and crying, and my arm is bleeding where I ripped out the canula.

'She does not look at all fine in your care.'

She turns to the security guard. 'Do not let them leave the building. I want legal down here right now,' she says turning to a nurse hovering behind. The nurse hurries off to summon someone from the hospital administration's legal team, who I pray can stop this from happening.

'Let my patient go,' Karuna orders the men.

The Crosshill staff exchange looks.

'She's bleeding,' Karuna says, gesturing to my arm. 'She's on an IV antibiotic drip. She's being treated for sepsis.'

'She ripped it out herself,' one of the orderlies protests.

'They were trying to spike me with something,' I bite back.

The security guard ushers the orderlies out into the corridor. They don't go without grumbling, but they do go. The cop replaces them, standing inside the room, feet planted firmly, as though to ward off any escape attempt I might make. Karuna helps me back onto the bed.

'Thank you,' I say to her.

'I found the blood test,' Karuna tells me in a hurried whisper, glancing quickly over her shoulder at the cop to make sure he can't hear. 'You were right. The original one shows no alcohol in your bloodstream. None whatsoever. No trace of any sleeping pill or anything else either. You were totally clean.'

I stare at her in shock. 'You need to give it to my lawyer. Please.'

'Who's your lawyer?'

'Isabel. Isabel Rodriguez.'

She presses a gauze to my hand to stem the blood flow. 'I'll try and hold them off as long as possible. But I don't know if the hospital's lawyers will be able to do much.'

Chapter Forty-Seven

Present

Karuna is right. The hospital's lawyers do what they can but inform us that the documentation has been signed by a judge – no doubt one who has links to Ryan's family – and that their hands are tied. Doctor Karuna takes as long as she possibly can to patch me up but when Detective Adams shows up with Lim, I know my time's up.

Adams orders the hospital to release me into the custody of Crosshill, and Karuna looks at me apologetically before she signs the piece of paper transferring me. I smile at her to reassure her that I don't blame her. She's done all she can, and I appreciate it.

She accompanies me, insisting on wheeling me in a wheelchair to the waiting ambulance. As she pushes me down the corridor, we pass several nurses and gathered staff, who watch the procession like it's a carnival parade. And we are a parade. The four Crosshill orderlies trail after us, along with two uniformed cops, the hospital security guards flank my wheelchair, and Detectives Lim and Adams head up the procession. I stare at Adams's broad back as he leads the way, wondering if he was the one who faked Doctor Thatcher's signature. Will I ever know?

We walk through the lobby waiting area and I catch sight of Ryan. I thought he had left, but of course he wouldn't go, not without seeing me safely off – witnessing me silenced once and for all.

He catches my eye, a smirk playing on his lips. I stare back at him, blankly. I won't give him the satisfaction. Abruptly, Doctor Karuna stops wheeling the chair. Adams looks back over his shoulder at us, frowning at the hold-up.

'Come on, let's get this show on the road,' he orders.

But Doctor Karuna is staring up at the TV on the wall of the waiting area. I follow her gaze. It's CNN news. The scrolling ticker-tape headline announces: 'RYAN REID ADMITS TO SERIAL RAPES'.

A commotion breaks out in the lobby and I turn to look at Ryan, wanting to savor the moment of his reckoning. He is staring at the screen and I watch as his face becomes ashen. The mask falls away and I see fear sweep across him.

Someone hits the volume button and I turn my attention back to the screen.

'An audio recording of Ryan Reid admitting to assaulting multiple women has been shared with multiple news agencies,' the newsreader announces with the tone of a man who knows he's gotten the scoop of the decade. 'In this shocking confession, caught on tape without his knowledge, Reid also admits to framing his wife. Reid had claimed that his wife was suicidal at the time of the accident in which their daughter was killed, and that she had deliberately crashed the car. But it appears that Ryan in fact forced his wife off the road in an attempt to kill her and cover up his crimes.'

I hear gasps all around me. Ryan looks like he's been struck by lightning.

I have set fire to his world and now I watch as it burns down around him. He locks eyes with me across the waiting room.

And I smile.

Chapter Forty-Eight

Past

Eight Hours Earlier

Isabel sits on the edge of my hospital bed in her nurse's aide uniform.

'I have to go,' she says, standing up. 'Stay safe,' she tells me.

'You too,' I answer, squeezing her hand.

She pauses as she starts to pull back the curtain that's around the bed, glancing through the little window in the door at the cop who's standing sentry outside. 'Here,' she says, taking something from her pocket and handing it to me. It's a phone. 'Take this,' she tells me. 'It's mine. Just in case you think of something else. Text my boyfriend. He's in there under Matt. He'll pass the message on.'

I nod and slip the phone beneath my pillow.

'Wait,' I say, as she makes to leave. 'I've got an idea.'

Isabel turns around. 'What?'

'Call Ryan's office. Pretend you're a doctor here, or my lawyer, and tell him that I want to see him.'

She frowns at me. 'Why do you want to see him?'

I hold the phone up. 'This has a record function.'

Isabel meets my eyes. She knows exactly what I'm getting at. 'You think he'll confess to you?'

I shrug. 'I don't know.'

'Will he even come?'

I nod. That's one thing I'm sure of. I'm betting on his ego. He'll take any opportunity to laud his triumph over me. 'He'll come.'

'OK,' she says. 'It's worth a try. And I'll track down this Diane woman in the meantime. It's our last shot.'

She leaves and I shove the phone under the pillow. The cop returns, taking up his position in the armchair and I pretend to sleep. Halfway through the afternoon I'm jolted by the phone vibrating under the pillow. I can't take it out to look at the message until the cops change shifts and stand chatting for a few minutes outside my room. Taking advantage, sneaking the phone out, I see there's a message from Matt, in other words Isabel. It says two words: 'FOUND HER.'

She must mean Diane. Hope soars in me but I work

hard to keep it in check. Just because she found her, doesn't mean that Diane will agree to speak up and even if she does, will it be enough?

I am on tenterhooks all day, waiting to hear more news, waiting to see if Ryan will show up before they transfer me. And then he does. He appears in the afternoon and I am grateful that Doctor Karuna is there and causes enough of a distraction for me to slide the phone out from under the pillow and hit record.

Everything Ryan says is caught on tape. The phone is hidden under my covers and I am terrified that it will be too muffled or that it won't stand up in court. I can't believe how he lets his guard down though, how much he admits to. But of course, it makes sense. He's so arrogant. He would never assume I was smart enough to outwit him.

When the orderlies come from Crosshill, I am utterly thrown and I fight tooth and nail because I cannot come so far and then fail. The phone clatters to the floor but in the chaos no one notices and I throw myself out of the bed, ripping out the canula in the process, in order to rescue it and to stop them from drugging me. I land on top of it, shoving it into my underwear before the orderlies manage to wrestle me into submission.

Once again, Doctor Karuna saves the day by stopping them from taking me, and when she fixes up my wrist I hand her the phone, begging her to give that and the blood report to Isabel. She takes it and nods.

It's only then that I dare to hope.

Chapter Forty-Nine

Present

'We're going to move now to a press conference that's being held with Rose Reid's lawyer, Isabel Rodriguez,' the newsreader announces. 'We understand she's the one who has brought these shocking claims to light with the help of her client . . .'

We are suddenly in the lobby of a building and I see Isabel on screen, wearing a suit, standing beside a woman I recognize immediately as Diane. Isabel did it! She must have convinced her to speak up.

One of the nurses standing in the lobby cranks the volume even higher, to drown out the buzzy murmur of voices.

I watch Diane move to a microphone set up behind a podium. She looks afraid but also defiant. I look again at Ryan who seems frozen in place, staring open-mouthed at the TV.

'I was raped by Ryan Reid,' Diane announces.

The words reverberate around the hospital waiting room. Everyone has turned to stare at Ryan.

He shifts his own gaze from the television and looks around at the crowd. I wonder how it feels for him to no longer have everyone eating out of his hand, to be the object of disgust and not the subject of admiration.

Detective Lim starts walking toward him, hand on his gun.

I see what Ryan is going to do before he does it. He grabs a nurse and shoves her toward Lim and then he takes off, running.

He pushes through the entrance doors out onto the street. Hospital security sprint after him, and the two patrol cops follow suit. I stand up and, still wearing my hospital gown and dragging my IV stand, I hurry after them. They can't let him get away. Not after all this.

I barrel through the doors in my hospital gown and catch sight of Ryan, the police and security guards hot on his tail. He looks back over his shoulder just as he steps out into the road.

He doesn't see the ambulance pulling in in front of him. He is thrown in the air like a ragdoll and smashes against the windshield before his body slams to the ground. A scream goes up from a bystander. Too late, the ambulance slams on its brakes.

I push my way through the gathering crowd of onlookers, stumbling but desperate to reach him. Ryan's lying in the road, broken, his legs bent at an awkward angle.

Snow drifts down, mingling with the spreading pool of blood around his head. He's still alive. His eyelids flutter open and he sees me.

His hand starts to lift. He's reaching for me. I ignore his groping hand and stand over him as he takes his last few breaths. Someone tries to pull me away, but I throw them off.

I want to be the last thing he sees. I want him to know as he takes his last breath, that we have won.

Chapter Fifty

Six Months Later

The typewriter clacks beneath my fingertips and the blank page fills. I don't know if what I'm writing is any good but I'm enjoying the process: feeling in control of the narrative and the journey that my character is going on. I'm writing a children's story. It's about two little girls – sisters – who must defeat an ogre by casting a magic spell. In order to gather all the ingredients for the spell they have to adventure through snowy forests and across icy lakes, and even through a haunted castle. Along the way they meet a kind fairy called Gwen and a woodcutter called Jake and a powerful sorceress called Isabel. A kind healer in the woods fixes one of the sisters up after the ogre attacks her. In the end the spell is cast and the ogre is defeated, transformed into a mouse that is then eaten by a passing bear.

It's the second thing I've written so far, the first being my application to Columbia. I'm going back in the fall part-time to finish my undergrad degree, which both terrifies and excites me in equal measure.

The cabin is filled with bright summer sun, pouring through the brand-new windows and onto the freshly varnished floor. It's summer, so there's no need for a fire, but there's a pile of chopped wood by the fireplace already, on stand-by for the winter.

The only times I leave the cabin are for my long daily hikes along the lakeshore or when I kayak across the lake to the store to see Gwen or to do my community service in town. I was given a suspended sentence for my charges of absconding and framing Ryan for my murder, the judge offering leniency due to all I had been through, and because public sentiment was on my side. I asked to do my community service at an organization in town that supports survivors of domestic violence. Gwen drives me there each week as I'm still too scared to get behind the wheel.

I get up from my desk and stretch and Toby, who's been lying at my feet, stands up too and pads his way toward the kitchen, a clear hint that he wants me to feed him.

I follow him, pausing briefly to look at the

photographs I've just hung on the hallway wall – a dozen or so of Sienna as a baby in my arms, as a toddler crouching on the beach reaching for a shell, another of her holding an apple in her hand the day I took her apple picking, and one of her the day before she died. It still makes my heart ache each time I see her face, but it hurts less than the thought of her face fading in my memory.

The cabin is not a mansion in Westchester with eight bedrooms and a swimming pool, but it's the first place I've lived that's felt truly like a home. It didn't take much to convince Isabel's boyfriend and his family to let me buy the place. They were happy to know it had been my refuge and that it would continue to be. I have started to redecorate and, this time, I really did choose everything myself, all the furniture and all the colors and I like it.

In the kitchen I find Jake Myerson, busy finishing the last of the new cabinetry. I hired him to fix the place up and install a kitchen and bathroom, and he's been working on it full time, putting in a new heating system too, as well as a brand-new shower and a bathtub, with piping hot water. This winter won't be anything like last, that's for sure.

'Looking good,' I say, taking in Jake's handiwork.

He grins at me over his shoulder.

'I meant the cabinets,' I tell him, trying not to smile in return.

It was only two weeks ago that Jake came clean and told me he had feelings for me. It shocked me, because I hadn't seen it coming. I'd been too focused on recovering from the trauma of the last few months and dealing with my grief. While I enjoyed his company around the house, I wasn't ready for a relationship. I like Jake but I'm still learning how to trust people. How do I know if he's wearing a mask like Ryan?

I told him that I didn't want to start anything with anyone and he was gracious and said he understood.

I do like having Jake around though; I can't deny it. We have an easy banter and a lot in common – both of us grew up poor and had to fend for ourselves as kids. His father abandoned him when he was little, and he has a sister who's also struggled with addiction. He makes me laugh, and he's perceptive too. He's the one who bought me the typewriter ribbon and told me to start writing after I mentioned one day that it had always been my childhood dream to become a novelist. And he's the one who encouraged me to reapply for a third time to Columbia.

'I need to go to town,' I inform him now, after I've finished pouring food into Toby's bowl. 'I have to pick some things up from the store.'

'You want a ride?' he asks, and I see both a glimmer of hope in his eyes and also concern. But I shake my head at him. 'I'll take the kayak.'

I like rowing across the lake. I love being on the water, beneath the open sky. There was a time I thought I might never see sky again so every opportunity to be outside, I take.

Jake nods, looking a little disappointed. 'Say hi to Gwen,' he says, turning back to his work.

I move to the door and then pause. 'Do you want to come over tonight?' I ask. 'I've got some friends coming for dinner, including Gwen.'

'I'd love to,' he says, beaming ear to ear.

Later that night, as I cook dinner on my new stove, I hear someone calling my name. I turn down the heat and rush outside. Isabel is walking toward the cabin, hand in hand with Matt, her now fiancé.

We hug each other tightly, laughing, and I lead them both inside the cabin. She hasn't visited in a while, and Matt hasn't been since he was a child, so they both are wowed by the work that's been done on the place, and I feel proud showing them around my new home.

'It's a new beginning,' Isabel says to me, squeezing my arm.

We open a bottle of wine and Gwen joins us, together with Jake, who ends up being a surprisingly joyful addition to the party – making everyone laugh with his stories.

'What do you do, Isabel?' Jake asks.

'I'm opening a legal aid center,' she replies. 'Here.' She reaches into her bag and takes out a flyer.

Jake takes it from her. 'The Women's Legal Aid Center,' he reads out loud. 'Domestic abuse. Sexual harassment. Sexual assault. We offer free advice and unparalleled expertise in women's legal issues.'

He stops reading and looks at me, cocking an eyebrow in surprise. 'Funded by the Rose and Sienna Lewis Foundation.'

I pick up my wine and, smiling at him, take a sip.

Chapter Fifty-One

Past

Six Months Ago

The funeral is sparsely attended, with barely a handful of people. The only person I recognize is Gloria, in a black suit with a veiled hat. She stands by the graveside, head held high, watching as they lower Ryan into the ground.

At least it's the family plot, I think to myself, and not the churchyard where Sienna is buried, so I won't have to see him when I visit her grave.

I watch from a distance. I am not here to say goodbye to Ryan. It's a private funeral anyway, and I wasn't invited.

Since he died ten days ago, I have been occupied giving statements to the police and the FBI and the press. Isabel has stood with me through all of it, as both my friend and my lawyer. All the most serious charges against me have been dropped and Isabel has negotiated community service instead of prison time for the rest. Detective Adams has been arrested for accepting a bribe in exchange for falsifying evidence against me.

A DA at Ryan's old office and a doctor at Crosshill are also under investigation as it's believed someone in the administration there was taking financial bribes in exchange for altering my medical records and misrepresenting my mental state.

After Diane came forward with her story about Ryan it unleashed a tidal wave of other accusations. Twenty-three women have so far come forward – perhaps encouraged by the fact that Ryan's dead and not able to fight back. The cases are all under investigation.

The funeral finishes and I watch the mourners leave the graveside and scatter to their cars. Gloria stays where she is though, watching the workers fill in the hole.

She looks up startled when I come to stand beside her. 'Why are you here?' she asks. 'You weren't invited.' Her voice is serrated steel.

She doesn't look at me, but I take note of her. I see how lined and pale she is, though she's dusted herself with a layer of powder and painted her lips a bold dark pink. She is as put together as always, and every bit as intimidating. But I am not the same person that I was. She doesn't frighten me anymore.

I take a deep breath. I've rehearsed this but it's still difficult. She is his mother after all. And I know what it's like to lose a child.

'I'm sorry for your loss,' I say.

Now she whips around to face me. 'You don't get to say that to me, you bitch,' she snarls. 'You killed my son. And you destroyed his reputation!'

I stare at her, my jaw dropping open with shock. Destroyed his reputation? She can't possibly believe that he is innocent – can she? After all the evidence against him has come out, after the women he attacked spoke out in unison.

'He wasn't who you thought he was,' I tell her, stumbling a little. This isn't how I imagined the conversation going and it takes me a few seconds to recover my train of thought.

She gives me a bewildered look. 'What do you mean?' she says. 'I knew exactly who he was. I saw it from the beginning. I'm his mother for God's sake!'

My mouth falls open. She knew what he was like all along? She knew that he ticked all the boxes for psychopathy and didn't think to do anything about it?

'If you knew, why didn't you try to stop him?' I gasp. 'Say something? Get him help?!'

She waves a hand at me dismissively. 'You've never had a son. Boys are different to girls.'

My eyebrows shoot up in disbelief. Is that really going to be her excuse for his behavior? Boys will be boys? I stare at her, anger momentarily obliterating my attempts to stay calm around her.

'How can you defend him?' I shout. 'After what he's done?'

'Look at what he achieved,' she interrupts, her eyes flashing with fury. 'What he could have gone on to achieve. You took that away. You ruined it!'

I let out an incredulous laugh. 'I suppose with a mother like you, I shouldn't be surprised how he turned out,' I say, shaking my head.

Gloria looks as though I've slapped her. I've never spoken back to her in all these years, and it feels great to finally tell her how I feel.

'Leave!' she commands. 'What are you even doing here?'

I don't budge. 'I'm his wife,' I answer.

Gloria snorts at that. 'No, you're not. He divorced you. About damn time too. He should have done it years ago if you ask me.'

'You're not hearing me,' I say again. 'I'm his wife.'

A frown line etches across her powdered forehead. 'Ex-wife.'

I shake my head and allow a small, triumphant smile to spread across my lips. 'I never signed the divorce papers. Which, technically, means I'm still Ryan's wife. Or, should I say, widow.'

Isabel brought me the divorce papers to sign at Crosshill. It's the excuse she used to get in to visit me, but she told me not to sign them, and so I didn't. She took the unsigned papers back to the law firm and filed them, and no one bothered to check if they'd been executed or not.

'Without a signature,' I tell a visibly horrified Gloria, 'they're invalid.'

'What?' Gloria gasps.

It's hard to suppress the smile. 'I guess you know what that means?' I say, still smiling. 'I inherit everything.'

She blinks rapidly, gaping at me with her mouth open, as her world reorders in front of her. 'There's a prenup,' she stammers.

'That was only in the event of a divorce. My lawyer has checked. Ryan died without a will. So, everything that wasn't wrapped up in the family trust, all his assets – the house, the cars, pension, savings, everything in fact – goes to the surviving spouse.'

Gloria must have assumed all Ryan's assets and wealth would revert to her. And she was right. He put it in his will that all his assets would go to any surviving children, and in the event of having no heirs, they would go to his mother – not to me at all.

But I removed Ryan's will from the safe on the

night of the accident. It was in the car. And Isabel located and destroyed the copy held by Ryan's law firm. She magicked it out of the file and shredded it, along with the electronic copy. So for all intents and purposes, there is no will.

Gloria has turned quite pale at the news. Her face begins to sag and she ages a decade in an instant.

'I wanted to let you know, in person,' I tell her.

She stares at me dumbfounded. 'You can't,' she stammers.

'I can. It's mine now. Everything is mine. Don't worry,' I add, patting her arm. 'I'll be spending it wisely.'

Chapter Fifty-Two

Present

'To the Rose and Sienna Lewis Foundation,' Gwen says, holding her glass up in a toast.

Everyone clinks their glasses against mine. It feels good to have been able to make some recompense to his victims, even though money will never be enough.

I have given almost all of Ryan's estate away to the women that he hurt, holding back several million, which I gave toward drug rehabilitation and drug outreach projects. The rest – an endowment of five million – I gave to Isabel to open the center.

The money I used to buy the cabin is money that I earned from an exclusive interview that I gave after Ryan's death, and I'll be able to live off the proceeds for a while, until I have finished my degree, and hopefully figured out what I want to do with the rest of my life. Right now, just getting through each day and enjoying my freedom feels like enough.

After dinner we head outside and sit on the steps of the cabin, watching fireworks erupting over the lake.

'What's left to do on the reno?' Matt asks in between whizzes and bangs.

'I'm almost done,' Jake tells him.

'Not quite,' I say.

Jake turns to me, pushing his unruly dark hair off his face. It's a joke between us that the work will never be finished. I'm always finding him a new task, and I've been thinking of building out the veranda and adding a treehouse, someplace I can lie and look up at the stars.

'I think you just like having me around,' Jake jokes.

I inhale deeply. 'I might,' I admit, unable to hold back the smile.

He grins at me in reply and his fingers brush mine against the wooden steps. I don't move my hand and we stay like that, our hands just touching, a spark jumping between us.

Gwen catches my eye and winks, grinning with delight.

It's a beautiful evening – full of laughter and love – and as I look around at everyone, I realize these are the first friends I've ever had. It is also the first time in months that I have felt even the smallest glimmer of happiness. Maybe, I think to myself, as the last firework explodes brightly against the sky before fading slowly away, everything is going to be OK.

Acknowledgements

An author does not birth a book alone, but with a team of midwives, and this was no exception.

My editor, Molly Walker-Sharp, went above and beyond in helping shape this novel, patiently digging through various drafts, first to help structure the myriad timelines to make the book as good as it could be, and then, to painstakingly ensure that all the dates added up (not my strong suit).

Thanks also must go to Helena Newton, my brilliant copy-editor, who was indispensable, spotting inaccuracies in the timeline, correcting errors – and even pointing out that it's Anna, not Elsa, who wears the red cape in *Frozen*.

Avon's team are the very best in the business and huge thanks go to Becci Mansell, Ellie Pilcher, and Ella Young in the marketing and publicity team, and everyone else who works so diligently behind the scenes to make the book a success.

Since my very first baby, *Hunting Lila*, was born, my agent Amanda Preston has been something of a fairy godmother to me, shepherding my career and supporting me, especially when I feel like throwing in the towel.

I started writing books on a whim and it was the encouragement of a few friends who helped me finish my first book. So, Sara, Nichola and Vic – thank you for helping push me down the path toward where I am today, and for sticking with me through the subsequent books.

I'm also indebted to my other friends who regularly cheerlead and keep up my spirits: Alby, Laurie, Lauren, Rachel W, Rachel G, Lynn, Jessica, Becky, Claire, Clarissa, Deepa, Carly and Karthi. And of course, the ladies of the lane – Tessa, Denise, Sandi, Dana and Brenda – the best neighbors anyone could ever dream of having.

And, finally, the most thanks to my babbo and bro, and to my two biggest loves (besides Melvin), John and Alula.

Two friends go on holiday.
Only one comes back.

Now a major Netflix movie starring Leighton
Meester . . . be sure to read it before you see it!

You're being stalked.
And they won't stop until you're theirs.

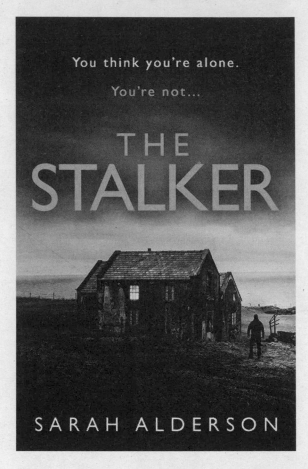

You think you're alone.

You're not...

THE
STALKER

SARAH ALDERSON

If you enjoy reading twisty psychological thrillers
that leave your heart racing, then you'll love
The Stalker.